Jenny's Law

Jenny's Law

a novel by Bobbi Loney

ONION RIVER PRESS
Burlington, Vermont

Onion River Press
191 Bank Street
Burlington, VT 05401

ISBN: 978-1-957184-08-1

Library of Congress Control Number: 2022911754

Editing by Louise Watson
Book Design by Jenny Lyons
Cover Illustration by Claire Tebbs

this book is dedicated to the youth who are working on
preventing suicide by gun and making this country
safer from gun violence and accidents

Never doubt that a small group of thoughtful, committed citizens can change the world; indeed, it's the only thing that ever has.

—Margaret Mead

Jenny's Law

Lemon Fair, Vermont
Spring

Chapter 1

Ruby Brown loved the bells, especially the ones at noon celebrating that half the school day was over. The bell from St. Sebastian's, her church, rang first. Then the Baptists, and then the Catholics, like they'd all agreed to take turns for maximum effect—10, 11, 12. She let out her breath, not aware she'd been holding it.

She returned to her list of names for Maple's calf.

Taffy
Caramel
Butterscotch

She was glad her family had Jersey cows; they were the prettiest.

Jess dropped a scrap of paper in Ruby's lap on her way up the aisle. Ruby watched her take the bathroom pass and go into the hall.

She looked down: *BBB*.

Boring Beyond Belief.

Ms. Moynihan stirred her finger in the basket and plucked out another name. It wouldn't be Ruby's. She'd already read her report.

"Kenny," Ms. Moynihan read.

Ruby watched Kenny shuffle up the aisle and turn to face the class. She started another list.

Favorites

Girls – Jess + Tisha
Boys – EF
Color – scarlet
Animal – sloth
Bird – saw-whet owl
Book – Anne of Green Gables

"Ethan Allen," Kenny said.

"Kenny, please lower your paper so we can see you."

Tina giggled. She giggled at everything.

Goals – grow out bangs

"Ethan Allen is famous for leading the Green Mountain Boys to capture Fort Ticonderoga on Lake Champlain from the British in 1775." Kenny's nose poked out over his paper. "We can see it from our farm. 'Ticonderoga is an Iroquois word that means meeting of two waterways.'"

How do you spell Iroquois? She'd skip that part. Ruby wrote **Ticonderoga means two waterways.** Complete sentences, that was the rule. For each report they had to write three sentences: something they hadn't known before, something interesting, and a question.

She almost didn't come after the hike got cancelled. Her mom would have let her stay home, with Maple about to calve. But this was her last Friday *forever*, after seven years! Next Thursday she'd march across the stage and get her certificate. It was important to remember milestones. There really were mile *stones*; she'd seen one by the Robert Frost Trail.

It wasn't fair they cancelled the hike.

Her graduation dress was in her closet waiting. And her shoes! An inch and a quarter wedge! She wouldn't wear the sash; it was babyish. She'd have a French braid.

Visit Grandpa every day!
Give half of egg money to charity

The shouts of the little kids came through the open windows and she imagined her little brother, Cooper, and his friend Seth running down the ramp of the play structure the town built before she was born. Her dad's and uncle's and grandfather's names were on the list of builders by the office.

"He was born in Connecticut," Kenny droned on.

It is interesting Ethan Allen was born in Connecticut. She didn't actually think so, but liked showing she knew that Connecticut was "connect" and not "connet."

Kenny had gotten to Influences.

She wished they'd been allowed to be more creative with their reports. She'd have written hers like a play, with Dorothy Canfield Fisher interviewing authors of the DCF books. But if her person hadn't had to be from Vermont, she would've picked Ruby Bridges. And under Influences she would've written Racism.

A sudden buzz pierced the room. A fire alarm.

The sound broke off, and their principal's voice came through the speaker.

"Attention please. We are sheltering in place. Proceed with secure mode protocol. We are sheltering in place. Proceed with protocol."

Ruby heard a whistle and swung her head toward the windows. Shouting. Another whistle. And again. More shouting. And then silence, like somebody had shut off the sound.

Goosebumps broke out on her bare arms.

Don't be stupid; it's a drill, just not for fire.

Ms. Moynihan put her finger to her lips, making a sweeping motion toward the wall to remind them of what to do. She mimed opening a book.

That girl in the magazine popped into Ruby's mind.

Don't.

Those kids at that school were in first grade, like Cooper.

Stop.

Ms. Moynihan turned the lights off.

Ruby opened her desk and took out her silent reading book. She followed Isabel on rubbery legs to the wall between their classroom and the hallway. Crisscross applesauce, that was the rule. The protocol. She tried to stretch her skirt over her knees.

Cooper's class would hide in the big art closet where the school kept the big jars of paint and the fat rolls of colored paper that were taller than he was.

Kids in that high school hid in a closet *two hours* before the police found them.

Could paper rolls stop bullets if they were fat enough?

Ms. Moynihan locked their door and pulled the shade down.

Those kids in the magazine were walking in a line, holding hands with their eyes closed. She'd thought for a second that it was a game. She'd never forget that girl's face.

Jess!

She started to get up.

"What are you doing?" Isabel hissed, pulling her down.

A siren. Their heads jerked up. Another. And another, like waves, getting closer. Then they all shut off. They hadn't come for the drill last winter.

What had that girl seen, before she closed her eyes?

She leaned out to see Ethan. He looked like he was reading, but his face was frozen and stiff. She gave up crisscross applesauce and wrapped her arms around her knees, pressing her face into her skirt, breathing in the smell of her mom's laundry soap. The smell of home.

She covered her ears.

Which was worse, to see or hear?

What about their friends?

What about their *brothers*? Cooper didn't know about that school or the other one either. He'd think the sirens were exciting.

See. See was worse.

But you can't cover your ears if you're holding hands.

Her heart jumped into her throat and her head started shouting *jump*, jump up! Run, run, *run*! Find Cooper! Stop it!

She opened her book. It didn't matter where; she'd read it before. Just read.

Not to see a man burst through the front door shooting. Not to not to not to. Kenny's uncle said somebody could kill their whole class in one minute with the right gun. Except he said firearm, which was just a gun with a fancy name.

The second door from the main entrance was Cooper's.

She clamped her lips against crying out at rolls of paper falling like those cardboard soldiers at the fair. That's what Mr. Larson at the mini-mart said—"My God! It must have been like a shooting gallery in there! They never had a chance!"

Ms. Moynihan shut the last window and pulled the shade down. It snapped back up. Everybody gasped. Ms. Moynihan pulled it again, slowly, up on her toes, like if she tiptoed it would stay put. She saw Ruby watching and smiled stiffly.

Jess! Ruby leaned forward.

Isabel flung her arm across her.

They sat in twilight. Nobody was reading. Ms. Moynihan sank to the floor with her back against the door. Sweat curved along her jaw. Ruby's fear sprang into terror.

She knew the sound of guns. They all did, in their woods and fields. At parades and the fair. From movies and TV and video games. The room was taut with listening.

Ruby slid her book to the floor in slow motion and got to her knees, pushing Isabel's hand away. She could get to Cooper in two minutes, tops. Hadn't she won the sprint at Harvest Festival her whole life?

She wanted her mother.

When her mother had read the handout she was angrier than Ruby had ever seen her.

"'Shelter in Place Protocol?' What does that even mean? Mind your manners while you hide? Keep your elbows in? The adults can't solve the problem so let's terrify the kids! Won't! Won't solve it! Instead of stopping selfish men who want to buy any gun they see, like kids at a toy store, they—we! Us! We make our children hide? God, it makes me furious! I'm going to tell Mrs. Fitch to give me notice, and you'll stay home! 'Protocol!' God!"

"But, Mom, Cooper wouldn't know what to do if it happens!"

"I can't believe this is a decision we're having to make! What kind of world is this? God!"

Ruby was dizzy from being Ready.

Someone wiggled the door handle.

Their world went on hold.

Isabel grabbed her hand. Her fingers were like icy claws.

Ms. Moynihan looked down the line of students and shook her head.

He was outside their room.

Wiggle, wiggle.

Knock-knock.

Ruby smelled pee.

Tina started crying.

Isabel's fingernails dug into Ruby's palm.

Nobody breathed.

KNOCK KNOCK KNOCK.

Wiggle, wiggle.

"It's me!"

"It's Jess!" Ruby burst out.

Ms. Moynihan lifted the shade and peeked out. They could hear her breath whoosh out. She twisted the door lock and bent back to open it, and Jess slid in. She handed the bathroom pass to Ms. Moynihan and looked around with wide eyes.

"It was just somebody turkey hunting!" Jess said. "In the woods at the top of the hill!"

Ms. Moynihan gripped Jess's arm.

"Who told you that, Jessica?"

Jess's eyes got wider. "Mrs. Cooke did! She said I should go back to my room. It was just Taylor McGraw, hunting!"

Everyone turned to stare at Richie McGraw.

"There's no turkeys in them woods!" Richie said. "Everbody knows that! He was just walkin' along, I bet! Nothin' wrong with walkin' in the woods!" Richie looked at the floor, getting red in the face. "He's gonna get switched, sure," he added.

Everybody burst out laughing. They all started talking at the same time.

"I knew it wasn't anything!"

"I wasn't scared!"

"I was! I thought we'd all get shot!"

"Your brother's a jerk."

"Your brother's a *turkey*!"

"Nobody should hunt anyway!"

"It's a sport, stupid!"

"Hunting's okay if it's for food."

"The geese poop all over the baseball field. Somebody should shoot *them*!"

"That's mean!"

"My dad says people wanna take away our guns!"

"Guns are bad!"

"We need 'em to protect ourselves!"

"Yeah, from Taylor!"

Kenny and Max pointed their fingers at each other. Pow! Pop!

"I'm a vegetarian," Isabel told Ruby.

Jess sat down cross-legged facing them.

They swung around at a squawk from the loudspeaker. "The drill is over. Thank you for your cooperation."

"See, he didn't do nothin'!" Richie said.

"Well, that's what Mrs. Cooke said," Jess defended herself.

"And the police came!" Kenny said. "You're lucky they didn't shoot him! They shot a boy dead in a park and alls he had was a BB gun!"

"Yeah, because he was Black."

"That's prejudiced!"

"*I* didn't shoot him!"

"It was because the *police* was prejudiced."

"A policeman shot a white boy with a BB gun in Montpelier."

"Sheriff St. Francis would never do that!"

Ms. Moynihan clapped her hands. "Okay, that's enough. Read your books for a few minutes more while I take care of a couple of things."

"But they—"

"It's okay, Richie, it will get straightened out. Open your book. And Jess, get your book from your desk, please." Ms. Moynihan whispered to Tina and helped her to her feet.

Jess got her book and squished between Ruby and Isabel.

"Were you in the bathroom the whole time?" Ruby whispered.

"I stood on the toilet seat. You know, so no one could see my feet. I sat on the top part."

"Were you scared?" Isabel asked.

"I was so scared I'd've peed if I hadn't just! Oh! I didn't mean—"

They looked over and saw Ms. Moynihan wiping the floor with a towel. And Tina was gone; she'd been allowed to break the stay-in-place rule. They scooted closer, their heads bent until they were touching.

"Then what happened?" Isabel asked.

"I was thinking about leaving but then somebody opened the door. I could hear breathing! All I could think was he'd look under and see me!"

"Who was it?" Isabel whispered.

"I don't know. They left."

"So you just finally left?" Ruby asked.

"Mrs. Cooke came in. When I heard her—you know, I got down and peeked and it was her clogs."

"Girls!"

They clapped their eyes on their books. Ruby was at one of her favorite parts, where Anne of Green Gables and Gilbert Blythe kiss. But all she could see was Cooper.

"Why are you crying *now*?" Jess whispered. "Ruby, I was never in danger. It was just Taylor the whole time."

Ruby wiped her face on her skirt. She should've worn shorts or leggings. You should always wear pants just in case.

In case there might be a shooting.

Laughing made her cry more.

"Ruby? Would you like to step out for a minute?" Ms. Moynihan asked.

"No thank you. I'm okay."

Jess held her hand until Ms. Moynihan let them go back to their desks.

Kenny was told to pick up where he left off, and everything went on as if it were a regular day. But Ruby didn't write something that was interesting about Vermonters John Deere or Ann Story, even though she'd been to the Ann Story cabin and there were three John Deere tractors in their shed at home.

The whole school went outside before bus time. The playground was a kaleidoscope of twisting, jumping, running, screaming kids. Ruby found Cooper in the middle of a gang of little boys. Pow! Bang! Aaa! There was a rule against toy guns at school, but fingers worked fine. She and Jess sat down at the picnic table.

"Want to play four-square?" Jess asked.

Ruby shook her head.

"It'll take your mind off things!"

"Maybe I don't want my mind off things!" Ruby looked at Jess's startled face. "I'm sorry, Jess! You go play."

"You sure?"

"I'm fine."

"Okay."

Jess got up and ran to the paved area by the bike racks.

Most of the time the boys played kickball and soccer or ran around swinging stick swords, and the girls played four-square or jumped rope. When she was younger, they pretended they were wild horses. But it was as if the school had been hit by a meteor or something. Ruby ran her thumb across letters carved into the picnic table. *Harold.* Harold Able from the feed store went to school with her grandparents, but she didn't think the table could be that old.

Would her kids go here?

Pow! Pop! POW!

Screaming boys ran past her, intent on killing each other. Pow! She drew her feet up to the bench. How could they, after what happened?

But she knew. Everyone had been scared like her. She'd seen it on her classmates' faces, and her own teacher's. And her class was the oldest.

Pretending they had guns made the boys feel big and safe.

She'd never forget the feel of Isabel's hand or the smell of pee or the sound of the doorknob.

Everybody had been scared, just like her, but at least they'd been scared together. Ruby Bridges had been scared all by herself when she walked into that horrible school, even when she had police around her—*especially* when she had police around her. She was the only Black child there. People *spit* at her. Someone showed her a *coffin.*

Ruby watched Ethan duck behind the climber and aim his finger at Kenny. Kenny clutched at his chest with both hands.

Ruby looked over at Jess. She wasn't playing four-square. She was standing with Grace and Isabel and they were talking, their heads bobbing up and down. Like the chickens after a fox walked across the field.

Ruby Bridges didn't have any friends to talk with. She was alone.

She, Ruby Brown, wasn't alone, so why did she feel like she was? She turned her back on the school, her second home for the last seven years. She looked at the top of the sliding hill, where Taylor McGraw had been hunting turkeys. The grass on the hill was a deep emerald green but the trees on top were pastel, as if Mother Nature had brushed color across and across, each stroke fainter as her paint ran out. The hills in the distance were just budding out with new life. Like the chicks. And Maple's baby, any day now.

"I know why we name the calves and not the chickens," Cooper had said at breakfast. "It's because they come when we call."

But Ruby did name the chickens and they came when she called. They knew her job was to keep them safe.

Why did she want to cry?

It was just dopey Taylor McGraw trying to get a dopey turkey.

They were safe. Safe as houses, Grandma Jenny would say.

Nothing had happened.

Nothing at all.

Chapter 2

VERMONT IS SO SMALL that in the puzzle Henry Cooper Brown put together in first grade, it had to share its piece with New Hampshire and Maine so it wouldn't get lost. But to seven-year-old Henry Cooper Brown (called Cooper so as not to confuse him with his grandfather, Henry Robert Brown), Vermont was their farm—which his dad, Wally, called No Frills Farm.

And it was plenty big, with two houses and two barns and two chicken coops, the summer one and the winter one, and a pond and a stream and two woods—the sugar maples and the evergreens where they got their Christmas trees. And two meadows, the high one and the low one. Everything in twos, although someone looking down from an airplane would just glimpse a patch of roof and dots that might be cows, or maybe they were deer, against a green background.

Cooper didn't think about things like that. But his sister, Ruby, sitting eight rows behind him on the bus, did think about such things. She had wondered how the road might look to an eagle, how the tops of the orange school buses might look like newts, and how the kids getting off with their backpacks might look like turtles. And she marveled every spring how her home burst into life like a surprise present, each of her twelve years so far.

And so it had been and, God willing, would continue to be—their grandpa, who was driving the bus, had said more than once. Just not lately.

He turned on the warning lights and stopped the bus to let off Remy LaFountain, their nearest neighbor and the last one off before Cooper and Ruby.

"Bye, Cooper!"

"Bye, Remy!"

Ruby peeked, but kept her head down. Jess thought Remy was cute. He was already in middle school.

"Grandpa, want to hear a joke?" Cooper raised his voice to be heard over the engine.

"*Grandpa*, want to hear a *joke*?" But their grandfather didn't hear him.

Cooper lurched back to sit across from Ruby, his winter-white legs sticking into the aisle.

"Ruby! Why is the letter A like a flower?"

Ruby pushed her glasses up. It was her fourth time reading about Ruby Bridges, and it was a gripping story. And true. But this time when she turned a page, her thoughts skipped to her heifer, Maple, so she might as well skip to Cooper instead. She saw that sometime during the day he'd skinned his other knee, but at least he didn't seem bothered by the shelter-in-place.

"Why *is* the letter A like a flower?"

"A bee comes after it! Get it? B and bee? Buzz? What do you call a girl with a frog on her head?"

Ruby imagined a fat spring peeper on top of Jess's blonde hair. Jess loved amphibians and reptiles. Even snakes. Especially snakes. "Jess."

"No! It's Lily!"

"Lily?"

"You know, like a lily pad? I'm hungry."

Their mom said Cooper was on a growth spurt and their dad said he had two hollow legs but she thought he just liked her snacks better than his own. She pulled her stained old canvas lunchbox from her backpack. She'd get a new one for middle school, and a new backpack, too. Only a week until Moving Up Day. But actually, and she was glad, she had the whole summer before she really moved up.

She gave Cooper her cookie. He dropped the baggie on the floor.

"Cooper!" she said. "Be your best you!" She stole a glance at their grandpa's back. It was what Grandma Jenny had always said. *There's only ever going to be one of you, so while you're here, be your best you.*

Cooper stuffed the baggie into his shorts pocket. He bit off half the cookie, and a raisin fell to the dirty floor. He picked it up and stuck it in his mouth.

"Ew!" Ruby stuck out her tongue.

But Cooper didn't care. It was Friday and an extra-long weekend, and he was marching with his Little League team in the Memorial Day parade. He would throw Tootsie Rolls to the little kids watching. First, he'd take some for himself. Four—two in each pocket. Or six.

But best of all, Cooper thought, nobody got shot at school, like what had happened to those other kids.

"Close your mouth when you chew," Ruby said.

Cooper stuffed the rest of the cookie in, went to wipe his hand on his T-shirt, and switched to his shorts.

"Did your teacher put Neosporin on that?" Ruby asked, pointing to Cooper's knee.

"It's okay. Maybe Maple will have her baby when we get home."

"She better wait for me! I told her!"

~

Up in the driver's seat their grandfather, Henry, hadn't registered Cooper's riddle, but Ruby's voice saying "be your best you" yanked him back to the present. Just a year ago his wife, Jenny, had been putting in her garden and greeting every green shoot like they were her grandbabies.

Sometimes, he'd been thinking, a person's gotta stop and look back before he can go on; sometimes a person should get to have a do-over. It just swept over him sometimes, and his soul convulsed. He'd been given a life sentence when Jenny died. No...that happened before, when she was given hers: pancreatic cancer, stage four. A year, they said. But she'd done it her own way like always, slipping away before he'd have to endure her pain, while he lay sleeping all thick-headed next to her.

Had she kissed him on her way? He was sure she would've, but he wished he could remember. There were so many things he wanted to remember—everything. *Everything.* He tried, but it felt like all the pictures of their life got stripped of color in the rooms in his head he'd been filling for sixty-three years. Did Jenny take his memories with her? They'd shared most of them. He should've paid attention better. Especially when Jenny wanted to talk about their son, Robbie.

She was sure Robbie would be in some Heaven, waiting for her. Henry wished he believed it. Instead, he was sunk in a well of grief, small crumbs of other people's happiness floating down now and again. The trillium would bloom any day now. Spring's stars, Jenny called them, and she wouldn't be there to see. That very morning he'd cried about it in front of the herd as they lined up to be milked. Looking sympathetic, like cows did.

Or Cooper would tell one of his jokes. Knock knock. Who's there? Swarm. Swarm who? Swarm enough to go swimming! Jenny was missing it all.

You got just this one life and it broke your heart.

That morning after the bus run, he'd walked to the library where Hazel, his daughter-in-law, Ruby and Cooper's mom, worked part time. She waved but didn't interrupt his path to the poetry section.

He'd pulled out his old friend Robert Frost and gone to the chair by the back window, where his butt had made a place for itself over the years. The book had fallen open to the one about the calf tottering when it's licked. He *knew* that calf, he'd seen it with his own eyes and even helped it into the world, and when he'd read it to Jenny in high school, he'd been opening his world to her.

The road in front of Henry wavered like it was underwater. Where did they live, all these feelings? It was like a game of Whac-A-Mole, popping up and whack, going back down before another popped up.

Jenny had loved Whac-A-Mole.

This damned life kept moving on. The trees were leafing out, the lilacs…the calves…Ruby graduating graded school…everybody was raring to go. If it weren't for the cows he might never get out of bed in the morning. What was left of them after Wally sold half of them off and went organic!

"Might as well," Wally had said three years ago. "With the new laws about runoff and chemicals we'll be ahead of the game. And they're getting twice as much for organic at the co-op." Henry felt like he was losing the farm, too.

The words of another poet popped into his mind.

> *For we are only the rind and the leaf.*
> *The great death, that each of us carries inside, is the fruit.*
> *Everything enfolds it.*

Rilke. *Book of Hours.* Jenny gave it to him the Christmas after Robbie got killed in Afghanistan.

He saw the top of Ruby's head in the big mirror. He needed to make an effort.

"I heard there was a false alarm today," he called back.

"It was Taylor McGraw turkey hunting," Ruby said. She got up and walked to the front seat. "Grandpa, did Daddy call?"

"Nothin's changed since the last time you asked. That baby will come when it's ready. No sense worrying."

Ruby fished Henry's cell phone from under a Harry Potter book and a squirt gun on the console. "Was the phone here all day?" She checked for a message.

Cooper slid into the other front seat.

"You two gotta stop moving around. It's against the rules and don't you know it," Henry said, changing the subject. He'd never figured that phone out.

"It's just us," Cooper said.

"That's no never mind."

Ruby put the phone back. "Grandpa, did they tell you? The reason they cancelled the hike today was there's a place by the trail where people shoot. It's not fair!"

"That's National Forest land. People have been target-shooting there my whole life," Henry said. "No reason to—"

"There's a turtle in the road! Grandpa, stop!" Ruby yelled.

Henry swerved, stopping with a jerk.

Cooper pressed up to the windshield. "Is he under the bus? Is he dead?"

Henry opened the door and grabbed the back of Cooper's T-shirt. "It could be a snapper, you stay back."

He went slowly down the steps. Cooper and Ruby scrambled after him. The ditch by the road was filled with water. They tip-toed around the front tire, hanging onto the mirror.

Henry saw that it *was* a snapper, a female. Probably chock full of eggs. "You two stay back."

The snapper lunged her head around, hissing. Cooper leaped back into the ditch and Henry grabbed him, but it was too late. Cooper's sneakers were caked in mud. Hazel wouldn't be happy about that.

"She's got just one thing on her mind, and that's to get to a good spot to lay her eggs. Best not get in the way."

Cooper had found a long stick and stretched to poke her.

"Cooper! You know better!" Giving the turtle a wide berth, Henry walked along the road to the back of the bus and opened the emergency door. He tugged the snow shovel out from behind the sand bucket. When he got back to the front, he tapped the turtle gently with the handle. She twisted and snapped at it.

"Are you gonna pick it up?" Cooper asked hopefully.

"Toby Pearson picked up a turtle by its tail and Jess made him put it down," Ruby said.

"Jess is right. That's a sure way to break a turtle's shell." He tapped the turtle again, and her legs and neck accordioned in, her nose sticking out. If you could call it a nose.

"Why doesn't she put her whole head in?" Cooper asked.

"Turtles can't have both a big jaw and a roomy shell. It's how nature made her." Henry slid the edge of the shovel under the turtle from behind and lifted it slightly. Her front legs poked out and started to walk, and he followed, like the wheelbarrow race on the Fourth of July.

When they got to the other side, he pulled the shovel away, feeling like a boy scout who'd helped a lady cross the street. But the turtle didn't say thank you or give him another glance. She thrust her head into the cattails, her shell waddling behind, and was gone, just a gap in the tall grass to show she'd been there. And then that was gone too.

Ruby looked at him, her eyes shining.

His heart turned over, and he was looking at Jenny in sixth grade.

"I'd like you all to welcome Jennifer Bilodeau," Mrs. St. Clair said, her arm around the prettiest girl Henry had ever seen.

B for Brown. B for Bilodeau. Harold Able had to move up to make a place for her in the desk in front of Henry. She smoothed her cornflower-blue dress under her legs as she slid into the seat. She flipped her hair back. She turned and smiled at him. And he was a goner.

"You did it!" Jenny said.

"Grandpa! You did it!"

It was Ruby.

"We have to go! Maple might be having her baby!"

It was *Ruby.*

They turned at the sound of an engine, and Ruby yanked Cooper out of the road.

The sheriff's car stopped behind the bus, and the sheriff got out. He walked along the bus, peering in the windows.

"Everything okay?" he asked Henry.

"Grandpa moved a snapping turtle!" Cooper said. "Want to see?"

"She's gone," Henry said. "Best get on the bus, and home to Maple."

"Maple?" The sheriff asked.

"My heifer! She's going to calve!"

"You kids get on the bus, then. I want a word with your grandpa."

Cooper and Ruby looked at Henry.

"Go on, then!" Henry said. Embarrassed, he didn't look at them.

Once they were on the bus, the sheriff pointed back at the road. "Geez, Henry, what were you thinking? Somebody could come around that curve any minute! You don't even have your hazards on." He leaned in. "I can see it in your eyes. And I can smell it. You know it takes one to know one." He shook his head. "Look. I know how hard Jenny's death...but you and I know it doesn't make a lick of difference. You will *not* drive this bus if you've had a drink! For God's sake, Henry!"

Henry looked away.

"I'm not gonna shame you with a ticket." The sheriff hitched up his belt. "There's what—a week left of school. You're gonna call Superintendent Dubois and make your excuses. You came down with a stomach bug. Or something. You will *not* drive this bus next week. And if I don't see you back at AA, well—you won't be driving it come fall, either."

And then Sheriff Tommy St. Francis, Henry's friend since they were five years old, put his arms around him and squeezed hard, and let go. "You can do this, Henry. You did it before and you can do it again. I'll give you a call in a couple of days."

Inside the bus, Ruby and Cooper looked at each other. Ruby put her finger to her lips.

The sheriff stepped up into the bus. "You kids come on. Today's your lucky day! You get a ride in the squad car!"

Henry stood there.

You did it before and you can do it again.

But everything was different now. Before, he had Jenny.

Chapter 3

Cooper finished clearing the wrappers and baggies, and crumbs from under the bus seats, holding his baseball T-shirt in his teeth to keep it off the floor. He'd only gotten to wear it by promising his mother she wouldn't have to wash it before the parade. With the sheriff driving them home, he'd thought he'd gotten out of cleaning the bus until Ruby said she'd tell on him. He picked up the squirt gun from the console. Pow! He whirled around. Pow! Pow! He fell across the front seat, twitching, and went limp. He sprang up and, peering towards the road where his grandpa had gone to get the mail, stuffed the squirt gun into his backpack and picked up the trash bucket.

"You about done?"

Cooper jerked. His grandpa was looking up through the open door. He had a handful of catalogs. That's all that came anymore, Cooper's mom complained. And bills. Nobody wrote letters anymore. That's when Ruby would jump in and ask for a cell phone. Everybody at middle school had one! "When pigs fly," Cooper would quote their dad, and Ruby would chase him and hit him with whatever she had in her hand, usually a book.

"Grandpa! Grandpa! Daddy says come quick!"

Cooper and Henry looked up the hill to where Ruby was waving her arms.

"Maple's having her baby!" she yelled.

Cooper jumped down the bus steps and took off, tossing his backpack toward the house. He ran into the barn, but the only sign of life was a cat napping in a spotlight of sun. Then suddenly his sister was there, babbling.

"Maple's having twins! She needs calcium! One's born, but her labor's stopped. Get towels and a bucket of water, and tell Grandpa we need calcium! I'm getting the disinfectant. We're in the birthing pen behind the barn!"

When Cooper finally got to the pen, his father had his hand inside Maple and was talking to her softly. "It's gonna be fine. Just one more time."

Ruby was on her knees next to a tiny calf, talking in the same gentle tone. The calf was slick and still.

"Hey, little baby. C'mon now." She grabbed a towel. "Cooper! We need to get her circulation going!" She began to rub. "See, like how the moms lick their calves."

Cooper had always been warned to leave the new calves alone, because their mothers felt protective. But this calf wasn't moving, and Maple was gazing off as if it wasn't even there. She didn't seem to care about his father's hand sticking into her, either.

"Cooper! Help me!"

Ruby and Cooper rubbed and patted, patted and rubbed.

"Daddy!" Ruby said. "She's not moving."

"Dribble a little water in her ears," Wally said. "That'll wake her up." Maple switched her tail into his face, and he grabbed it like a rope and held it away.

The calf's skin suddenly quivered. "Ruby," Cooper whispered. He felt like he was bringing the calf to life. Ruby dipped her hands into the bucket and dripped water into the calf's ears and on her head, like baptizing a baby. And just like babies do, she shook her head and cried.

Henry came through the gate. "Any action?" He was holding a syringe.

"It's presenting right, just she's quit on me." His arms occupied, Wally pointed with his head. "She's still ignoring her firstborn, too."

"Well, let's give her a jumpstart." Henry slid the needle under the skin in Maple's neck.

"Ruby, stick that calf in front of Maple," Wally said.

But Maple went down on her knees and then onto her side, Wally still attached.

"Maple!" Ruby crawled to Maple's side. "Maple, try!"

Cooper wiggled his arms under the first calf and pulled her to her feet. Her back legs wobbled, and she pitched into him. He fell onto his back, his arms abruptly full of warm, wiggly calf. He laughed. She turned and looked at him. There were drops of water on her long eyelashes.

A swoosh of yellow gunk gushed down Wally's arm, and Maple shivered from tail to head and back.

"That-a-girl!" Wally said, pulling his arm out. Two tiny hooves peeked out, slid in, and slid out again. In, out. In, out.

"Come on, Maple! You can do it!" Ruby duck-walked to Maple's head and petted her neck. "You're doing great!"

Wally and Henry each grabbed a hoof and pulled. It looked to Cooper like it would hurt Maple *and* the calf, even though he'd been told it didn't. How could they know for sure?

Maple gave out a long moo, and the head was born.

"Ruby," Wally said quietly.

She ran over and dipped her hands into the disinfectant, then broke the membrane around the calf's head and scooted back as the calf slid out onto the straw.

Maple craned her head to see her new baby—the only one she had, as far as she was concerned. Henry took the first calf from Cooper and held it up to her, nudging. Maple pushed back, but not like a mom.

"We might have ourselves a bottle calf," Henry said, nudging again.

"What's a bottle calf?" Cooper asked. He scrambled away as Maple heaved up onto her feet. His calf—that's how he thought of her, he realized—stretched her head toward her mother and mewled.

"Maple, look!" he said. But Maple wouldn't. She was busy licking her other calf.

"All the calves used to be taken away from their mothers and bottle-fed," Henry said.

"That's mean!" Ruby said.

"It was to get the most milk out of them. You could show that calf at the fair, Cooper, like Ruby did with Maple," Henry said.

"But Maple's mother took care of her!" Cooper said.

"I did *lots* of stuff. I trained her to her halter and made sure she was healthy and…I kept records of everything," Ruby said. "You have to do all that to show."

Cooper petted the calf, and she snuffled at his T-shirt.

"She wants to nurse on you, Cooper," Ruby said, laughing.

Cooper pulled back, appalled. But the calf ducked her head against him and snorted.

Wally turned to Ruby. "That calf needs colostrum, and she's not going to get it from her mother. There are a couple of bags in the cellar."

"Can't Cooper?"

Wally stopped her with a look. "It'll need thawing, and should be brought to warm."

Ruby sighed.

"Let's get this little girl situated," Henry said. He scooped up the calf. She looked at Cooper and gave a plaintive cry.

Cooper ran his hand over her head. "Don't worry, I'm coming."

~

Ruby could see that her mom was home—her book bag was on the table, next to Cooper's backpack and his open lunchbox. He'd still had his own cookies all along.

"Maple had twins!" she called down the hall.

She turned on the hot water and stuck a pot under the faucet. She got a bottle and nipple from the mudroom and tossed them in.

The sweat and straw on her arms and legs cooled and prickled as she descended into the cellar. She breathed in deeply. Apples, potatoes, and squash. Two lonely jars of her grandmother's apple butter sat on a shelf. It made her sad to see them. Her grandma's old aluminum lawn chair sat in the corner where she used to read on the hottest summer days. That made Ruby even sadder. Did chairs miss people?

Ruby opened the freezer. This was the emptiest time, most of last year's garden eaten. The bags of colostrum were easy to spot. She gripped one between her thumb and finger, shut the lid of the freezer, and looked again at the apple butter. They could have it at Thanksgiving with her aunt's homemade rolls. Last year's Thanksgiving had been *horrible*, everybody pretending it was okay to have it after Grandma Jenny had died just two weeks before.

The water was piping hot when she got back. She turned it off, plopped the colostrum into the full pot, and weighted it down with a mug.

Now she had to wait. She was missing everything!

She wet a dish towel and wiped her arms and legs. She picked up her backpack and tugged her book out.

The screen door slammed and Rowsby padded in.

"Rowsby, Maple had twins, but she doesn't want one of them. *Cooper's* going to take care of it." The dog raised his eyebrows as if he agreed that was a cause for concern. He was so old he spent most of his time under the kitchen table, on his worn patch under the porch, or on Grandpa's bed, which wasn't allowed when Grandma was alive. But he always knew when Ruby got home.

Ruby took a cookie from Cooper's lunchbox and gave half of it to Rowsby, biting into the other half. She looked down the hall at the sound of footsteps. Her parents' bedroom used to be the parlor, although only the minister had ever sat there, Grandpa said. Pastor Lori, their minister now, sat in the kitchen like everybody else when she visited.

"Did I hear you right? Maple had twins?" Hazel kissed Ruby's cheek. She noticed the pot. "Oh, sweetie! Is Maple okay?"

"Mom! She won't even look at one of them!"

"It'll work out. Remember Minnie-moo? And she wasn't a twin. But your dad got Bettyboop to nurse her baby. He'll get somebody to take Maple's."

"Grandpa asked Cooper if *he* wanted to raise it."

"Cooper?" Hazel's surprise was obvious, and Ruby abruptly changed sides.

"I took care of Maple when I was his age."

"As I recall, Maple's mother helped. And you might have been his age in years, but …"

"He cleans the bus."

"A bus isn't a living creature. And your grandpa's not as strict as he was with you."

"Nobody's as strict with Cooper."

Ruby gave Rowsby Cooper's other cookie.

"That's not good for him," Hazel scolded.

"It makes him happy."

"For the blink of an eye."

Rowsby thumped his tail.

Hazel sat down, adjusting one of the lilac stems she'd picked that morning. The kitchen was the center of their family life, with its large table and big well-worn couch, the place for meals and homework, farm business, games, and school projects. The front door was never used, and the dining room was only used for holidays and Cooper's

Lego constructions. The main stairs had become shelves over the years, each step half-filled with books and puzzles and board games.

"Now that you won't be waiting for Maple, let's go shopping tomorrow. You need a new bathing suit, and let's get something Vermonty for Tisha. We'll make a list!" Hazel said. She loved lists as much as Ruby.

Ruby poked the bag of colostrum. It was taking forever!

Hazel picked up Ruby's book. "I remember this," she said.

"Mom?"

Hazel looked up.

"Why did you name me Ruby?"

"You know why. It's your birthstone. Besides, I knew I better be quick before you were named Henrietta."

"*Really*?"

"What do *you* think? Henry Thomas, Wallace *Henry*? There was some talk of naming you Roberta after your uncle."

"You didn't name Cooper after him."

"You were born before he died. Later, your Grandma Jenny said no, it wouldn't be fair to Cooper."

The screen door slammed, and Cooper ran in, excited.

"Is the colostrum ready? Mom! I'm gonna take care of Maple's other calf! I have to feed her! I need the milk stuff! Is it ready?" He took a pear from the counter and bit. Juice ran down his chin. He peered into the pot.

Ruby threw the dishcloth at him. "Wipe your face. Then stir the pot. It will thaw it faster."

Hazel opened the book. "*Through My Eyes*."

"It's all true!" Ruby went to look over her mother's shoulder. "Her name is Ruby Bridges. Her grandparents had a dairy farm just like us. She had to go be the only Black child in a school that was supposed to integrate when they made that law. People were *horrible* to her! Grownups! And she was younger than you, Cooper. She was only six!"

"Ruby." Cooper said.

"What?"

"Like you."

"I know! Even the same initials, R.B. She was really brave, though. I can't believe someone could be so brave and be so little."

"You can be brave at any age," Hazel said. "A hard thing's in front of you and you do what's called for, even when you're scared." She sighed. "But it's a crime to make a six-year-old child do what the adults should do."

It was like what her mom said about sheltering in place. Ruby hoped Cooper wouldn't mention they'd done one that very day.

What would it be like to have dark skin, Ruby wondered. Like Tisha, and Sally. Nobody in her class was Black, and hardly anyone in her school, but almost all of the summer Fresh Air kids from New York City were. And the migrant workers, but they were from another country. Not like Rosa Parks or Martin Luther King Jr. Had white people been mean to Tisha too? Ruby looked at her arm. She got tan every summer, but never as dark as Tisha.

If her aunts Maggie and Sally had a baby, they'd have to decide between white and Black.

Was she prejudiced?

But she loved Tisha and Sally.

"How can people be so mean?" she asked.

Her mother touched a photograph of five little girls; only Ruby Bridges was dark-skinned. "Fear. That we're not enough. Treating somebody like they're less makes people feel like we're more. And everybody feels safer in a herd, not just cows. And doing the right things doesn't just come out of the blue. It needs to be taught. And practiced." Hazel stroked Ruby Bridges' cheek and sighed. "But some meanness…even with our awful history of racism, I just don't understand."

Hazel closed the book. "Cooper! I think if you're old enough to be a calf daddy you're old enough to wash your baseball shirt."

Cooper looked down. His shirt was filthy with dirt and straw. "I'm *not* old enough! I can't! I have to take care of my calf!"

Ruby met her mother's eyes, careful not to laugh.

Hazel stood up and walked to the refrigerator. She took something from the top of it.

"What can you tell me about this?"

Cooper looked from her hand to his backpack, where he'd stuffed the squirt gun.

"It was on the bus," he said, hoping that might be enough.

"Doogie Thirsten was shooting it," Ruby said. "Grandpa took it away from him."

"Well, what's *our* rule?" Hazel asked.

"No guns that look real," Cooper said. "I'm going to paint it!"

Ruby laughed. "What color? Baby blue?" she teased.

"Did Grandpa give it to you?" Hazel asked.

Cooper shook his head, looking at the floor and holding the baby bottle against his shirt. His dirty shirt.

Ruby took pity on him. "What will you name your calf?" she asked.

"I can *pick*?"

"I picked 'Maple'," Ruby reminded him. "Because of her color. How about Butterscotch?"

But without a second's thought, Cooper said, "Jenny. Her name is Jenny, after Grandma."

Chapter 4

COOPER BRACED HIMSELF AS Hawk Costello slapped his big hand down on his shoulder.

"Cooper and Wally Brown! You're a sight for sore eyes! What're they feeding you? Looks like you grew a foot! You gonna march in the parade today?"

Cooper nodded. "With my baseball team." He looked around. He and his dad were the only ones there. The way he liked it.

"So what's it gonna be this year? I just got a VW bus you might like to take on."

Mr. Costello ran a target-shooting range. Cooper's dad came to the range every Memorial Day in memory of Cooper's Uncle Robbie, and Cooper had gotten to go along the last two years. It was the only time they came. Cooper had never met his uncle, but he knew that Hawk's had been his favorite target-shooting place. The targets were rusted-out cars, trucks, and vans; most were veterans of demolition derbies at the fair. Barrels of water filled in the gaps, but that didn't mean the woods behind them were spared. A lot of trees were busted up and barely clinging to life, or to each other. When a car crumpled and collapsed or, as happened sometimes (the best!), caught fire, Hawk's son, Birdy, sprayed it down and hauled it off and brought in another wreck. When Birdy was around he always gave Cooper a lollipop as if he were a little kid, but Cooper didn't mind. Birdy was kind of like a little kid himself.

They always went to the center stand. Cooper pulled on his ear protectors while Wally clicked in a magazine and wiped his hands on the raggedy towel nailed to a post. They always shot a water barrel first.

Wally pulled Cooper tight up against him. Cooper opened his eyes wide. Last year he'd shut them at the first shot and almost missed the whole thing.

"Ready?"

Cooper nodded.

Wally pulled the trigger.

Ack ack ack ack ack ack ack ack ack ack ack ack ack ack ack ack ack ack ack

Cooper loved it, feeling terrified and safe at the same time. It was the best ride ever, better than anything at the fair, rattling him inside and out, so much that his teeth clicked together. Water burst out of the holes and the barrel fell on its back like a beetle.

Cooper laughed.

Wally reached for another magazine. "What's your pleasure?"

Cooper pointed.

He was sure they could kill the Chevy van.

~

"What's taking Mom so long?" Ruby complained to her father.

"I hear it!" a little boy called out from the middle of the street.

Main Street was closed, so there wasn't any danger of the boy being hit by a car. Ruby used to love standing on the center line and looking downstreet for the pulsing light of the sheriff's car leading the parade. The second she saw it she would drag Cooper to the curb.

People were lined up two and three deep, sitting on lawn chairs or perched on the curb and standing on the sidewalk behind, munching on muffins and donuts. Like she would be if her mom would get back!

After being cooped up all winter, Memorial Day felt more like a town reunion than a "dedication to those who died in foreign wars," even though her own uncle had died in one of them. She took comfort that the same thing was happening all over; that there were families like theirs in other towns all over America, holding their own secret griefs like her father and grandfather did.

"I see the sheriff's car!" somebody shouted.

Ruby had known Sheriff St. Francis her whole life, and not just because he was her grandfather's best friend. He'd be the master of ceremonies in front of Town Hall later and run the town meeting in March. He was Smokey the Bear at school every April, handing out posters reminding everyone to bring their bird feeders in because the bears would be hungry coming out of hibernation. He'd ride the fire truck to the library dressed up as Santa Claus and listen to what kids wanted. She'd always known he was just "one of Santa's helpers," but told him what she wanted until she was eight. Cooper still did. Cooper would take hunter safety classes from him, just like her dad and uncle had done. Not her!

And there was what happened that day of the turtle, but she tried not to think about that.

The middle school band marched behind the sheriff's car in their yellow vests and black berets. Next year she'd be marching with them.

Ruby looked forward to getting a band uniform next year, but she didn't like the mascot on the vest. A cartoon cat. Not a catamount, which at least lived in Vermont, or had. At least they could make it a barn cat.

Her tiny class would be scattered into a class of over one hundred seventh graders. What if Jess wasn't in her homeroom!

Watching the parade with her parents was another last thing. But it was a first thing too; Grandma Jenny wasn't there.

"Finally!" Hazel squeezed through the crowd and handed Wally two coffees. She gave the bakery bag to Ruby and slid into her canvas chair.

"You wouldn't believe the line," she said. "Lydie was there, Tyler begging for a frosted donut." She laughed. "It's weird being Cooper-less, kind of free, but I keep wondering how he's doing."

Ruby spread a napkin on her lap and another on her mom's and put a sticky bun on top of each. Hazel plucked a walnut off Ruby's. It was always the same—her mom got no nuts and ate half of Ruby's.

Ruby sighed with satisfaction.

Wally pried the lid off his coffee and took a sip.

Something struck him in the forehead and plopped into his cup, splashing coffee onto his fingers. "Ouch! Hot!" He fished out a Hershey's Kiss.

Ruby laughed. "Save it for Cooper," she said. Cooper had come down that morning in his Spiderman underwear and announced he wasn't going to march in the parade.

"Your team is counting on you," Wally said.

"I can't, I'm too tired!" He was close to tears. "If I'm marching, I won't be able to get any candy!" Then his last appeal, looking at their mom: "I didn't get all the dirt out of my baseball shirt!"

But their mom didn't budge either. "We keep our commitments in this family."

"There's Jess!" said Ruby, waving. "She looks cute." Jess was dressed as a spotted dog. She threw out a handful of Hershey's Kisses and kids scrambled to get them. One little girl stood back. Wally handed her his Kiss and was rewarded with a shy smile.

"Say thank you, Lindsey," the child's mother said.

"Thank you," she said softly to the pavement.

Hazel leaned over and kissed Wally on the lips. "You're a good guy," she said.

Ruby looked down, embarrassed.

They waved to every state representative and senator. Republicans or Democrats, it didn't matter, they were their neighbors. Ruby's father's side of the family had always been Republican, but after her uncle got killed her dad stopped voting unless it was local.

Ruby saw Jess's dad and called out to him. "Hi, Senator Somers!"

"It's the Brown family!" The senator wove his way over and shook her dad's hand. "Guess I'll see you later!" He was back in the stream of walkers before Wally could answer.

Ruby could tell her dad didn't have a clue what the senator meant by "later."

"The cookout," Hazel reminded him. "You like Jack and Lydie—you'll enjoy it once you're there."

Behind the politicians was a string of convertibles, and Wally and Hazel got to their feet, their hands on their hearts. Her dad gave her a look and Ruby stood up too. American flags were draped over the sides of the cars and men in uniforms were perched on the backs of the back seats. Someone asked Ruby's grandfather to ride in one of the cars every year, even though he always said no.

Behind the convertibles came Ethan Allen's Green Mountain Boys in tri-cornered hats. They stopped and lifted their muskets. Ruby plugged her ears.

BANG!

There was always just enough time while they reloaded for her to dread the next one.

BANG!

A cloud of gunpowder hung over the float behind them, a flatbed truck rigged up to look like a playpen. The daycare teachers shook rattles, and pacifiers hung from their necks on ribbons.

"You couldn't pay me enough," Wally said.

"That's true. They barely make minimum wage," Hazel answered.

Ruby loved the Beaupre family's beautiful draft horses, which came next. They were decked out in bright garlands, their tails braided with red ribbons, and Willy Beaupre followed with a shovel and a little red wagon, just in case. The high school band followed after a long gap, playing "The Stars and Stripes Forever."

Wally broke into song: "Be kind to your web-footed friends, for a duck may be somebody's mother, be kind to the denizens of the swamp, where the weather is very very dawmp. You may think—"

"Dad, stop! Everybody's looking!" Ruby whispered.

A million songs, songs Grandma Jenny sang when she was baking and canning and weeding, were stuffed in her father's brain and you never knew when they'd pop out, like Grandpa's poetry.

Her mom listened to books on tape when she baked, and that was hardly ever.

Here came the fire trucks.

"Farmer Brown!" shouted their neighbor, Arnold LaFountain, who was driving the hook-and-ladder. Remy was hanging off the side. Somebody could be a junior fireman at thirteen, but Ruby thought he looked like he was dressed up for Halloween.

"I don't see how they take care of that big herd and still go to fires, much less all those musters and meetings," Hazel said.

"They have the migrant workers," Wally said.

Miss Vermont was waving from the back of another convertible, wearing a crown and a pink strapless dress. The girls' hockey team skated behind her on roller blades wearing helmets and carrying sticks. Ruby thought Miss Vermont and the hockey team couldn't be more different, like opposite ways to be a girl. She didn't know which she'd choose if she had to.

"There's Cooper!" Hazel pointed.

Cooper's blue shirt said CO-OP CREEMEES under the number 42, Jackie Robinson's number. He'd been thrilled when he got it. And CO-OP. "Like Cooper! C-O-O-P, see?"

He dashed over and flung his arms around each of them, his bag of Tootsie Rolls banging Ruby in the neck. It was as if the morning had never happened.

"I gotta go!"

There was another long gap in the parade and when the couple next to them started to get up, Ruby said, "There's one more group."

And finally an old-fashioned red tractor came putt-putting down the road. Ruby knew it was an Allis Chalmers RC and that it had been delivered to the McGraw farm in 1940 in parts, to be assembled. Her mom said more tender loving care was given to that tractor than to all the wild McGraw boys put together.

Right behind it was Grandpa, driving the John Deere her great-grandfather had bought new in 1946, using money saved from his army pay in World War II. Every year since he'd stopped getting into uniform, Henry had polished it up and taken his place behind Mr. McGraw. He said he was biding his time until either the Allis Chalmers or Pete McGraw didn't have what it took anymore. Then he'd get to lead the line of tractors, each one bigger than the one in front of it, ending in the latest. "With an ice machine, no doubt, and surround-sound," Henry joked.

Grandpa waved his cap at them, grinning, and something inside of Ruby let go. She'd been worried he wouldn't have the heart to come without Grandma watching.

Then, just like that, the parade was over for another year. They folded their chairs and joined the stream of people heading to Town Hall, where she'd have to listen to "In Flanders Field" and try not to cry in public.

And then "Taps."

It seemed to Ruby like the whole world stopped to be sad for that. Even little kids and babies. She imagined the haunting notes rising up to the Heaven Grandma Jenny believed in. Maybe the men and boys who'd lived in Addison County and died in Flanders Field and Afghanistan waited every year to hear the beautiful lonely sound of Davy LaSalle's trumpet. Uncle Robbie had been just nineteen.

All she could remember of him was bouncing on his shoulders.

"Hazel!" It was Jess's mom, tugging Tyler behind her, a lollipop in his mouth.

"I forgot to say about the cookout. Come about five?"

Tyler popped the lollipop out, jiggling from foot to foot. "Mommy!"

Lydie gave Ruby a quick hug. "I better go! Tyler can only hold it for so long."

When she was out of earshot, Wally said, "Five is my busiest time."

Hazel got in his path so he had to stop. "She's my only town friend. Be a good sport and do it for me. You know full well Henry can handle everything."

"I'm not in the mood for another rant about gun-safety laws."

Ruby hated when they argued about guns.

"Well, you signed that petition for background checks."

"Yeah, and when he was at Miller's Feed getting dog food for those monsters of theirs, he thanked me right in front of Jonas Miller."

"Oh no!" Hazel said. "You've been outed as a peace-loving hippie!"

Wally laughed. "You've lured me over with your crunchy granola."

They found Cooper playing tag on the green. When they got to him, Wally took out his handkerchief. "I guess you didn't throw out *all* the tootsie rolls," he teased, wiping chocolate from Cooper's face.

"I just had four."

Ruby raised her eyebrows.

"Maybe six. We got coupons for CO-OP creemees!" Memorial Day was opening day at the creemee stand. "Can Seth come home with us? His mom said okay."

"We're going to Jess's later for a cookout," Ruby said.

"Do I have to? Tyler will want me to play cars."

"You like cars," Ruby said.

"They're baby cars."

"If I have to go, you have to," Wally said.

"Daddy!" Ruby objected.

"I can stay with Grandpa," Cooper said.

"No, you can't," Hazel said. "Seth can come and we'll drop him off later on the way to the cookout, but we're staying for the ceremonies first."

Cooper flung his arms around Hazel's waist. "Thanks, Mom! We'll go to the playground! You can pick us up after," he added hopefully.

"You'll stay with us and pay respect." Wally pointed to the plaque in front of Town Hall. "A lot of people died defending our rights, including your own un—"

"I *know.* Uncle Robbie's name is there," Cooper interrupted. He looked over at Seth, waiting at the gazebo. "I never knew him," he mumbled.

"What's that?" their dad asked. But he wasn't asking.

"Yes, sir," Cooper said.

Wally ruffled Cooper's hair. "Go get Seth. After the ceremonies we can get cremees."

"Yes, sir!" Cooper grinned and took off. "Seth, they said okay! And we can get a creemee!"

Wally put his arm around Hazel. "He's a good kid," he said.

She went up on her toes and whispered in his ear. "Want to know a secret?"

"Sure."

"I'm in love with his father."

Ruby groaned. So embarrassing!

She smiled.

She loved Memorial Day.

Chapter 5

Lemon Fair Links

This month's appeal is for the Frank and Ellie Lucas family on Quarry Hill Road, who were burned out of their home last week and are staying with relatives. They've lost almost everything. You can pick up a list of their immediate needs at the library or Paulsen's Market, and drop off your donations at the school. Sally is size 2, but Ricky, size 12, and Fran, size 10, would enjoy getting gift certificates to choose some things themselves.

And a reminder: Our salamander neighbors are migrating, so keep a lookout for people near Lemon Fair River who are helping them cross at night.

Hazel pressed SEND. She'd taken over Links in the local paper from Jenny back in October, just a few weeks before she died. She liked how it made her feel connected and useful, but it often made her sad. She kept imagining Frank and Ellie—and the kids—being struck, over and over throughout the next year, by the absence of things they couldn't replace, like their baby and wedding pictures or a special picture book or stuffed animal or blanket. She thought of the marked-up cookbook Jenny got as a wedding shower present half a century ago and Wally's one-eared elephant from when he was a little boy. And the letter Robbie wrote to be sent to Wally if he died in Afghanistan. Or her old English papers she'd saved, in case one day they'd spark a novel.

Hazel had gone to Burlington Wednesday for a state library meeting that happened to be at her old high school. Walking down the hallway she'd felt diminished, like her life was smaller than she'd thought it would be. Her whole world used to be rocked by what happened there, or even what she just imagined might happen. She vividly remembered carrying on at lunch about whether Tommy Laduc would invite her to the winter carnival dance and then going to history class and finding out about the internment of Japanese Americans during World War II. Everything skidded to a halt. Or she thought it should have.

Back then, everything—anything—was still possible: what brave thing she might do, what distant land she might go to and how she'd make people's lives there better, the important book she might write. And of course she would live forever, and so, too, would her yet-to-be-found lean but hunky husband—not Tommy Laduc, who was just a placeholder—and her so-beloved beautiful children, one of each, a boy and a girl. She'd gotten the lean and hunky husband and the two kids, but the only thing she wrote anymore was "Lemon Fair Links."

The night before, they'd watched Ruby, all dressed up and solemn, graduate from the same elementary school Wally and his father had. How they'd missed Jenny! Hazel missed her every day, and lately, planting out the seedlings that she'd started inside like Jenny always did, she needed her. Hazel was always the apprentice and Jenny the master gardener. And it was still Jenny's garden, every morsel of dirt, every slug, worm, butterfly, and bee.

And snakes! Early that morning an innocent garden snake had done such a good job being invisible that she'd stepped right up to it, then leaped away, right on top of the tomato seedlings she'd just tucked in. When she'd looked back, the snake was gone. But where?

Jenny said gardens were blessed when snakes come to them, so Hazel had stood there a long time, trying to think welcoming thoughts—Jenny thoughts—while her toes curled inside of her Crocs.

She was trying to cultivate the joy Jenny felt every spring, but the plants and animals must be worried. She was worried—that the broccoli and Brussels sprouts and cabbages and all their little plant cousins wouldn't thrive, wouldn't reach their full potential, might even go into mourning when they realized that Jenny wasn't going to show up. And that the darn snake wouldn't return to bless them.

Maybe she should read them a poem, like Toad did in *Frog and Toad Together.* Or sing the lullaby that Jenny sang to Ruby and Cooper when they were small. The other day she'd overheard Cooper singing it to his calf. "Cowboy Bill, Cowboy Bill, shiny black pony too-oo, I saw you go riding over the hill, I wish I could ride with you."

Hazel closed her laptop and blinked and blinked to keep from crying, and failed. It seemed like she was on the brink of tears a lot lately.

It wasn't just missing Jenny. It was feeling like a phony. She *was* a phony. She didn't know how to be a farmer's wife. Jenny was the farmer's wife on this farm, and Hazel had gotten to go along in her wake, doing a bit of this and a bit of that, but never seriously taking it on. So here she was, bumbling around, bluffing. And she was a snob, too, trying to hang onto some city-girl writer persona with Links. Which had also been Jenny's baby.

She pushed off with her foot, making the chains attaching the swing to the porch ceiling creak. Every once in a while, Wally would say he'd oil it, but Hazel never reminded him. The swing's voice was as much a part of the farm as the haunting voices of the mourning doves and the horny bullfrogs and the spring peepers and the calves and their mothers and Cooper and Ruby. She pulled up her T-shirt and wiped her cheeks. How would it go with Cooper and his Jenny? She hoped Ruby wouldn't be too bossy, or worse, do everything for him when he didn't do it her way.

And Ruby. Hazel had found herself standing over the sink two nights ago, scrubbing at the crusted tuna casserole dish and sobbing, remembering Ruby turning around on the step of the school bus to wave goodbye on her first day of kindergarten, wearing her checked pink and white seersucker dress that Jenny had made and new sneakers that blinked at the heels. Her dark hair stuck out in stiff braids ending in pink bows. When she'd returned at the end of the day, her ribbons and shoelaces were untied. She was clutching "homework, Mommy!" There was a smudge of green paint on her forehead as if she'd been baptized or given a third eye. Hazel pretended she was thrilled as Ruby told about her big day out in the world, where she, Hazel, had no control and would have to depend on others to stop her baby if she ran toward the edge of it like Holden imagined Phoebe doing in *The Catcher in the Rye.*

Find five things that start with the letter A. "Abidail does, right Mommy?" as she held up her doll. It took Ruby five minutes, and then she fell asleep against Rowsby on his bed under the kitchen table after tucking her list into her backpack. For her teacher. Up to then everything she'd made had been for them.

Standing at the sink scrubbing, Hazel tried to remember. Abigail and apple and apron…

Jenny had once shared how she'd cried over the dishes the day before Wally went to the university. Just an hour away. But still. Probably generations of women had wept over dishes or while hanging up laundry or scrubbing a floor, doing their other job of letting go at the same time. Women were good at multitasking.

BANG!

Hazel jumped.

Turkey season.

Cooper had been nagging about going to deer camp, but at least Wally said no, not until he'd done hunter safety. When Ruby first heard about deer camp she begged to go. She thought it was a place kids fed and petted deer. How could her gentle father kill a deer? She'd refused to do hunter safety, and secretly Hazel was glad.

Suddenly lonely, she jumped up to go and find Wally. Skirting the house, Hazel heard the buzz of the chainsaw in the woodlot. Henry would be cutting firewood for next year's sugaring. He spent too much time alone and brooding. She detoured through the barn to say hello to Jenny. The little calf teetered over, and Hazel stroked behind her velvety ears. Jenny looked up at her. Those eyes! So sweet.

Jenny was lonesome too.

Hazel slid the gate open and got down and pulled Jenny onto her lap. So soft. She was rewarded with a soft moo—Ruby called them coo-moos—followed by a rough lick on her arm. She rubbed her cheek against the calf's soft face.

"You are *so sweet*."

Just then Rowsby entered the barn and walked stiffly and oh-so-slowly down the aisle. He had arthritis. The vet said to keep him moving, but Rowsby didn't like moving. At least he'd gotten over avoiding the new barn. Wally thought it had been the carpenters bringing their dogs. Every one of the workers had a dog. It was as if when anybody bought a truck a dog came with it, like an add-on.

Rowsby and the calf stared at each other.

"Rowsby, have you met Jenny?" Would the name be confusing?

But Rowsby wagged his tail and plopped down next to the box.

She moved Jenny off her lap and stepped out of the pen.

"You're in charge, Rowsby. Tell Jenny all about the farm!"

She glanced back from the doorway. Their eyes had followed her, and their expressions were exactly the same, like she'd abandoned them.

"Make friends!"

She took the path along the edge of the woods and stopped to watch the chickens pecking around their summer coop. They were in their third year of "free range," the chicken poop fertilizing the fields as the coop got moved around, but they'd lost one named Amelia Bedelia the week before to a fox. Jenny had never named the chickens. She said naming a creature gave it a place in your heart, and life brought enough heartbreak without adding chickens. She was right, but now it was too late. Ruby had named every baby born that spring after a character in a book.

Hazel walked along the alfalfa field, fuzzy with green buds, breathing in deeply, like she'd been starving for chlorophyll. She ducked into the woods and walked along the path. She stepped into the clearing and blinked, dazzled. The trillium blossoms glowed against their dark leaves. Jenny's stars. And Wally was just where she'd pictured him, sitting with his back against the big oak that had been there for generations of Browns to lean on.

He'd been crying.

She'd seen Wally cry when the kids were born and when those men in their stiff uniforms came about Robbie. When Jenny died, he'd kept it private, going off like an injured animal.

"Hey, there."

"Hey."

She picked her way, careful not to crush any blossoms. When she got across the glade she sat down and leaned her back against his knees. He wrapped his arms around her. He smelled like the barn, but she liked it.

"I've been checking every day for them to open," he said.

"I'll bet your dad has too." She imagined each of them sneaking off as if the trillium was their own private secret.

"I miss her almost more here, but it's a better kind of missing. But it's also...Ruby graduating. She's growing up."

BANG!

Hazel stiffened and sat up.

"It's not fair! Spring *finally* comes and our children can't be free on their own land! I wish you'd post it!" It was her old complaint, and it was like talking to a wall. Or a Vermont farmer.

"We'd still keep the cows and kids from being in the high meadow during hunting."

The cows and kids, she thought, as if they were the same. Except the cows came first.

BANG!

"Well, I wish Arnold was a better shot and would get his dumb turkey! Maybe when Ruby and I are in town we can pick one up at the supermarket and drop it off. Betty might like not having to pluck it and all." Then she felt terrible. It was Jenny who'd done "pluck it and all" at their house.

"Might be Remy shooting."

"Remy!"

"He's thirteen. I got my first turkey when I was ten."

"I don't want Cooper—"

"Cooper will be fine," Wally said. "And it's his right."

"What kind of right is it to kill something!"

"Hazel. Stop." Wally sighed. "Do we have to do this now?"

"I'm sorry. Sometimes I just get…" She leaned back against him. "I'm sorry. I miss your mom too."

"Sometimes I talk to her."

"She's probably mending angel wings and watching us all. But I'm worried about your dad. Do you think he's depressed? It can happen with grief. He forgot to feed Rowsby on Saturday."

"How do you know?"

"Rowsby told me."

She felt his laugh through her back, and was abruptly happy.

BANG!

I'm such a sissy hypocrite, Hazel thought. Isn't it better for a turkey to have a free life and have it end under a beautiful sky? And deer, too. She was proud that their meat came from their own cows and chickens and what her own husband brought home, and not from some awful factory.

Wally pulled her scrunchy out and ran his hand up her neck and under her hair.

She turned and kissed his neck. Salt and sweat. She nosed in like the calf, and turned around until she could wrap her legs around him.

Like old times when they still shared the house with his parents and snuck off to the sugarhouse or the high meadow, and even the hammock that time. And still did, now and again. She pulled his T-shirt off over his head, and then her own.

Summer

Lime green shorts
Bathing suit – 2 piece!!
T – shirts – pink, yellow, lime green
flip flops
Tisha - Ben and Jerry T-shirt
Ruby Bridges biography
Glow sticks
Flashlight batteries

Chapter 6

COOPER DUG IN HIS heels as Jenny grabbed on and gulped; milk dribbled down his hand. It was just seconds before the calf finished and the nipple popped out of her mouth. She licked his hand. She was always sucking and licking and nibbling at him. He liked it.

He picked up the brush gingerly. His palm was still tender from the splinter Grandpa took out. Rowsby nosed the brush as if to get him started. Next to eating, brushing was Jenny's favorite thing.

"Rowsby's old," he told her, moving the brush in a circle over her side. "Older than Grandpa in a dog's years, almost a hundred." What were cow years?

Jenny turned her head to study Rowsby, as if to see what a hundred years looked like.

"You're named after my grandma. She died. She—me and her—we played UNO all the time. That's a card game. And puzzles. We did a puzzle of Vermont with a thousand pieces. She made all the birthday cakes. I had a baseball cake last year. I mean, when I was six. Now I'm seven. How she did it was three round cakes stacked up and vanilla frosting and red licorice cut up for the stitches."

This year he had cupcakes his mom made from a mix.

He moved the brush to Jenny's neck.

"Ruby graduated. Grandpa gave her a rose, a *bought* one! Red for Ruby, he said, from Grandma." Did Grandma tell him to do that before she died? He couldn't ask.

He searched for something happy to talk about, brushing around and down, around and down, thoughts tumbling. But he'd been keeping Jenny pretty up to date. The parade, his last game, did that turtle lay her eggs yet, stacking wood and the splinter.

"Seth is coming over today. And my dad—you know, Wally—we're gonna build a pen outside for you!" Jenny hadn't been outside or seen his house or the pond, or anything. It was like she'd been in jail her whole life so far.

"Seth has a crow named Truman Whitby. The crow has a cage, but he doesn't use it except for sleeping. He collects shiny things. He took Seth's sister's ring and it's still lost! Seth lives in a house that was a church. It has a high ceiling and Truman Whitby likes to fly up there. Seth's bedroom is where the choir sang. There's a round colored window. Mom sings in our choir but there's not a special place."

He crawled to Jenny's other side. She moved too.

"No. You stay, *I* move."

He tried walking backwards, but she still followed.

"Jenny! Stay!"

She tugged at the bottom of his T-shirt and he fell into Rowsby. Jenny went down on her front knees and then her back ones and stretched out next to him. She nuzzled his face. Cooper laughed.

"Oh, Jenny." He lay on his back between Jenny and Rowsby and watched a swallow dart through the window, landing on the rafter next to her nest. She hopped up and disappeared. Strands of straw drifted down. How many babies? He'd found one of the eggs broken on the ground, its insides eaten out.

Pretty soon they'd be ready to fly on their own. It worried him.

"Falling, they'll learn to fly," Grandpa said.

But what if they fall too fast? One time his mom tried to save a baby robin, but it died. And Ruby found baby rabbits that died. Mom said a fox must've gotten their mother, or maybe Rowsby.

He was sure it wasn't Rowsby.

"Want to hear a joke? What do you call a rabbit with fleas?"

Jenny cocked her head.

"Bugs Bunny!"

Jenny licked his neck.

"Mom braided Ruby's hair with a ribbon for graduation. It was pretty. Ruby said she'd braid your tail for the fair."

Jenny's eyelashes tickled. Taking care of her would be fun if he didn't feel bad that she couldn't be with her mother. If he couldn't be with his mom, he'd feel awful! He scrambled up and took down his clipboard with his list.

Fresh straw. Check. Clean bucket. Check. Fresh water, clean trough, fresh grass. Check. Wipe ears, nose, mouth. Wipe butt. Clean and brush coat. Check, check, check.

Ounces of milk: 24.

Halter, lead rope.

The halter was easy for Grandpa. He just held Jenny's head with one hand and slipped the loop over her chin and the other loop over her ears with his other hand. After three days, it had been Cooper's turn. Jenny had shaken her head, and her ears went every which way, but Grandpa held her, and Cooper finally got the halter on. He'd rewarded her with a chunk of apple.

But today he was on his own. He took down the halter.

Jenny rolled her eyes and shook her head.

"Come on, you know it doesn't hurt!" He reached into his pocket for a piece of apple. "Apple, Jenny! Apple, Rowsby!"

Rowsby got to his feet. Rowsby didn't like apples, but Jenny didn't know that.

She looked from the apple to Rowsby. She staggered up, and then got her footing.

Cooper held the halter behind his back. "Good girl!" When she reached for the apple, he moved to pin her between his legs.

But Jenny ducked, and stumbled to the other side of the pen.

"Aw, Jenny! You have to learn this, or we can't go to the fair!"

He approached her with his arms out wide. But she ducked under again. They did this again, and again, and on the fourth round, Rowsby jumped into the game, ducking and running from side to side with Jenny. At least Rowsby was getting some exercise.

In the end, Cooper lunged and held Jenny down by lying on top of her and, with a lot of head shaking and struggling on both their parts, finally got the halter on. Cooper leaned against Rowsby, breathing hard, and took a time out.

Because they weren't done yet.

For the time being, the lead rope was Rowsby's leash. Cooper held it out and Rowsby took it in his mouth the way he did when there was a "leash law" somewhere. Rowsby stepped out of the pen and Jenny followed him, not to be left out.

"Good boy, Rowsby!"

Cooper clipped the leash to Jenny's halter, and she took it in her mouth just like her friend did. Then Rowsby led the way down the aisle of the empty barn, Cooper and Jenny behind him.

"Coo-per!" Ruby stepped through the far door. "Mom says get ready for church!"

"I'm staying home with Dad!"

"He's coming! Remember? Mom's singing." Ruby walked toward them. "Is that Rowsby's leash in Jenny's mouth!? That's so cute!"

"Rowsby showed her how. This way I don't have to tug."

"What do you mean?" Ruby stooped and stroked behind Jenny's ears. Jenny dropped the leash and leaned into Ruby's hand.

"At the fair."

"Well, you'll still have to lead her."

"No I won't. Jenny follows me!"

"Cooper, it's the rule. And besides, she could take it into her head to follow another calf, or she might get spooked." Ruby picked up the end of the leash and handed it to him. "Show me."

Cooper walked forward, pulled, and Jenny dug in her heels.

"See?"

"Give her a push."

He went behind her and pushed.

She bent her knees. Her backside followed, and she was down.

"See!"

Rowsby plopped down next to her.

Ruby laughed.

"It's not funny! Why will she follow me without it, and not with it?"

"Jenny's a herd animal. And you and Rowsby are her herd. She feels safe following you. That's where she thinks she belongs. But the lead is confusing her. It's always that way with calves, not just Jenny. Maple was the same. It just takes practice." Ruby petted Jenny's neck. "She's plenty smart, that's for sure!"

Cooper sighed and unclipped the leash. "C'mon, Jenny." And she followed him into the pen as easy as pie. He hugged her.

"You did fine, Jenny."

Rowsby watched Cooper and Ruby disappear through the big door. Cooper hadn't closed the gate latch, so he nosed it down.

Jenny studied every move.

~

Ruby loved their church. She loved the creak of the old pews and the smells of furniture and candle wax. She loved how the stained-glass window burst into color when the sun came out. When that happened, she felt like she believed in something. Her father didn't believe. Not in God. He believed in people. Her mother said she didn't know about God, but she believed in prayer.

"But who do you pray *to*?" Ruby asked.

"It doesn't matter," her mother answered. "It's the praying that matters."

But it mattered to Ruby. She'd never been able to pray to Jesus, like Grandma Jenny. Being the son of God didn't make you God. If there even was God. How could Jesus be God's son when he was Joseph's? It was like Joseph was made to be a stepdad.

Her grandmother had been Ruby's first Sunday school teacher. Ruby had especially loved hearing the story of Noah and making animals for the felt board. She'd made more than two cows, though, because how could she leave the rest behind?

Grandpa didn't come to church anymore; it made him feel lonesome. But when Ruby was in church it was easy to think her grandma might be close by, watching over them. And she'd be happy to see Grandpa and Daddy there today. They'd come because her mother was singing a solo. Ruby felt nervous for her mom.

The choir rustled to the front like a flock of bluebirds, their silky robes drifting around them. Mr. Lundrigen lifted his arms. Her mother stepped forward.

"Amazing grace! How sweet the sound
That saved a wretch like me
I once was lost but now am found
Was blind but now I see."

Ruby loved the word "wretch," imagining herself in a patched dress with a pocket hanging off and high-top shoes like Anne of Green Gables. But no laces.

And here came her other favorite part—

"When we've been here ten thousand years, bright shining as the sun."

Her heart seemed to rise, and her eyes stung as she met Jesus's sad eyes in the stained-glass window.

She felt Grandpa's rough fingers on her knee and looked at him, surprised. Tears were streaming down his cheeks. She leaned against him, but then away. Even in his good clothes he smelled like something sweet and sour that stung her nose. She thought it might be whiskey.

She still hadn't told anyone about the sheriff and that day on the bus, and she hoped she would never have to.

Pastor Lori went to the pulpit.

"'Amazing grace! How sweet the sound! I once was lost but now am found.' Such wonderful words! *Amazing* words." Pastor Lori said it again, whispering. "Amazing words." Her gaze traveled over them and for a second it touched down on Ruby.

Pastor Lori sometimes called them her flock. Ruby had imagined them all wearing bonnets and little vests like in Beatrix Potter, with little gray goslings running around under the pews, pecking at their feet. Her toenail polish would look like berries.

"The man who wrote those amazing words was John Newton. He was an English ship captain, sailing from Africa to the Americas, and you can guess what his cargo was."

Ruby tried to guess. Was it drums, like the ones sold at the International Craft Fair in Burlington?

"Human beings. Human beings like you and me and everyone we love."

Ruby flushed with mortification. So stupid! How could she have thought it was drums?

Pastor Lori continued. "Babies. Little children. Children just coming into their teens. Mothers. Fathers. Grandfathers and grandmothers, sisters and brothers. Packed against each other in darkness in the bottom of a rocking, stinking ship and not knowing where it was going. John Newton was a businessman, and the more people he could cram into his hold, the more profit for him. They were merchandise, like livestock. Except we treat our livestock more humanely."

Ruby thought of the lady who spit at Ruby Bridges.

"One day his ship nearly sank in a storm. Fear brought him to his knees, and he called out to God to save him and all the souls aboard! And they survived. When he became a minister many years later, he realized the horror he'd been inflicting on those souls at the very same time he was praying for their safe passage. He joined the fight to end slavery, and the Slave Trade Act was passed in England in 1807, the year he died."

Pastor Lori held up a hymnal.

"Some say 'Amazing Grace' is John Newton's prayer for forgiveness. When he'd called out to God to save the souls on his ship during that storm, they'd lived, but to be enslaved. Did he deserve forgiveness?"

Ruby Bridges' mother had told her to pray for the horrible people who spit and said awful things. One lady even yelled that she was going to poison her, and Ruby Bridges was scared to eat at school. Did she pray for *her*?

Maybe it wasn't John Newton's prayer that made him see, Ruby thought. Maybe it wasn't John Newton's prayer that made him want to stop slavery. Maybe it was somebody down below in that ship in chains who, like Ruby Bridges, prayed for her enemies. Maybe it was somebody like her father, who believed in the goodness of people. Maybe it was someone who prayed without it mattering who she prayed to, like her mom. Maybe it was the praying that mattered.

Pastor Lori smiled. "We all have good in us. We all have bad. We all have been blind and will be again. When, with God's amazing grace, you are given the eyes to see the wrongs in your world, be they injustices, ignorance, or just plain meanness, you must pray, and then do what you can. Once you see, you cannot turn away. You are my flock! I expect you to speak out! I expect you to act!" She stepped out from behind the pulpit. Light from Jesus's window lit her from behind.

Like an angel, Ruby thought.

"There's a quote from Margaret Mead on the wall in the Sunday school," Pastor Lori continued. "Her work as an anthropologist supported the idea that all human beings share an underlying humanity. She said, 'Never doubt that a small group of thoughtful, committed citizens can change the world; indeed, it is the only thing that ever has.'"

Pastor Lori lifted her arms. "And now, may the peace which passeth understanding, the peace of God, which the world can neither give nor take away, be among us, and abide in our hearts."

Ruby loved that.

US Forest Service
1400 Independence Avenue SW
Washington, D.C.

June 10

Dear Sir or Madam,

My school was supposed to go on a hike but it was cancelled because the trail goes by a gravel pit where people target shoot. My grandfather said the land belongs to the public, but you make the rules. I think there should be a rule against shooting near places where children go for recreation or education. People need a permit to cut down a Christmas tree in the Green Mountain National Forest, but they don't need a permit to shoot there. That isn't right. My pastor said if we see something wrong we need to pray and do something, so I prayed and now I am writing to you, and now you see too and should do something.

Yours truly,
Ruby Brown
Lemon Fair, Vermont

P.S. You can pray if you want. It might help you never know.

Chapter 7

Lemon Fair Links
This week's appeal is for the Lane family, whose four-year-old Sally needs a bone marrow transplant at Boston Children's Hospital. There will be a potluck and contra dance at the Grange Hall Saturday, July 11th, at 5 pm, suggested donation $5 a person, children under five free. Please come, and bring a dish and a card for Sally! (She likes foxes!)

Hazel pressed SEND and went to find Ruby. They were meeting the Fresh Air bus in an hour and welcoming Latisha back for her fourth year.

She couldn't even imagine how Evan and Susan Lane were handling it. Sally was only four years old! It made her want to grab Cooper and Ruby and examine every inch of them.

Before hearing about the Lanes, she'd been counting her blessings, which were surprisingly many that almost–Fourth of July. After they'd worked at it for four years their farm was certified organic, and it felt good. Even the grass seemed happy, and the chickens seemed excited to be eating it, though how do you know, with chickens, when they were so nervous-acting? She was sure they knew she felt skittish around them and went after her toes on purpose, especially the one called Matilda. She should be renamed Attila.

But the garden! So far, the vegetables weren't holding Jenny's absence against her, and even the kids were doing their due diligence, weeding their rows with minimal complaining. She'd have kale and early peas to sell alongside Ruby's eggs at the farmers' market, and a sprinkling of radishes to pretty the table up. Ruby had helped Cooper make two rhubarb pies to sell, money toward his new lead for the calf. He finally had a pet of his own! How many barn cats had he tried to bring into the house, only to get scratched before they took the first opportunity to escape. Cooper sang and talked to the calf constantly and she talked back in the sweetest voice, like a mourning dove's. A couple of nights ago they'd been sitting at the table over rhubarb pie and heard Jenny and Rowsby at the back door. They'd come for dessert. And they got some, too, though Jenny really shouldn't be rewarded for getting out of her pen.

Was that the phone?

"Hazel, are you there? *Please, please* be there!"

It was Jess's mom, Lydie. She sounded like she was crying.

"Oh, God! I can't *do* this on a message!"

Hazel dashed back to the kitchen and picked up the phone.

"Lydie? What's wrong?"

"Oh, Hazel! Oh, God!"

But then she was silent.

"Lydie?"

"Listen, can you have the kids for a couple of days? I know it's terrible timing, with Tisha coming, and the Fourth, but...Jess wants to stay here, and...I can't take Tyler, I—"

"Lydie, what's wrong? But of course they can stay, Tyler can have Ruby's room. She has the tent up for Tisha coming."

"We have to go up to St. Albans. It's my nephew Peter, my brother's—Oh, God! Hazel!" Lydie began to cry. "Oh, God, Hazel! He shot himself!"

Hazel gasped. "Will he—"

"He's dead! He's just sixteen!"

Hazel groped for a chair. "What have you told them?" She fell onto the seat. "Uh huh. No, I think that makes sense."

She jumped up and started pacing. "I won't say anything to Cooper, then. Oh, Lydie, how can anybody *bear* something like this? I can't imagine!"

She went to the door. "No, no. It's the *least* I can do, I wish I could do more. Just take care of yourself and Jack, and we'll take care of Tyler and Jess. Please try not to worry about them. I'm so, so sorry."

She hung up and covered her mouth.

She walked outside. The house was too small for such a thing.

She remembered how she'd tiptoed around with Ruby after Robbie was killed, and when it became too much, quietly snuck outside to look at the sky. The sky seemed big enough to hold it all.

And Ruby laughing and growing, new words every day, but feeling like she needed to hide it. Ruby learned to climb up to the counter and open cupboards those first awful weeks and Hazel had child-proofed the whole downstairs behind their backs without any of them noticing, keeping her head down until they began to get used to living with their lives torn apart.

But that was a war.

Sixteen.

How did anyone get over that?

They didn't.

Stupid *stupid* guns!

~

The Fourth of July was coming to a close. Ruby stepped outside, careful not to slam the door while trying to keep the lemonade from spilling over. Lights were on at her grandfather's. She hoped Rowsby was keeping him company, but lately the dog had been sleeping with Jenny. Everyone thought it was cute. They thought Cooper was cute too.

She felt strange around her grandfather, and it wasn't just her feeling that way—he was acting different. He'd been avoiding the whole family, and not eating supper with them. When she dropped off a plate for him it was like he was impatient for her to leave. And he'd called her Jenny more than once. It made her feel like he didn't see her. It made her sad.

The grass was wet with evening dew and stuck to her bare feet. Her toes glittered like little jewels. Tisha had bought a half-used bottle of silver nail polish at the Humane Society's tag sale and she and Jess and Tisha had polished each other's toenails at Cooper's baseball game, but they ran out before getting to their fingers. Then they did the races and Jess won the sack race like she did every year. Ruby was glad, because it made it seem like a regular Fourth of July.

Was Jess missing her mom and dad? Tyler had cried, so Hazel took him into their bed, and Cooper got jealous, so he ended up there too, so her dad went upstairs to sleep in Ruby's room. She was glad she could escape to the tent.

Peter's funeral was tomorrow. She hadn't asked Jess anything, just hugged her. She didn't know what to say anyway. Did Peter *know*, just before? Was there a time *in between*, when he *knew*? Did he want his mom? Ruby looked at the sky, crowded with stars. How could God let it happen? But maybe there wasn't any God, maybe there was nothing. What was it like not to *be*? Was Peter just...*erased*? She shivered.

Jess used to say stars were souls who'd died and were waiting to be born again. Did she still think that?

Maybe one of those stars was Peter.

It was an accident, so maybe it was fast, not like those kids in the schools. *Shooting gallery.* She stumbled and lemonade spilled out.

Jess and Tisha had moved the lawn chairs to face the pond as if they were on a beach. The plate of Rice Krispie bars was on the ground, only one left. Ruby came up behind them.

"More lemonade," she said.

They whipped their heads around. "SHHH!"

"What?"

"A skunk!" Tisha whispered.

Then Ruby saw it, meandering along by the water's edge; its white stripes seemed to be glowing. "It smells your Rice Krispie breath," she said.

Tisha slapped a hand over her mouth.

"She's teasing," Jess said. But she moved the plate away.

Ruby handed them their cups and sank into her chair. "It can't see you. They're practically blind."

"You sure?" Tisha asked.

Ruby wasn't, not totally, but said anyway, "Blind as a bat!" She kept her eye on the skunk until it was halfway around the pond.

"Is Tyler asleep?" Jess asked.

"Sound asleep, like a bug in a rug."

"He's cute as a bug," Tisha said.

"He's annoying as a bug," Jess said. "Brothers!"

Ruby glanced at Tisha. Would she say anything?

"I have a brother, he's fifteen." Tisha cleared her throat. "He's a paraplegic."

"You mean...he can't walk?" Jess asked.

"He's paralyzed from his waist down."

"Why?" Jess asked.

Jess always just went ahead and asked when Ruby wouldn't.

"It happened when he was my age. An older boy found a gun and was aiming it around the park and it was loaded."

Jess gasped.

"Lots of people have guns. They put a metal detector in school," Tisha added.

"Aren't you scared?" Jess asked.

"Sure, but...at least they can't bring them *into* school."

"What happened to the boy who shot the gun?" Jess asked.

"He was just sixteen but got sent to prison upstate. His mom is an aide at my school. She visits him for holidays."

"Just holidays?" Ruby asked.

"It takes six hours each way on the bus, for just an hour visit. His sister only saw him twice since it happened, even though kids are half price."

"They make them *pay* to see him?" Ruby was outraged.

"No, the *bus*. The bus is half price."

Ruby hadn't known about the boy. She'd never even wondered.

"If I tell you something, do you promise not to tell?" Jess whispered.

They leaned in.

"Pinky promise."

They hooked their fingers together.

"Peter wasn't cleaning his deer rifle. It was my uncle's. A handgun. He did it in the woods. On purpose." Jess began to cry. "In his head!"

Ruby wanted to cover her ears. But it was too late. She got up and squished next to Jess. Jess started sobbing, her face on her knees. "Why *would* he?"

Ruby wished her mom was there. She'd know what to do.

Who *found* him?

Jess had known about Peter the whole day.

The whole day—all Fourth of July—Jess would've been thinking about it.

Watching the parade. Making s'mores. Doing their nails. While Tyler and Cooper ran around with glow sticks that looked like darting fireflies. Passing around Skittles, the taste of mosquito repellent on their tongues, and then the fireworks, her favorite part, and all the time...

"I should've *gone*," Jess wailed.

Ruby thought of her grandma's funeral. Her grandpa cried. Her mom cried and that made Cooper cry and then she cried. It was horrible. But she would have felt worse if she hadn't gone.

Tisha jumped up. "We can do a funeral! We can sing, and I know a Bible verse. Each of us can say a few words. Then we'll have a moment of silence."

Jess straightened up. She wiped her face and blew her nose into a red, white, and blue napkin.

"I know where." Ruby led them across the grass to the weeping willow, where she and Cooper had their funerals. Their cat Fitz, who lost a leg from a combine but lived to die of old age, was buried there, and at least three barn cats. And her turtle, Rosie, her place marked by the rock she used to climb up on. And the baby rabbits that Rowsby dug out of their nest and hurt so badly her dad had to kill them. She never let on that she knew, but she shut Rowsby in the house during the burial.

Ruby joined hands with Jess and Tisha. The grazing cows in the low meadow seemed to be bowing their heads too. The pond sparkled with reflected stars. Maybe Heaven was like this, Ruby thought. Nothing could be more beautiful. Maybe going to Heaven was like walking on water like Jesus. Walking from star to star like stepping stones. She liked that better than souls waiting to be born.

But she didn't know a few words. She squeezed Jess's hand, wishing she knew poems like her grandfather. Then Tisha began to speak, and Ruby recognized the words. She'd heard them at church.

"The Lord is my shepherd, I shall not want, he maketh me to lie down in green pastures, he leadeth me beside the still waters, he restoreth my soul, he leadeth me in the paths of righteousness for his name's sake. Yea, though I walk through the valley of the shadow of death, I will fear no evil, for thou art with me, thy rod and thy staff they comfort me. Thou prepareth a table before me in the presence of mine enemies, thou anointest my head with oil, my cup runneth over."

Ruby loved the last part.

"Surely goodness and mercy shall follow me all the days of my life, and I will dwell in the house of the Lord forever."

Then Tisha sailed right into a song.

"Amazing grace, how sweet the sound that saved a wretch like me."

The words had new meaning for Ruby. Wretch was real. It was her friend. It was Jess's family and Peter's family and Tisha's brother, and it was the boy in jail and his family.

It was her Uncle Robbie and her grandfather and her father.

"I once was lost and now am found, was blind…" Tisha stopped and pointed. She took two steps back.

The skunk had made its way back around to their side of the pond.

Jess snorted. "Oh, God! 'Was blind! Was blind!'"

"Stop it!" Tisha hissed. Ruby and Jess collapsed against each other, trying to muffle their laughter.

Then Tisha stood over them, her hands on her hips. "I'll never take you two to another funeral, that's for sure!"

Ruby and Jess shrieked.

"Oh, God! I'm going to pee my pants!" Jess gasped.

Finally, they all lay on the grass looking up into the tree. The long, drooping branches swayed, and starlight popped in and out between the leaves.

"It looks like fairies live there," Tisha said.

"For fragrant air and cooling breeze, for beauty of the blooming trees: Giver of all, we thank you," Ruby said.

"What's that?" Tisha asked.

"It's from a song we sang at my grandma's funeral," Ruby said. "She used to sing it."

"Do you think there's Heaven?" Jess asked, and sat up. She suddenly reached out and put her arms across them. "The skunk!" she whispered.

Ruby sat up.

The skunk was walking in a circle, as if it were following its own scent. Ruby frowned—and then a thought came to her. She put her finger to her lips. She motioned with her arm toward the house.

They walked backwards until Ruby grabbed their hands and took off to the dooryard. She leaned over, breathing hard. "That skunk might have rabies."

"Rabies! Don't they, like, foam at the mouth?" Jess asked.

"I'm getting Grandpa. Wait here."

When she got to the door, Ruby knocked and walked in. "Grandpa?"

She walked into the living room. He was asleep in his chair. There was that sweet and sour smell. She saw the bottle on its side. She looked for the glass. Had he spilled?

She stooped and screwed the top on the bottle. It was sticky, like lemonade.

"Grandpa, wake up. I need you." She put her hand on his shoulder. "Grandpa!" She shook him gently. His head bobbed up and down like the bobble-head in the truck. "Grandpa, wake up!"

But he didn't. He just bobbled.

Ruby suddenly felt sickened by him; he'd turned into a stranger. She wanted to shake him. "Wake up!"

Rowsby came out of the bedroom. He walked over and licked her sticky hand.

She turned. "Rowsby, stay!" When she got out of the house she ran. She found Jess and Tisha huddled under the eave outside the mudroom door.

It was easy to wake her dad up, and as soon as she said why, he headed downstairs. In his underwear! But he just waved at Jess and Tisha standing there, took his coverall off its hook and pulled it on.

Then he hoisted himself up onto the freezer and pushed back a ceiling tile. His hand came out holding a rifle.

A squeak escaped from Jess.

"It's okay, it's not loaded," Wally said. But then he took his tackle box off the shelf and took out two cartridges, shoving them into his pocket. He looked around. "Where's Rowsby?"

"At Grandpa's."

"You went there first?"

She nodded and looked away, feeling like she had a secret. "He was asleep."

Hazel came into the kitchen, holding her robe closed.

"What's going on?"

"Might be a rabid skunk," Wally said.

"Oh, is everybody—" Then she noticed the gap in the ceiling. She looked at Wally, confused. "But the guns are at your dad's."

Wally didn't meet Hazel's eyes. Instead, he stepped into his barn boots and went out the door.

Hazel walked stiffly to the counter. "We might as well have hot chocolate."

Ruby could tell by her back that she was mad.

They heard a thumpity-thump-thump, and Tyler burst into the room, saw Jess, and scrambled onto her lap. He stuck his thumb in his mouth, his eyes at half-mast.

"Why's everybody up?" Cooper asked, following, rubbing his face.

"Daddy's gone to shoot a skunk," Ruby said.

Cooper made for the door.

Hazel scooped him with her arm. "You're not going anywhere. Help Ruby get down the mugs." She poured milk into the pot.

"Can I have a marshmallow?"

"I guess just one won't hurt."

"Can Tyler?"

The sound of the shot froze them in place.

Ruby squeezed her eyes shut, waiting for another.

But what came instead was the unmistakable stink of skunk.

"He got 'im!" Cooper said.

"Jess is crying," Tyler said in a tiny voice.

Hazel turned around. "Jess? Sweetheart?"

"It's just—I thought of—" Jess pressed her chin on top of Tyler's head and pinched her lips together.

Hazel picked Tyler up and put him on his feet. "Go help Cooper put the marshmallows in the cups." She sat and put her arm around Jess. Jess cried harder.

"Come on, baby," Tisha said, taking Tyler's hand.

"What's wrong with Jess?" Cooper whispered to Ruby.

But Ruby shook her head. There were so many things wrong she wouldn't know where to start. And besides, Cooper was too young to know.

She wished she was too young. But for now, there was Tyler, watching his sister and wondering if he needed to cry too.

"Open up." She popped a marshmallow into his mouth like a pacifier.

Chapter 8

HAZEL STOOD AT THE foot of the bed watching Wally pull his T-shirt over his head.

"Can't we talk about this later?" His voice was muffled.

"You lied to me!"

"I never said I'd moved every gun."

"You never said you were keeping one in my ceiling, either! What were you thinking!"

"I was thinking about keeping my family safe."

"Safe! From what? The people breaking into our unlocked house to steal the Legos?"

"You've never seen a rabid animal. They're dangerous and unpredictable." He went to the dresser to fill his pockets, his back to her. Keys, change, knife.

Handkerchief.

Under normal circumstances it would have made her smile. "You've said that before. I'll bet they're not as dangerous and unpredictable as guns and little boys."

"He better not hear you calling him little."

"I'll call my son whatever I want!"

"I have to get to the barn."

"Of course you do! I'll be gone when you get back. But go ahead, go to your precious cows!"

"Oh, you're leaving me now?" He tried to get her to smile.

"We're going to Montpelier. Henry's taking the kids to see the statehouse and I'm having lunch with my sister. I told you!"

He put his arms around her. "I didn't forget. I was just teasing."

She shrugged him off.

"Are you crying?" He took out his handkerchief.

"It's just so...so hurtful! Why didn't you tell me the gun was there?"

"Because of this kind of thing."

She sagged onto the bed. "We don't have secrets."

"Hazel, I need you on my side in this."

"Well, I need you on *my* side!"

He sat down next to her and wiped her cheeks. "Hazel, please."

"I miss our old life. I never took in all your mom did, and how much work it was, or...and...I'm not any good at it! I wasn't raised into it like you. I feel like I'm always doing something the wrong way, or forgetting to do something."

"It's hard work, farming, I'd never deny it. And Dad. He's barely pulling his weight." He rested his chin on her head. "I guess we're the grownups now."

She leaned against him.

"Does growing up mean having a gun in the house?"

"You're like a dog with a bone." He sighed. "*Not* having a gun in the house is as unnatural to me as *having* one is to you. Do you get that? It's my job, to take care of this family, and this farm, and our life—"

"I just don't see what that has to do with guns."

"It's how this country started—clearing the land, feeding ourselves, defending our rights."

What about the people who got cleared *from* the land, who were here first, who *lost* their rights, she thought. But this wasn't the time to bring that up. She examined Wally's face. He was brown from the sun, except for his forehead. The same startling whiteness was hidden beneath his T-shirt.

"Is this about Robbie?"

He frowned. "Robbie?"

He turned his head away, the way Cooper and Rowsby did if they'd snuck something. She felt a rush of tenderness. He looked so vulnerable.

"Did he die for this country?" She hesitated. "For your rights, like the Second Amendment?" She tried to keep judgment out of her voice.

"What if—"

She could barely hear him.

"What if he died for nothing?"

She took his hand between hers and rubbed her thumb along the palm. Rough, from hard work and leaving his work gloves everywhere. "I wonder what *he* would say. What *Robbie* would say he died for. Maybe in the end we remember—have a second to know—what we love most in our life. And maybe that's what counts."

"This. He loved this."

"Like you do."

They sat silent, not saying the rest. *Like she didn't.*

He stood up. "I'll lock it up at Dad's for now, and get one of those trigger locks. But I really have to get going."

"To your precious cows."

"You're a close second, though."

"Second to a cow. What I always wanted."

~

"Jenny! And Rowsby, you know better!" But the sight of them made Ruby laugh. It was like Rowsby was bringing his friend for a playdate. Jenny pushed against her dress and licked. Calf drool.

"Oh, Jenny! And don't you give me that innocent look!" But she rubbed the calf's neck and side. Rowsby nosed her hand, wanting his share.

"I'm ready!" Cooper banged out the door. "You look pretty."

"I *did*. Look what your calf did! Go get a leftover sausage from breakfast."

With Cooper waving the sausage to entice them, they finally got Jenny and Rowsby to the outside pen, where the gate stood open.

"Oh, Cooper!"

"I didn't do it! Jenny's smart."

Ruby closed the latch. "Rowsby, you're in charge, and no shenanigans."

After changing, Ruby found her mom and Grandpa and Cooper in the car.

"We've been waiting *forever*," Cooper said.

When they got to Montpelier, Hazel dropped the three of them at the statehouse. Cooper bounded up the steps as if they were nothing, but Henry had to work to get his breath. He knew Wally wanted him to go see that new lady doctor. But even if he couldn't go uphill so good didn't mean he was going downhill. He was like the old John Deere. He just needed a tune-up, was all, an oil change. He snorted.

"What's funny?"

He jumped about a mile. Jenny had snuck up on him. She looked so pretty with her hair up in one of those...he had the word somewhere.

"Do you need help, Grandpa?"

It was Ruby.

Jenny was gone.

He wished he could go there.

"I'm not some cripple! I can get there on my own steam!"

"It's Ethan Allen!" Cooper ran up and tagged the statue by the big doors, sounding proud, like Ethan Allen was a relative of his. "He doesn't look like my book."

"Nobody knows *what* he looked like. They made him up, like Jesus," Henry said. "But he looks darn silly with his arm raised like he's waving to somebody downstreet. It's not dignified."

They followed him inside, and Cooper's mouth fell open.

"It's like a palace!"

"But it's called the people's house," Ruby said.

Cooper went to the center of the vaulted space and, arms out, began to spin.

Ruby grabbed his arm. "Stop it! We have to be dignified! What if the governor saw you?"

Cooper switched to hopping from square to square on the chessboard floor.

Henry heard sounds like whispering up under the dome. Were they voices from the past? If he stayed stock still, maybe he'd hear himself and Jenny on their high school trip.

"Grandpa, come see!" Ruby called out.

A wall was covered with words.

"It's Dorothy Canfield Fisher! She started the kids' book contest we vote in but they changed the name because she was prejudiced. Now it's called the Vermont Golden Dome Book Award after this very building!" Ruby pointed. She read out loud, "The Vermont Tradition grapples with the basic problem of human conduct, how to reconcile the needs of the group, of which every man or woman is a member... with the craving for individual freedom to be what he really is."

"I wonder if Robert Frost and this lady met. I bet they'd get along," Henry said.

"What's reconstile?" Cooper asked.

"Recon*cile.* It's like if you and Ruby have a dollar to share for a snack and she wants chips and you want candy. So she goes along with the candy but gets to choose what kind. You each lose but you each win," Henry explained.

"I'd get Butterfingers." Cooper stretched to touch a place high up on the wall. "It's Ethan Allen! What does it say?"

Henry spread his legs apart, swept an invisible hat off his head, raised his arm, and read. "I am resolutely determined to defend the independence of Vermont, as Congress are of that of the United States, and rather than fail will retire with hardy Green Mountain Boys into desolate caverns of the mountains and wage war with human nature at large!"

"Uncle Robbie was a Green Mountain soldier, Cooper," Ruby said.

"But did he? Did Ethan Allen have a war?" Cooper asked—eager, Henry knew, for the answer to be yes, and a bloody one, too.

"It was the Revolutionary War, Cooper!" Ruby said. "Remember Fort Ticonderoga and the Green Mountain Boys?"

Cooper began to skid along the floor brandishing a sword. Whoosh and whoosh.

"Ticonderoga means two waterways," Ruby said.

Cooper stopped. "It's a snail!" He dropped to his knees.

Henry leaned over. "It's an ammonite fossil. Extinct. The ancestor of a squid. See the tail? It's gotta be half a billion years old."

"Were there people then?"

"No people—or dinosaurs yet either."

"You know a lot of things, Grandpa. I bet you know almost everything!" Cooper took his hand.

"I forget some."

"That's okay, Grandpa. You still know a lot more than me."

"Everyone starts out ignorant. We'd be pretty bored otherwise. Come around the corner. I want to show you both something."

Henry lifted Cooper up. "Look for Brown. It's alphabetical."

Ruby stretched and ran her fingers over the cool marble and stopped. Robert Thomas Brown. "Is it Uncle Robbie?"

Cooper wiggled to the floor. "I don't want to be in a war."

"Then don't," Ruby said.

"Why did they drop that bomb?" Cooper asked.

But it wasn't a bomb, it was a mortar, Henry thought.

"Everybody got killed. Kids and babies. And *animals.* A whole city! They shouldn't have done that!"

Hiroshima. Cooper was talking about Hiroshima.

Last summer was the first time he and the kids had gone to the commemoration vigil with Jenny and Hazel. They'd made paper boats and helped Pastor Lori pass out candles. No one was talking; even Cooper went silent from the sadness and the beauty, as people lit one candle from another. Henry held Cooper's boat while he put his candle in, worried he might catch it on fire. But it seemed important that he do it on his own. Ruby put her boat in the stream and Cooper copied her. Their boats rocked against each other and then suddenly, as if they'd decided, they turned into the current and were off.

Henry had looked across the water to where people were lined up, watching. He looked up at the steeple of the church, where a light burned high above the trees. He looked back to the river, the boats almost invisible now, their tiny flames looking like flickering fish.

He'd seen the photographs of Hiroshima. He'd read that people were blown into nothing, and had wondered if the spaces in the pictures had been people. Did their souls leave all at the same time? He'd been told his father would have had to fight in Japan if it hadn't been for the bombing.

But this small clump of silent people in their small town in their small state, what good did it do? He'd said as much to Jenny. "What does it matter?"

"Of course it matters," she said. "Love always matters."

He cleared his throat to clear away the memory.

"No, Cooper, they shouldn't have dropped it, and it's a lot to make up for."

A wall in the Cedar Creek Room was covered with a mural depicting a Civil War battle. The horses were life-size, and men swung swords under a cloud of gunsmoke poked by ragged flags. Henry hated it.

"Did the horses get stabbed?" Ruby asked.

Cooper walked from one end to the other, studying it so closely his nose almost touched the wall.

"See anybody who looks like me?"

"Are you joking, Grandpa?" Cooper asked.

"Your great-great-great grandfather lost a leg in the Civil War. But over half a million men died, so you could say he came out easy," Henry said.

Cooper brought an imaginary rifle up and aimed at Ruby.

"Cooper!" Ruby batted his arm. "Stop it! Guns are real! You should be ashamed!"

Cooper looked stunned.

She turned to Henry. "*You* know! Tell him, Grandpa!"

"Let's move on," he said instead, and walked to the door, and they shuffled out behind him.

The next room was where the governor signed bills. When Ruby saw the lamp, she remembered the story Mr. Somers had told her and Jess. "See that lamp?"

"It's a naked lady!" Cooper said.

"A governor had a dress made to cover her up."

"Where is it?"

"I guess the current governor doesn't mind a little nudity," Henry said.

When they stepped into the House Chamber, Ruby gasped, and Henry could see why. He felt small, too, looking up at the chandelier in the dome where its leaves sent out shards of light into the huge space.

"How d'you think they clean that thing?" Henry asked, pointing to the ceiling.

"A ladder?" Cooper asked.

"There's no ladder in the world that tall!" Ruby said. "Do they use a hose? I guess all the desks would get wet, though."

"Now there's a thought, clean out the whole place. No, they lower it down and every single leaf gets dusted. And those desks are for our representatives. They meet here and argue how to spend our money, and make laws."

"Like speeding?" Cooper asked.

"Not speeding!" Ruby said. "*Important* laws. Like so Aunt Maggie and Sally could get married!"

"Your aunt spoke at that. The place was packed to the gills, filling the hall and balcony."

"What about Sally?" Cooper asked.

"Sally wasn't in the picture yet."

"Anybody could speak?" Ruby shook her head. "I'd be so nervous! But if it was important you'd have to."

"Like you told Cooper, it's the people's house."

When they got to the gift shop, Henry gave them each a dollar.

"Look! They're selling cookies from Aunt Maggie's bakery." Cooper held up a cellophane-wrapped maple leaf. "Two dollars! And we can have them for free!"

Ruby finally chose a pencil with Vermont facts on it and Cooper chose one with the Vermont coat of arms because it had a brown cow.

They walked out into blazing sunlight and heat.

"What's the state bird?" Ruby asked, looking at her pencil.

"Hermit thrush," Henry said.

"What's the state flower?"

"Red clover."

"What's the state song?"

"You can't fool me. There isn't any state song."

"There is too! Look!" Ruby held out her pencil.

"'These Green Mountains'," Henry read. "Never heard of it."

"Can we get a drink?" Cooper asked, pointing across the street.

Henry pulled out a dollar.

"It's going to be more than that," Ruby said apologetically.

He handed her his wallet.

She took Cooper's hand and looked both ways before running across the empty street.

Heat radiated through the soles of his shoes, and Henry looked for a place to sit. He spotted a bench shaded by a big maple. He sank down with relief and pulled his shirt away from his body. He reached into his back pocket for the flask and took a sip. He closed his eyes. Ah.

Just one more. Ah.

He slid into a memory.

He was lying on the grass watching Jenny chain daisies. Her face was bent down, in shadow. The tips of her fingers were green. His senior class ring slipped down her finger. She'd wrapped string around the inside to make it fit, but it was still too big.

"I'll never take it off, until—" She said, and grinned at him.

He watched the chain grow into a crown. She reached to place it on his head, but he sat up and took it from her and put it on hers and tucked her hair behind her ears. A daisy fell into her lap and she picked it up.

"Loves me, loves me not, loves me, loves me not, loves me," she said, plucking petals and placing them in the palm of his hand. "Do you, Henry? Do you love me?"

"Grandpa? What's this?"

Henry opened his eyes and blinked, dazed.

Cooper and Ruby were standing in front of him. Cooper was licking a purple popsicle and holding his flask.

Henry looked at Ruby, but she wouldn't meet his eyes.

Chapter 9

WALLY PARKED BEHIND THE 4-H barn. As he stepped out of the truck the rising sun washed over him. He grabbed the bag of egg sandwiches. The air was crispy clean, the usual fair dust tamped down by the rain that had passed through overnight. There'd been a spell of lightning too and Hazel had fretted, but she and his dad would arrive in a couple of hours, and she'd see the kids were fine. This was the big day. Cooper was showing Jenny.

Kids were coming down the ramp, precariously balancing wheelbarrows mounded up with dirty bedding or struggling with their heifers and cows. It took a lot to get a stubborn dairy cow to go your way if she had a different plan, especially when her herd wasn't there to follow. Many of the young handlers were the kids of kids who'd been with him and Robbie back in their day, part of the cozy band of overnighters who got to feel special and superior to the town kids this one time of the year.

"Good morning, Wally."

"Mark! You're showing this year?" Wally asked, shaking hands.

"My youngest. Your calf made the night inneresting, I'll say that!"

"Our calf?"

"When the thunderstorm came through she started bawling until the whole place was bawling, all the cows tryin' to come to her rescue.

Your boy had to take his sleeping bag and sleep with her to get her to settle. Like Little Boy Blue asleep in the hay!"

Stepping up into the barn, Wally was assaulted by the roar of the giant fans at both ends. And walking down the aisle he was plunged into the familiar business of pre-show morning—kids hauling fresh water, mucking out and spreading fresh straw, some beginning to groom their charges.

"Daddy!"

"No running!" Wally held his hand up.

Cooper's hair stuck up, pieces of hay in it and sticking to his sweatshirt.

Wally scooped him up.

"Daddy," he said again, and put his arms around Wally's neck in a way he hadn't for a long time.

"So, how'd it go?" Wally asked, curious what Cooper would tell him.

Cooper slid to the ground and took the sandwich bag. He fished one out, unwrapped it, and gave the foil to Wally.

"Fine."

"You look like you slept in a barn, that's for sure."

They'd gotten down to Jenny's box. Empty. A full wheelbarrow stood next to it.

"Where's Jenny?"

"Ruby took her for a walk."

"She took her for a walk?"

"She said Jenny needed to see the show tent and all before—" Cooper looked down at his feet. "See, she kind of made a fuss last night." He took a big bite out of his sandwich.

"I heard about that. And chew with your mouth closed."

Cooper stuffed the crust in with his finger and closed his mouth.

"What I heard was you took good care of Jenny."

Cooper swallowed. "But I wasn't supposed to sleep with her. You said."

"Oh, well. The best laid plans..." Wally combed his fingers through Cooper's hair to get out the bigger pieces of hay. "Go get fresh bedding. Then clean yourself up."

"But I have to change later anyway!" Cooper whined.

"You can start by changing your tone."

"Yes, sir."

Wally sat on a cot and watched Cooper stagger down the aisle behind the wheelbarrow. He lay back. The wooden sign Robbie'd made in junior high shop hung on a nail above the stall, the words No Frills Farm burnt into it. His mom complained that it made them look like hippies—or worse, hicks.

"We *are* hicks," his dad would say, and do the chicken dance.

The posterboard under the sign had the photograph of Cooper and Jenny in its center, Jenny's name and date of birth above, and Cooper's age and full name below, printed painstakingly in capital letters that took a significant slant down. Henry Cooper Brown. When the fair was over Hazel would put it up in Cooper's room, and at some point it would disappear into the bin where she kept everything the kids made. His mom had done the same thing, and someday he should sort through it. But the box held Robbie's stuff too, since everything was mixed up.

Robbie had never taken to showing, and said the prettying up with the clipping and the combing and the hoof polishing was cheating. But he loved the fair. He had a maple creemee twice a day and spent the rest of his savings losing at midway games. The demolition derby was his favorite event. He'd planned on entering when his deployment was over.

Wally was used to his little brother being missing; he was missing everywhere. But in some places, he was missing more.

"Morning, Mr. Brown!" It was Remy LaFountain. "A big day for Cooper!"

Wally sat up quickly, rubbing his hand down his face to erase his feelings. "Sounds like it was a big night, too."

"Cooper did good." Remy shuffled his feet. "Can I ask you something?"

"Of course."

"You've gone organic, right?"

"Just got our certificate."

"No antibiotics, Dad said."

"Well, we had one heifer treated last winter, but keeping the calves with their mothers means fewer vet visits overall. Milk production's gone down, naturally, but we're thinking we'll make up for it with the higher price of organic."

"We've been talking about it in 4-H. Do you think you could come talk about it sometime?"

Wally felt uncomfortable. "Well, sure. But you maybe should call NOFA in Richmond, and get connected to Vermont Organic Farmers. They'd send somebody, I'd bet on it."

"Oh. Okay." Remy put his hand out to shake, looked at the dirt, and stuck it in his jeans pocket.

"But if you want to see for yourself, just come over," Wally added.

"Thanks, Mr. Brown. And if you ever need a hand, I'd be glad to help."

"Doesn't your dad need you?"

"Just in the morning. The afternoon is usually done by the workers."

"I'll keep you in mind, then. The kids can milk in a pinch, but Ruby's got the chickens too."

Alone again, Wally lay back with a sigh and looked up at the rafters, suddenly and vividly seeing Robbie at Remy's age, as if he might fly in like Peter Pan, looking for his boyhood shadow. Instead, a sunbeam flared through a crack between the roof and the siding, grain dust swirling along its path to where a big Holstein calf was nursing on her stolid mother. The best nativity scene in the world, bar none.

This was his children's heritage, a part of their inheritance. It had been his and Robbie's, and their dad's, and their grandpa's, and Wally was flooded with gratitude that this safe little world was still bustling and humming along. He couldn't wish for anything better for Ruby and Cooper.

~

Cooper was finding out what people meant when they said they had butterflies in their stomachs. He had a bunch of them for sure. But Jenny didn't, at least so far. Her head rested on his shoulder and her breath was wetting his clean white shirt, but he didn't move her. She was being good.

He'd hosed and brushed every inch of her and scrubbed her knees and cleaned her ears and butt. He'd slipped on the halter and clipped the new blue lead to it. He'd painted her hooves with shoe polish, but she wouldn't stand still for Ruby to braid the ribbon into her tail.

There were eleven calves in their class, and Jenny, being the only Jersey, was the smallest. The calves in the group before his rushed out of the tent like it was recess time. Jenny wouldn't do that.

"Peewee class," came over the loudspeaker.

Ruby had said, "Look straight ahead, not at Jenny."

His dad said, "Look the judge in the eye." His mom said, "Tuck in your shirt."

Grandpa just smiled.

He dared a quick glance to the bleachers. They were all looking at him. He waved.

"Number three is Jenny, nine weeks old, led by Henry Cooper Brown, age seven. His parents are Wally and Hazel Brown from Lemon Fair."

Cooper looked straight ahead and stepped forward. The girl in line in front of him had to tug hard to get her calf started, but Jenny walked right next to him, holding the lead in her mouth, his hand on the halter, just like they'd practiced. The two judges, a lady and a man, stood in the middle of the tent and watched the line circle around them. They were supposed to go around two times.

It was stop and go as one calf or another dug in its heels and needed to be persuaded. One plopped on her side and had to be tugged to her feet by a judge. Another one turned all the way around and went the wrong way.

It was kind of a mess.

Jenny shook her head to get Cooper to let go of her halter, and finally he gave up and let go, even though it was against the rules. But then she dropped the lead and turned to suck on his sleeve.

"Jenny!" he whispered. "We still have to walk!" He grabbed her halter, and she walked in a circle.

"Jenny! Be good!" She licked his hand. He waved the lead in her face and she took it, but they were having to stop to wait for others every other step, and every time they did she dropped the lead and turned to nuzzle. Finally, going in fits and starts, everyone made it back to where they started.

Jenny dropped the lead, like "Thank goodness *that's* over," and put her head on Cooper's shoulder.

"She's darn cute. Did you teach her that trick with the lead?"

It was the man judge. Close up, Cooper saw that what he'd thought was an American flag tie had Holstein cows instead of stars on it.

"Our dog did."

"Your dog!" The judge ran his hand down each of Jenny's legs. He lifted up her tail to take a look, and she looked around as if to say "Hey!" Cooper covered his mouth not to laugh. Then he saw from her expression she was going to go. And there was nothing he could do to stop her.

Plop. Plop. Plop. Right in front of the judge!

The judge stepped back as if he was used to it, but Cooper was mortified when a girl came and raked it up and put it in a wheelbarrow.

The judge laughed. "I guess everything's in working order!" He rubbed Jenny's face and behind her ears. Jenny licked his hand and tried to grab his finger to suck on.

"Is she weaned?"

"She's bottle fed. I stopped giving her milk two weeks ago."

"Was she on formula? Any calf starter?"

"It was her mother's milk in a bottle." Cooper didn't want to explain about Maple. Would the judge think Maple was a bad mother?

"Grain? Beet pulp?"

"Just fresh grass; she grazes outside. And six quarts of water."

Jenny butted the judge's stomach. The judge knew what it meant and rubbed behind her ears again.

"Is she with other calves?"

"She'll go with them when school starts. But she's not alone, she's with Rowsby."

"Who's Rowsby?"

"Our dog."

"Oh! The dog who taught her the lead trick." He leaned in to peer inside an ear.

Jenny grabbed his tie.

"Oh no you don't!" The judge squeezed her nostrils and she dropped it. "That's a first!" He put his hand out. It took Cooper a second to realize he was supposed to shake it.

"You've done a good job, Henry," he said, and walked forward to the girl in front of Cooper.

Henry.

"You did great, Jenny," Cooper whispered. He looked over to the bleachers. His whole family was looking at him. He knew they would be. And they were smiling just like him.

~

"Here's for lunch and your ride bracelets," Hazel said, giving Ruby two twenty-dollar bills. "And no junk food or sweets until you've had protein and fruit. And I don't mean a candied apple."

Hazel went to kiss Cooper and he stepped back, embarrassed. He wasn't a baby! But when he looked back to where she stood at the top of the ramp, she waved, and he ran back and hugged her.

They started at the Vermont Pavilion, and Ruby gave him his twenty-dollar bill like she'd promised. First, they picked up Emmett Hardware bags to put everything into. Then, at the end of the aisle, they got plastic hard hats from Green Mountain Construction and next, giant pencils with dogs and cats on them from the Humane Society. Then Valley Electric for a light bulb and Vermont Soap for a hunk of soap. Cooper always got pine, but Ruby had to smell them all before she chose lavender, as usual.

Then around the corner, free milk from the Future Farmers of America booth. Ruby got plain and Cooper got chocolate. If their grandpa were there he would say, "We gotta get one of those chocolate cows!"

They picked up rulers from Kingdom Lumber, and in the next booth they pinned on Democrat buttons because of Jess's dad.

Daggett's Cheese gave out cubes of cheese on frilly toothpicks.

"Take two," Ruby said.

Champlain Orchards was in the third aisle. Free apples.

Having had their protein and fruit, they took a chunk of maple sugar from Monty's Maple to nibble on.

Next to the maple booth was one they'd never seen, "Vermont Kids Safety Network" printed on a bright blue banner across the back wall. There was a basket of safety plugs for electric outlets and a bin of clear plastic tubes. Cooper picked one up and stuck his finger into it.

"Anything that fits in that tube a baby could choke on," the lady said. She smiled. "Unless, of course, it's attached to something bigger, like a person."

Ruby was reading a pamphlet. There was the outline of a gun at the top, a red line across it.

"People can get trigger locks at the doctor's?" she asked.

"Not yet, but we're working on the funding for it. And we want the legislature to make a law that every doctor has to ask patients if they have a gun in the house, and give them information about safe storage."

The woman pointed to a clipboard. "That's what the petition is about."

"I'll sign it," Ruby said, picking it up. "Cooper, you sign too."

"Okay." He started pulling the tubes off his fingers.

"I wish you could, but you have to be eighteen."

Ruby frowned. "I can't sign?"

"Only registered voters. And for that you have to be eighteen."

Ruby had The Look. Cooper stepped back.

She slammed down the clipboard. "Did you know kids *my age* can *hunt*? So I can kill an innocent *deer*, but I can't sign a paper for my brother to be *safe*?"

If Ruby talked like that to their mom, or anyone in *front* of their mom, she'd be in big trouble. Cooper pulled the last tube off his finger and put it in the basket.

"I wish you *could* sign."

Ruby walked away.

"I'm sorry," Cooper said, feeling like somebody needed to be.

The lady handed him a tube.

When they got to the Vermont Fish and Wildlife booth, Ruby stayed back, frowning, and crossed her arms, her bag swinging from her elbow like it was angry too.

The table was covered with pelts, each one tagged with a number. First, people could pet them. Then they'd take the list of animals and numbers and try to match them up. Grandpa knew them all: beaver, muskrat, fisher, ermine, black bear, otter, woodchuck, snowshoe hare. The red fox was easy, and so was the skunk.

"C'mon, Ruby!" Cooper said.

She glared at the deer's head mounted in the back.

"You look old enough to do hunter safety," the man said. He picked up a paper and held it out to Ruby.

"She decided not to," Cooper said. "But our dad said I can, maybe next winter even."

"You're young for it."

"The man who does it is our friend."

"Well then." The man handed the paper to Cooper, and he stuffed it into his bag. He picked up the list to do the matching game.

"You *know* they were all shot!" Ruby said behind him.

Startled, Cooper looked up at the wall behind the booth and met the deer's glass eye.

"Actually, that's not totally true," the man behind the table said. "Some got hit by a vehicle or died another way."

"Yeah, like trapped. Let's go, Cooper," Ruby said. "I'm going," she warned.

They weren't supposed to separate.

"Then go!" he said. What did he care, anyway?

He got eight right, and the button to pin on his shirt. But it wasn't fun. He dropped the button in his bag so Ruby wouldn't see it.

She wasn't in the next aisle or the next or the next, and he started to get nervous. He saw a glimpse of purple, but it was a stroller. He rushed around a corner following a hard hat, but it was on a boy.

He wasn't lost. He knew the fairgrounds almost as well as their farm. But he felt lost.

If he ever got lost, he was supposed to tell a policeman or he was supposed to stay put. He hadn't seen any police, and he hadn't stayed put. But it was Ruby who was lost, not him.

The Fish and Wildlife man had a badge. He'd ask him.

"Have you seen my sister?" he asked.

"The anti-hunting girl who was with you?"

"She's not," he started to say. But he knew she was. He nodded.

"Sorry. Is she meeting you here?"

Cooper shook his head.

"Want to leave a message, in case she comes back?"

"I guess."

"What's the message, then?"

Tell her she wasn't supposed to leave! Tell her—he started to feel mad. Tell her she's a rotten sister! "Tell her I went to the barn." He was going to miss the rides.

He went through the big open door and turned in the direction of the 4-H barns. A mom and little boy went by, sharing a blue cotton candy. Two girls passed him, eating rainbow cones and laughing as they licked at the drips running down their hands. A bunch of older boys ran around him. As if he were just a rock in the path. He fingered the twenty-dollar bill in his pocket. So what if she wasn't there? What did he care, anyway.

He made an about-face.

There was a line for the ride bracelets. Two kids in front of him were debating.

"Let's go on the Zipper first!"

"You said we'd do the ferris wheel first!"

"You're just scared."

Cooper was too short for the Zipper.

He struggled to fasten his bracelet, and when he did it was crooked and loose.

He went on the merry-go-round first like he did every year. Some kids would say it was a baby ride, but he loved it still. But the whole time he found himself searching the crowd for Ruby. He got in line for the Tilt-A-Whirl. The man made him sit with a girl. They sat as far from each other as they could. When it got going, though, he couldn't help it, and squished up against her. Neither of them screamed or laughed.

Everyone was laughing and having fun.

He was like the eye in a *hurricane* of fun.

"Look where you're going!" A boy brushed around him.

He watched the boy thread through the crowd and go into the arcade.

Cooper wasn't allowed to go to the arcade.

It was like entering a cave. Shadowy figures hunched over glowing screens that were stabbing out lights and noise, ratatatatatat! He walked up behind one. Big-muscled men in camouflage darted and jumped, shooting fire and colored smoke. Ratatatatatatatatat!! Figures flew into the air, and legs and arms and heads rained down with bloody fireworks. The boy in front of him pumped his arm.

"YES!!"

"Cooper!"

Ruby grabbed his arm, and he wrenched it away.

"I've been looking *everywhere*!"

He turned away. "You *left*!"

"It was just a minute, I was talking to Ethan! Don't be a baby!"

She took his hand.

He flung her off.

"Come on. We're getting fried dough," she said. "I'll treat you."

He looked around her and saw Ethan watching from the entrance.

"Cooper, I'm sorry! I'm *sorry*! I'm sorry you were scared. C'mon, you can have whatever you want. Do you want cotton candy? Caramel corn?"

"I wasn't scared! I'm going back to the barn, anyway. I did enough rides, tons of them!"

"We'll walk you back," she said.

"I can go by myself."

She leaned down. "Are you going to tell Mom?" she whispered.

He gave her a look. Who did she think he was?

Besides, then she'd tell about the arcade.

She hesitated. "Okay. I'll see you back at the barn."

Outside, Cooper walked fast. When he looked back, Ruby and Ethan were gone. Probably lining up for the Zipper.

He saw his grandpa across the way, heading behind the bathrooms.

"Grandpa!" He ran over. "Are you looking for me?"

Henry shook his head, like the cows did to shake off flies.

"I was going to the bathroom."

"You went right past, Grandpa. Come on, I'll show you."

"Don't tell your dad I got lost. He'll think I'm losing my marbles."

Cooper gave him a look. Who did he think he was?

But now he had two secrets. He sighed.

Fall

backpack
lunchbox
purple high-tops
gym sneakers
3 pairs white tube socks
2 blue shorts
3 white T-shirts
2 sports bras, white and pink
binder, dividers, paper - college ruled
erasable pens
lip gloss
scrunchies
coconut jelly craft styling gel

Chapter 10

HAZEL SLIPPED THE KNIFE around the last muffin and balanced it on top of the others. She surveyed the table. It was just like Jenny would had done: the blue flowered plates, the yellow tablecloth and napkins, blueberry-banana muffins in the blue and green braided basket, and the blue vase stuffed with sunflowers, their stems distorted by the curved glass. Was it okay? The last thing she wanted to do was upset Henry, but these were good things, weren't they?

"It smells like the first day of school," Wally said, coming in from outside. He turned on the water, putting the pail of eggs under it, his first-day-of-school favor for Ruby. There was a shriek from above, and he hastily turned it off. "She's just now in the shower? She'll miss the bus."

"Oh, she'll be on the bus. It's breakfast she'll miss," Hazel said. She began to line the bacon up on a paper bag. Wally took a piece with one hand while swishing the eggs around with the fingers of his other one.

"That's one of yours," Hazel warned.

"Nope, it's Ruby's," Wally said, reaching for another one. "And she gets two."

Hazel laughed.

Cooper thumped down the stairs. When he got to the bottom he ran to Wally and grabbed his hand.

"Did you check Jenny?"

Jenny had barely looked back when she joined the herd in the big field the week before, kicking up her heels like she was going to a party. They'd planned it so she'd have a few days to adjust before school, and it had been hard on Cooper, and Rowsby too. But it was past time—she'd become an expert at letting herself out of her pen.

Wally ruffled his hair.

"Daddy, don't! It's got stuff on it!" Cooper slicked it down.

Hazel looked at Wally, sending a message. Don't say it smells like coconut. Do *not* say it.

"Stuff, huh?" Wally put his hand on Cooper's shoulder. "What grade are you in, again?"

"Daddy, you *know*! Second. Did you check Jenny?"

"I did. And she's perfectly fine."

Cooper bounced up on his toes, smiled, and went to the table. "Grandma's muffins!"

Hazel's heart lifted. For Cooper, it was like yesterday had never happened. Now if only she could forget. She leaned against Wally even though he smelled like a cow, and she would too, in her librarian clothes, if she stayed there too long. But she only pressed in harder. Everything was changing, it felt like, but not this. Not this.

Cooper grabbed the top muffin and bit into it.

"Cooper!"

He put it back.

"Put it on your plate."

She straightened the collar of Cooper's new polo shirt. "You look very nice. Go get Grandpa for breakfast."

But Cooper came back alone. "He said he wasn't hungry. I wish he was driving the bus!"

Ruby came down just as they were finishing up.

"Do I look okay?" She twirled.

"You look grand," Wally said. "Just grand. Is that a new dress?"

Hazel shared a smile with Ruby. "Grand" was Wally's best compliment, usually reserved for an extra-good milker. And it wasn't a dress; it was a tunic. "You look perfect. Go show Grandpa."

"There's not time."

"There is."

"I don't want to, okay? Mom, please."

"But...okay. Just this once."

Hazel went to tuck a couple of muffins into Ruby's backpack for the bus ride, and saw Jenny looking through the screen door. Not again!

"Cooper! Guess who came to see you off!"

"He *taught* her to open gates!" Ruby said behind her.

Cooper squeezed around them. "I'll bet she's smarter than Truman Whitby!"

"She could go down the road!" Ruby said.

"Rowsby would never let her."

And as if to prove it, Rowsby was there too, pushing at the door to let his friend in.

"Oh no you don't," Hazel said, pushing the other way.

"One of these days we'll come home to find them sitting at the table playing cards," Wally said, laughing.

"It's the bus!" Cooper said. "I gotta go! Daddy, will you take Jenny back?"

"This one time. And I'll remind your grandpa to change the latches."

Wally and Hazel watched them head down the driveway. Cooper began to run, but Ruby just walked faster. Not to mess up her hair, Hazel thought. She'd finally grown out her bangs and that came with a whole new set of problems.

The bus stopped at the end of the driveway, and Ruby waved just before boarding.

"It feels strange that it's not your dad driving."

Wally sighed. "I guess I'll check on him, see if he's eaten anything. I wish he'd put the kids first this morning instead of sulking."

"Oh, honey! He's not sulking, he's sad!"

"Well so am I sometimes, but Mom wouldn't want him to miss their first day of school. And Ruby—does it seem to you like she's avoiding him?"

She kissed his cheek. "Prepare yourself. She's at the age where she'll start avoiding all of us! When I was in seventh grade, I made my mother walk behind me so nobody would think we were together!"

"She might have been glad not to be seen with *you*, too. What're you up to today?"

"I have Links, and then it's time to take on the tomatoes."

He laughed. "You selling tickets? Hazel Brown versus the No Frills Farm tomatoes! I think I'll stay away from the kitchen today."

"Very funny."

He gave her a smacking kiss. "I'm on your side, no matter what. We can always buy tomato sauce, but you're one of a kind."

~

Lemon Fair Links
This month's appeal is for Project Back to School. They're asking for clean and new-looking backpacks and lunchboxes, or even better, new ones. Drop them off at the elementary school and the staff there will distribute them to those who need them.
Also, it's time to sign up for Harvest Festival! You can help organize, or run events on the day of the festival.
The more the merrier, and if you're new, someone will be there to help you learn the ropes. It's a great way to be part of the community! Contact Colleen McKenzie.

Hazel pressed SEND. She'd go to Nearly New to look for a backpack. Ruby's old one was too used up to give away, and Cooper's had a couple more years' wear. She'd washed it and bought him a new Toy Story lunchbox as a surprise. Watching him run to the bus that morning, she'd thought of him watching Jenny run to join the herd. After spending the summer giving his calf all the love and attention and teaching a seven-year-old has to offer, and spending the night before curled up in a sleeping bag in her stall, he'd stood and watched her leave him behind.

Cooper hadn't looked back that morning to wave, but he hadn't acted like he bore his mom a grudge from the day before, either. They'd gone to the Labor Day yard sales like they did every year, and she was rummaging through a box of books when Ruby yelled, a look of horror on her face. Cooper was standing by a makeshift table looking down the barrel of a handgun. For a second, she was confused. Was it a toy? Then she saw the long guns. "Put it down! Cooper! Put it down! Drop it! Drop it!" She screamed the words as she ran, and everyone turned to look. He dropped the gun but she grabbed him anyway and shook him. "What are you doing!? You know better! Never—never, ever—pick up a gun without permission!"

A man walked over. "He did ask, and I opened the chamber to show him it was empty. He did the right thing."

Hazel was embarrassed. And worse, she'd embarrassed Cooper.

"I'm sorry, Cooper." But he wouldn't meet her eyes.

"I think you know my wife, Lucille Gibson. She was your daughter's fourth grade teacher."

"Oh! Yes! They went to Shelburne Museum, and Fort Ti."

"Fourth grade means Vermont history. Lucille loves it, and has dragged me all over the state."

Hazel tried to smile, to be neighborly, but she felt shaken up. And with the connection to the school, she didn't dare say what she thought.

Now, filling the sink for the tomatoes, she wished she had. Selling guns at a yard sale? And he had no right to give Cooper permission! How dare he!

She should have a yard sale and sell the guns in Henry's gun cabinet! And while she was at it, she'd get rid of the ancient sprung couch in the kitchen that Jenny and Henry had bought when they were newlyweds. Just about everything in the house had been picked out by Jenny, or Wally's grandmother before that. She'd read about a day in Italy when people put things they didn't want out by the curb and everyone drove around and picked up what they wanted, like a big swap meet once a year. Kind of like their Labor Day weekend, except free. She should put it in Links next year. Or maybe she'd see a sofa at Nearly New when she looked for backpacks. And maybe she'd look for a desk to tuck into a corner of the bedroom and supply it with fresh notebooks and brand new pencils. She didn't have an idea yet, but maybe it would inspire her.

Everybody else was starting something new. Wasn't it time she did?

Chapter 11

RUBY STARTED DOWN THE aisle of the auditorium, searching for Jess. Who would she sit with if she couldn't find her? She hated that they'd been assigned different homerooms.

"Ruby!"

It was Emily Roleaux.

"There's a seat here!"

It wasn't that Emily was a bad person. It was just…she was so loud. And she said things right *out* loud, things Ruby would never say. It was embarrassing.

Kids pushed around her.

"Ruby, down here!"

It was Jess, waving from the front row.

Ruby breathed a sigh of relief. "I promised Jess," she called to Emily. As she hurried down the aisle, she could feel Emily's disappointment following her.

But she was safe.

Jess was sitting with Isabel, and Ruby sank down next to her and shoved her backpack under the seat. She made a face. "Emily Roleaux wanted me to sit with her."

The auditorium lights dimmed, and Principal McBride walked to the center of the stage. She held up a hand. Ruby raised hers in imitation, like they had in elementary school to show they were listening, two fingers sticking up to be ears. Jess poked her. She shoved her hand under her leg. So embarrassing!

"Good morning, everyone! It's fabulous to see you all! This first day is an important one for you, and for us as a school, too. And this year we have a special assignment. The Vermont Department of Education has given a mandate to all schools in our wonderful state, saying that each school must create a plan against bullying and a plan to increase awareness and inclusion of students who are isolated. That's a tall order. But I can't think of a better way to start a new year."

She paused, scanning the auditorium.

"Bullying. The word makes me think of Moe in *Calvin and Hobbes*, demanding Calvin's school lunch money." She smiled. "Maybe there *are* people like that, but for our purposes today I'd like you to drop any stereotypes and focus on *your* experiences and *our* school, and how we can make it a safe and kind place. I became a principal to help you fulfill your best potential. That's impossible if you don't feel safe, physically *and* emotionally."

A screen descended behind her.

"We'll watch a short film, and then you'll go back to your homerooms. Your task is to come up with one or more reasons people bully and one concrete suggestion for creating a safe community. We'll return here to share them. So, without further ado, I give you *It's Never a Joke.*

The words appeared in the center of the screen. Ruby slipped on her glasses.

Little kids sat in a circle, singing, and Ruby sang along in her head: *The more we get together, together, together, the more we get together, the happier we'll be, 'cause your friends are my friends, and—*

The circle twisted into a group of kids standing in a hallway. Another kid passed by and looked back, and they laughed. That picture twisted into three kids in identical shirts pointing at someone and whispering behind their hands.

—my friends are your friends

One scene followed another: an arm shoving a stack of books off a desk twisted into a hand pouring a can of soda on someone's shoes twisted into a leg sticking into an aisle and tripping someone twisted into fingers texting *you won't believe what I just heard.*

Then voices:

She did what?
He's a freak. He's a freakfest.
Did you see what she's wearing?
I was just teasing—teasing—teasing—
Get over it—over it—over it!
What are you, chicken—chicken—chicken?
It was just a joke—a joke—a joke!

The faces became shadows, and the voices became whispers.

Retard! Loser! Fag! Nerd! Freak! Weirdo!
What's wrong with you!

Ruby wanted to cover her eyes, but at the same time she couldn't tear her eyes away, like watching a snake. Was this what happened in middle school?

And then the song again, from far away. *Your friends are my friends, and my friends are your friends.* A face filled the screen. That face melted into another face, and that face dissolved into another and then another. And on and on. Fear. Sadness. Confusion. Hurt.

Each one was looking right at her.

Then the words "*It's Never a Joke*" filled the screen again.

The lights came up.

Ruby blinked. She looked at Jess, shaken. She felt like she'd just stepped off the Zipper at the fair.

"Jeez," Jess whispered.

They'd been best friends forever. They'd shared popsicles and beds and bathtubs and strep throat and secrets and fights and even underwear, that time at gymnastics.

But they'd also shared laughing at Susie Ford's lisp, and how Mrs. Fitch, the elementary principal, called everybody "kiddos," and how Lizzie Small's left eye wandered and she couldn't kick a ball, and how bad Doogie Thirsten smelled. And they'd left people out, safe in their best-friendness, and they'd known it. People like Emily Roleaux.

"Alright, everyone, may I have your attention? Attention, *please*!" Principal McBride clapped her hands.

It took longer this time. Something else was in the auditorium now besides the kids.

"Thank you! Before you leave, I just want to say one thing. When you get to your homerooms, *listen* to each other. We need everyone's voices, *especially* those we don't hear enough. Okay!" She clapped her hands. "Dismissed!"

Talk erupted as seats slammed up and everyone began to inch into the aisles.

Ruby watched Jess adjust her backpack on her shoulder and whisper to Isabel. Was it about *her*? She followed them up the aisle. She'd never doubted Jess before.

Her backpack! She'd left it under her seat.

By the time she got to the hallway it was almost empty. She hurried, worried she'd be late. Everyone would stare.

"I saw you go back! I waited!" It was Emily Roleaux. "I thought you might like company. I don't like to be the last one, I get embarrassed! Do you?"

Ruby peered around to see if anyone had heard, and Emily kept talking, as if she'd answered.

"I have this assignment, like homework? Except from my therapist, not a teacher. You aren't asking what it is, but I'll tell you because it's about you! I'm supposed to pick a person and be friendly. Because it's hard for me? I have a difficult time with social cues?"

"You picked me?"

"Because you picked me!"

"I picked you?"

"At art camp!"

"Oh." That was a whole year ago! And the counselor had told her to. "We better hurry, or we'll be late."

But when they got to the room kids were out of their seats, milling around, taking papers off Mr. Ritchie's desk, and talking. Ruby grabbed a paper and sat down just as Mr. Ritchie turned away from the blackboard and held up a hand for them to listen. Ruby almost laughed. His hand had two fingers poking up to be ears!

"I've been looking forward to this assignment, because it's a great way for everyone to get acquainted, including myself. By the time we go back to the auditorium none of us will see the others in quite the same way, and I hope you'll feel like you belong here, like you're among friends."

He rubbed his hands together. "So let's begin! May I have a volunteer to read the words on the board?"

No one raised a hand.

"Ethan Foley, thank you!"

Everyone laughed.

Poor Ethan. Ruby would have just died!

"'Never believe that a few caring people can't change the world. For, indeed, that's all who ever have.' Margaret Mead."

It was almost like what Pastor Lori said!

"Who agrees with that statement?" Mr. Ritchie asked.

Ruby thought of Ruby Bridges and her teacher. She looked around. Only Emily had her hand up. She began to raise hers, and then brought it back down.

"Shari, please read the words at the top of the paper you all have," Mr. Ritchie said.

"Everyone has a right to be safe in their school and feel like they belong."

"It's our job today to come up with one good idea to support that. That's a formidable task, but I agree with Margaret Mead. Let's be that small group of people, just for today! To begin, please look over the questions on your paper and jot down a response or two."

Ruby took her pencil out.

1. How did the film make you feel?

   Horrible.

2. When haven't you felt comfortable or safe at school?

   When people are mean to someone.

   When a teacher calls on me.

   When I make a mistake.

   When I can't find my friends.

She paused. Was it okay? But it was true:

When people are weird.

She erased "weird" and wrote "different."

3. When have you felt like you didn't belong?

She thought and thought, but couldn't come up with a time. She'd always belonged.

4. Have you been bullied?

She stopped. It wasn't exactly bullying, but still...what about the people who did target-shooting by the trail? They acted like they owned it, but they didn't.

5. Have you ever bullied someone?"

Mr. Ritchie, do sisters count?" Lucy asked.

Everyone laughed.

"Let your conscience be your guide."

6. Have you been in a situation when you didn't do what was right and knew it?

Ruby thought of the fair, how she made like it was Cooper's fault that they were separated and practically threatened him not to tell, when all the time she'd been looking for him and scared. She thought of how she hadn't wanted to sit by Emily.

Did Emily ever feel like she didn't belong?

She looked up at the board. After Pastor Lori talked that day about Margaret Mead, Ruby had imagined that one day she might go somewhere and study strange people. When she told her mom, Hazel had pointed out that the people Margaret Mead was studying would have thought *she* was the strange one. After all, they were the ones who were at home. Ruby had looked Margaret Mead up in the encyclopedia and found something else she'd said: *Always remember that you are absolutely unique.* That was the first part. But the second part was the important part:

Just like everyone else.

Emily was still writing, like she had a lot to say. Was she writing about *her*?

Mr. Ritchie clapped his hands. "Okay, then, who wants to be brave and share a response? Thank you, Emily!"

Emily read from her paper in her loud voice. "I get bullied because my brain is *different*. I saw a documentary about monkeys, howler monkeys *specifically*, where they ostracized a member of their troop who had a toe missing on each foot! Monkeys are safer in *groups*, and when someone is different that individual is a threat. *I'm* a threat to some people because I'm not good at hiding my inner thoughts, and they don't know what to expect. My therapist says middle school might be like the howler monkeys because everybody's bodies and brains are changing so everybody feels self-conscious and is scared they will get picked on! And underneath, *everybody* is scared they are a freak." She looked up from her paper. "I did home school last year because I got picked on, but I'm trying again."

Ruby looked at Emily in astonishment. How could she say all that, right in front of everybody?

"Emily, I'm so sorry you were picked on," Mr. Ritchie said.

"Well, the first day of school is hard for everybody but it's extra hard for me because I don't have a friend. I'm supposed to try to *be* a friend, and *not freak out.* My therapist calls it give-and-*take*, what friends do. I don't know *how* so I practice with her. I look at pictures to learn what people are *feeling* because I have difficulty with that. That movie was *very scary*, all the faces, and people being mean. Looking right at people is hard! And I need to *moderate*. I'm too loud! And say too many details. Moderate and give-and-take. It rhymes!"

She looked at Ruby. Ruby froze.

Emily's eyes skittered away. "You can tell me when I'm inappropriate. I'd rather people say how I *messed up* instead of calling me a *freak*."

Ruby felt ashamed. And awe. Awe at what Emily had just done.

Roger raised his hand. "People who get bullied a lot might become school shooters."

Ruby was appalled. Did Roger mean *Emily*?

"No, it's the bullies!" Shari said. "It's bullies who shoot."

Everybody snuck looks around the room, as if they were trying to figure out who might be *their* shooter someday, and maybe they could stop it before it happened.

"That could never happen here," Mr. Ritchie said. "You don't need to worry."

Ruby looked at him in disbelief. Why not? Why *not* here? A sixteen-year-old could take his uncle's gun and kill himself, so why not other people? Was Peter bullied? He was shy. And a little strange. He kept pet snakes. But so would Jess if her mom let her.

She raised her hand halfway.

"Ruby?"

She hesitated. It was the first time she'd have said the word out loud—would she say it wrong?

"I think Emily's right. Everybody is scared to show they are *unique*. Sometimes I try to be invisible—you know, like when a rabbit freezes, thinking nobody will see it? And sometimes I pretend I like something or know something but when I pretend like that it's like running away from who I am." She knew she was blushing. "Maybe we should try to *show* how we're unique, not hide it." Like Emily did. She was so brave!

Ethan raised his hand. "We did this game at scout camp that was kind of like that. Everybody wrote something on a paper that we thought nobody knew about us, something we were good at or liked to do..." He smiled at Ruby. "Something *unique*, and then we guessed whose it was. It was really fun."

"That sounds like a great next step," Mr. Ritchie said.

Ruby knew just what she'd write. If she dared.

~

When they returned to the auditorium, Ruby was happy to sit with Emily. Her stomach did push-ups while each homeroom took a turn to present ideas, until finally it was theirs. But she had started to feel excited, not just scared. Because all anybody was saying were ways to be nice. Her homeroom's idea was *much* better. And the *name* for it!

"Let's welcome Mr. Ritchie's homeroom," Principal McBride said.

They trooped up the steps to the stage and made a line across it. She looked out, searching for Jess, and saw Remy standing along the back wall with other boys. Was that a thumbs-up?

They'd divided their speech up. Toby went first.

"We bully to get our way."

"We bully to build ourselves up by knocking someone else down."

"We bully because we're scared."

"We look away when people are bullied because we're scared to be picked on too."

"We're scared to be different."

"But everyone *is* different."

"Everyone is *unique*."

"Everyone worries they're weird."

"But everyone *is* weird—in some way."

Emily's turn.

"With some people you can see! With others it's less *obvious*!" She pointed to her head and made a face. She laughed louder than anyone.

Ruby's turn. "What if we *celebrate* our uniqueness?"

She moved over for Ethan, stumbling in her relief to be done.

"Mr. Ritchie said that there will be seven Friday afternoons this year dedicated to the arts. We think all other Friday afternoons should be for activities *students* choose and lead also, to share what we like to do and try new things."

Ruby smiled in anticipation.

"To start, everybody could make a medallion to show an interest of theirs," Ethan finished. "We have a name for it, too!" He pulled a giant paper medallion out from under his shirt.

I am a freak! was written across the center, each letter a different color. Under that he'd drawn a stick figure on skis. He looked down the line. Everyone in their homeroom pulled out a medallion. For hers, Ruby had drawn a book with *By Ruby Brown* on its cover.

Mr. Ritchie wanted to jump from an airplane.

Emily wanted to fly one.

"And the name is...ready...set...go!" Ethan said.

They yelled it together. "Freaky Fridays!"

The boys in the back started whistling.

Principal McBride walked over. "What a wonderful idea!"

"It was Emily's. Emily Roleaux. She's a genius!"

This is going to be the best year ever, Ruby thought.

Chapter 12

COOPER KICKED HIS SNEAKERS under the gun cabinet in his grandparents' mudroom.

Don't leave your shoes for someone to trip over! He could almost hear Grandma saying it. He went into the kitchen and took an apple from the blue bowl. They'd built the house when Ruby was a baby, and the bowl had been there his whole life, but after his grandmother died it sat empty until Cooper told his mom. He bit off a chunk of apple and went into the bedroom. Rowsby was in the middle of the bed with his head on the pillow. He thumped his tail, but looked away. Rowsby thought if he didn't see you, you might not see him.

"Don't worry, I won't tell," Cooper said, leaning back on the dog's big warm body, chewing. He reviewed the pictures on the baby wall: Grandma holding a baby that was his dad; his dad in *Star Wars* pajamas holding baby Robbie; Uncle Robbie in his uniform holding a baby that was Ruby; and last, Ruby in the rocking chair, holding a bald baby that was him.

Looking at the pictures made him feel lonesome. He hadn't been there for most of it, and didn't remember being a baby. And now Grandma Jenny was missing everything too. He got up to study his uncle's baby face, leaving the apple core on the bed. He moved to the grown-up photo of his uncle with the medals on his chest. When he'd asked Ruby what the medals were for, she'd said, "I don't know" and "better not ask."

He went to the closet and pulled the vacuum out and pushed it into the living room. He crouched in front of the bookcase and pulled out the red album from under the stack of poetry books. His grandfather knew whole poems by heart. You never knew when he would say one.

Cooper plunked down on the recliner and pulled the lever to make the foot part spring up. The part that reclined was broken, and only Grandpa could make it work. *Don't you touch that now, what if it got stuck back there? I'd hafta glue the TV to the ceiling!*

He opened the album and turned the yellowed pages to where there was a picture of his dad dressed like a *Star Wars* storm trooper, cradling a blaster against his chest.

But it was his uncle, next to his dad, he wanted to look at. He was Cooper's age, wearing army camouflage pants and holding a long black gun. Cooper wasn't allowed either one, camo pants or a long black gun. When he'd demanded to know why, his mom just said it was complicated.

He heard the door open and she came in with the laundry basket. She frowned at the vacuum.

"Cooper! Have you done *anything*? We leave in an hour! I need your help burying the toys."

Cooper loved Harvest Festival, and the toy hunt was his favorite part when he was little, searching blindfolded through straw until he felt one that he wanted. Matchbox cars were the best. He was too big for it now, and the bounce house and ponies too. But he and Seth planned to do woodcarving, and of course the obstacle course. He'd gotten the best time for his age every year since he was five, the youngest you could do it.

He went to put the album back. "Do I look like Uncle Robbie?"

"Oh, honey, I don't know. I mean, I only met him those two times, when we got married and when Ruby was a baby. He was in Afghanistan."

Hazel lined up the pill bottles next to the pill sorter.

"He left his pills again! Two days' worth," she said, popping open the boxes one by one. "Am I going to have to dole them out like a nurse? I'll bet that's what your grandmother did."

"Why does he take so many pills?"

"Oh, for high blood pressure, high cholesterol, high blood sugar—high everything. Too bad they don't make him high, he could do with some happiness." She shook pills from a bottle into her hand and began to drop them into the little boxes, each marked with a different day of the week. "I wish he'd drive the bus again. I thought he liked it."

"Did you hang our scarecrow?" Cooper asked, to change the subject.

"Wait until you see where! The best spot on the green!" Hazel pressed the lids for each day down with a click. She picked up the laundry basket and went into the bedroom. "Rowsby! Get down from there! And what's *this*?"

Cooper unwound the vacuum cord, plugged it in, and turned it on. Rowsby slipped through the bedroom door and squeezed behind the recliner. Hazel came to the doorway holding the apple core. "See, this is the kind of thing that gets me worried! Your grandfather never would have left this before Jenny died."

Cooper pushed the vacuum back and forth and pretended he couldn't hear over its roar.

"Okay, be in the car in an hour," Hazel said, passing him. "And don't forget Rowsby's water."

When he shoved the vacuum back into the closet, he heard a clink. He got on his knees and stretched his arm out to the back, pushing away Grandpa's church shoes. A bottle. And another one next to it. He grabbed one. *Jack Daniels*. WHISKEY. He opened it and tipped it up for a taste. Yuck! He spit it out and wiped his mouth on his T-shirt. He put the cap back on, and the bottle back in, rolled in the vacuum, and shut the door against why Grandpa didn't drive the bus.

He felt sneaky, like he and Grandpa shared a secret, even if Grandpa didn't know it, and guilty too, like he had a secret *against* Grandpa.

When he got outside, Jenny was there waiting. She licked the front of his T-shirt. Did she taste the whiskey? "Jenny, you gotta stop doing that!" But he didn't move. He didn't *really* want her to stop licking him like he was her special boy. She butted her head into his chest, inviting him, and he hitched himself up on her back. She was getting so big that his toes barely touched the ground. She started to walk, swaying a little, and he pressed his legs against her sides. His mother was scared Jenny would buck, but she would never. And Ruby was scared it would hurt her, but he knew Jenny would tell him if it did. His dad didn't like it because "you just don't ride cows!" But kids rode bull calves in rodeos, so why not cows?

"I won't be back 'til late, Jenny! Today is Harvest Festival. And tonight there's a dance. In the *street*." One of his favorite times was watching his mom and dad dance under the lights strung across Main Street for Harvest Festival. His mom had talked his dad into lessons one winter and they'd learned how to swing dance. One was called Lindy Hop, but his favorite name was Jitterbug. He loved seeing his mom's dress swirl around her legs, and when his dad picked her up and swung her over his head, and she laughed, it was like his heart was swinging and laughing too. That was the best. The worst was when she got mad, like when he picked up that gun at the yard sale.

Cooper didn't want to think about that. He leaned against Jenny and wrapped his arms around her neck. "Grandpa told me a story about why there's Harvest Festival. See, there was a farmer who had very bad luck."

Jenny cocked her ears to listen.

"First there was a late spring frost and he lost half his seedlings. Then, as if that wasn't bad enough, there wasn't enough rain, and he lost half his plants. *Then* there was an early fall frost, and all he had left was one squash. And to make things worse, it was a zucchini."

Where were the cows, he wondered for the first time. Were they wild then? Did people hunt them? And what about milk?

"So the farmer lit up a pipe and offered it to the Great Spirit to ask for help. In those days, before they knew better, people liked to smoke, and so did God. Grandpa said it was called Secondhand Smoke, and God loved it."

Jenny nodded.

"The next morning there was a pile of seeds by the farmer's door, and he and his family planted them. And the *next* day they were already coming up! For a whole week the days were warm, and squash, *acorn* squash, and beans, and corn grew, like each day was a whole month. They picked it all and had a party to celebrate! That was the first Harvest Festival, and they did it just in time, because the wind blew winter in that very night. All the leaves fell to the ground in one swoosh, and it snowed."

They'd arrived at the low meadow. Cooper slipped off Jenny's back.

"And that's the story, morning glory! Hope you liked it!"

~

After he'd buried the last toy in the straw, Cooper turned in his can of tuna fish at the food shelf booth and went to find his and Ruby's scarecrow.

The town green was anchored by the fountain on one end and the gazebo on the other. Lights were strung above the food and craft booths that lined the wide sidewalk between. The gazebo was loud with screaming toddlers and parents talking over their heads. The space in front was a stroller parking lot. And tied to a post, where everybody passed by, was their scarecrow!

She wore an old gardening hat with straw for hair and was dressed in Grandma's apron with the pockets shaped like tulips over an old flowery dress of their mother's. They'd stuffed the front so the chest stuck out. She wore Mardi Gras beads around her pillowcase neck, and Ruby had drawn long eyelashes around her button eyes, and a big smiling mouth.

The scarecrow that raised the most money for the food shelf earned a gift certificate to the bookstore. He checked the envelope pinned to her pocket. Seven dollars! And it was just the start.

"Cooper Brown, you're just the person I need."

Cooper stuffed the money back. Would the sheriff think he was stealing?

"It's ours. Me and Ruby's," he said.

Sheriff St. Francis took a wallet from his back pocket and pulled out two dollar bills. He folded them and put them into the envelope. "She's a beauty! I hope you win! Meanwhile, I need help carrying the hay bales for the obstacle course. Want to give a hand?"

Cooper knew he couldn't say no, not after the two dollars, and not to the sheriff, even if he'd be late meeting Seth.

"Yessir."

"My truck's parked in front of the post office," Sheriff St. Francis said, beginning to walk. "Your grandpa says you're thinking about hunter safety next year, is that right?"

"Yessir."

"You're a little young, but when I had your dad, your uncle tagged on, and he was close to your age."

"Yes, sir, I know."

They made six trips, with Cooper hauling the hay bales in a wagon and the sheriff carrying the hurdles.

"A little token for your help." The sheriff handed Cooper two tickets. "I'll expect you back here for the race!"

Cooper looked at the tickets. They were for the wagon ride that went around town, led by Mr. Beaupre's big draft horses. Only old people and little kids went on it. Nothing happened, you just sat on itchy hay bales and waved at people walking by faster than the ones stuck on the wagon.

"Thank you, sir."

Cooper found Seth watching the cupcake walk, which was like musical chairs except you got a cupcake. It cost a whole dollar, but it was worth it because the cupcakes looked like Dr. Seuss made them, with candy sticking out and a zillion colors. There was a long line. Maybe they'd come back later.

The booths selling jams and honey and apple butter were on the way to the woodcarving, and Seth stopped to get a free chunk of sourdough and a sample of honey for dipping. But Cooper kept walking. Every year before, Grandma Jenny had been there to give him an extra-large piece spread with her homemade jam.

They passed Ruby painting little kids' faces with Jess and her new friend Emily. Ruby was painting whiskers on a little girl. Then he saw his grandfather by the fountain, sitting on a bench by himself. Just sitting there alone, while people all around were having fun.

"Come on," Seth said. His lips were shiny with honey.

"I gotta do something."

"What?"

"Never mind. I just have to."

"What about carving?"

"You go."

"Well, I'll meet you at the obstacle race then."

"I might skip it. You go ahead, though."

Seth stood there looking at him. "You might skip the *obstacle race*?"

Cooper looked over to where the sheriff was stacking a bale of hay on top of another one. He looked over at the ponies. Little kids were waiting in line, jumping up and down, excited. He'd done that. He'd sat on a pony, hanging on tight, and his grandpa had walked next to him, just in case. Except for riding Jenny, he'd outgrown it, along with the toy hunt.

He'd keep growing. Jenny would too.

He'd do the obstacle race until he got too big for it, and probably win, and someday he'd bring his kids to do it. Everything would go on the same, but everyone doing the things wouldn't be the same. Because people and animals died. Rowsby would, before Cooper grew up.

He felt hollowed out with loss. And most of it hadn't even happened yet.

"I gotta do something with Grandpa."

Seth looked to where Cooper was looking. "Want me to come?"

"No, thanks."

"You sure?"

"Yeah. You go ahead. Maybe you'll beat my time!"

Cooper walked the long way around, coming up behind the bench. He put his hands over his grandfather's eyes.

Henry jerked and turned his head. "Jeezum, Cooper! You about gave me a heart attack!"

"*You* do it."

"It's my prerogative."

Cooper sat down and took the two tickets from his pocket.

"Want to go on the wagon ride, Grandpa?"

"I saw you hauling that hay with Tommy. He give you those?"

"Yes."

"He's a good man. You couldn't ask for better if you're in a jam." He took the tickets and looked at them. "Truth to tell I've always thought the wagon ride was boring as hell—heck. I mean, what's to see? And it's itchy on the backside to boot."

Cooper grinned. "Yeah."

They watched the kids wading in the fountain. Cooper had done it himself, lots. Little kids could do it, but older kids got yelled at for some reason. He might get yelled at or he might not, depending on if he was the oldest or the youngest in the fountain at the time.

He was an in-between kid. There should be a name for it. And when did you become a big kid? With girls it was changing shape, like Ruby was. But with boys—was it when they shaved? Remy was older than Ruby but he didn't shave yet, Cooper was pretty sure.

With cows it was easy. There were the calves. Then there were the heifers. Then there were the cows.

"I wanna ask you something," he remembered.

"Shoot."

"How did cows come to Vermont?"

His grandfather stared at him, looking serious. "Well, now, Robbie, there's the facts as we know them, and there's the facts as we make them up. Which version do you want to hear?"

Cooper didn't say "I'm Cooper." And he didn't say which version, either. Grandpa always told the made-up story first.

And that's how Cooper liked it.

He bet Robbie had too.

Chapter 13

RUBY PEELED THE PLASTIC wrap off the ball of dough and cut the dough in half, exactly like her grandmother had. It should feel cozy, she thought. If she were writing a story, she'd make it cozy, a girl making pies before Thanksgiving with her mom while the cute little brother was out playing with his pet calf, and the faithful family dog snored under the kitchen table.

Pretty soon the yard light would come on and Remy LaFountain would come up the drive on his bike. The cows would line up to be milked, calling out as if maybe it wouldn't happen if they didn't make a fuss. After milking they'd have waffles with their own syrup, keeping Grandma Jenny's tradition when "the boys" were away at deer camp. Her mom would invite Remy to stay, and he'd say, "Thank you very much, Mrs. Brown, but Mom will be expecting me."

Every time, she wished he'd say yes, but then was relieved when he didn't.

And she didn't feel cozy; she felt sad. Grandma Jenny had been their family's pie maker her whole life, even the year before, making them early as if she'd known she wouldn't be there.

Jess's family got their pies at the co-op. They were still made at a home, just someone else's.

Ruby sprinkled flour on the counter.

BANG.

Her hand jerked. "I wish hunting was over."

"It's that the shots aren't predictable," Hazel said from the table. "It puts me on edge too." She rubbed Rowsby with her foot. "How come fireworks scare you, but not gunshots?" she asked him.

Ruby slapped the dough down. A deer might be dying at that very minute!

She picked up the rolling pin and rolled. She turned the dough and rolled, turned and rolled, measuring with her eye.

Hazel walked to the counter. She took a pinch of dough.

"This one's cherry," Ruby said. Cooper's favorite. "Maggie's making a lemon meringue." Grandpa's favorite. "And the rolls, of course."

Ruby folded the piecrust once and then again, placed it in the pie plate, and unfolded it. She tucked it in. She began to roll out the lattice.

"Can you prompt me? I think I almost have it." Ruby spooned the cherry filling into the bottom crust. She dipped her finger in and licked. Yum. She took a fingerful. Double yum.

To be a delegate at the seventh grade Constitutional Convention you had to memorize a part of the Constitution. Because there were no female roles, Ruby wasn't going to do it—until Emily pointed out that that would make it so men and boys *still* got to run things.

Hazel picked the paper up from the counter. "I loved learning about the Constitution. Especially the Bill of Rights," she said. "Go ahead."

"'We hold these truths to be self-evident'… " Ruby spread the filling out to the edge of the pie with the back of the spoon. She cut strips of piecrust and placed one across the pie. "'that all men'—it should say all *people*—'are created equal.'" She crossed the strip with another one. "'That they are endowed by their Creator with unalienable rights'…"

"Certain," Hazel corrected.

"'*Certain* unalienable rights, among them'—no, '*that* among *these* are life, liberty, and the pursuit of happiness.'"

The lattice and the Preamble finished neck and neck.

"Thanksgiving's going to be too sad without Grandma Jenny," Ruby said. "Just like last year's."

"Maggie and Sally will be here," Hazel said. "They always cheer things up." The phone rang. She picked up the receiver. "Hello? Speak of the devil!"

"Is it Maggie?" Ruby wiped her hands on a towel. "I want to talk."

"What? *What*? Oh my God! Oh, Maggie! How long? Do you know—uh huh. Oh, Maggie! I'm so happy for you! Have you—uh huh, uh huh—no, I get it. Oh! It's so great! So, so good! Give Sally a big enormous hug! Listen, Ruby's right here, so I'll let you tell her."

"Aunt Maggie?"

"We're having a baby!"

"What? When? But *who*—I mean—how?"

"The what is a baby, the when is early June, the who is me and the how is a donor who is Black."

Ruby wondered. Was it like the cows, when the vet came and stuck—she could never ask.

"How do you feel?"

"The first weeks weren't fun, but the worst is over. And everything is shipshape."

"Tell Sally congratulations!"

"I will! Listen, a customer's waiting. Give each other a big baby hug from us, and we'll see you next week!"

"Okay. Bye!"

Hazel flung her arms around Ruby. "Baby hug!" They swung around in a circle.

Ruby stopped. "Why didn't they have it be Sally who got pregnant?"

"What?"

"I mean…Maggie had the miscarriage."

"Oh, honey, that could have happened to anybody, to Sally too. It wasn't Maggie's fault."

"I just...it was so sad! I think they're brave to try again. Do they know if it's a girl? If Grandma was here, she could give them the dress she made last time."

"I don't know. They might wait this time, to find out when the baby's born. We did. But if it is, we can still give them the dress. Jenny would want us to."

"Can I go tell Cooper?"

"You *may.* And remind him he's helping Remy and you with milking."

Hazel slid the cherry pie over and sprinkled flour on the counter.

Ruby grabbed her fleece.

"Wear your parka. And a hat. And your mittens."

"Mom! I'm not a baby!"

The storm door slammed.

Rowsby scrabbled out from under the table and whined.

"You're leaving me too?"

Hazel opened the door for him to slip out and rested her back against it. "A baby!" she whispered. She did a little dance.

~

The cows were bunched up by the fence, complaining. It was weird. It was too early; the sun was just dipping below the tree line on the ridge. Ruby climbed up and ran her palm down the closest face.

"You're a half hour early, doofusses."

She jumped down. "Listen!"

They stared at her.

She put her hands on her hips. "We hold these truths to be self-evident! All cows are created equal! They are endowed by their creator with un—with *certain* unalienable rights!" She swept her arm out. "Among them, a pond!" She swept her other arm out. "A barn!" She pointed to herself. "Nice humans! And life, liberty, and the pursuit of good pesticide-free grass!" She bowed.

Then, starting with Peony, they took up their complaining again.

The calves were bunched up too, but Jenny wasn't there.

"Cooper! Cooo-per!" She slipped through the narrow opening between the post and the gate and slid the barn door open enough to squeak through. The barn was warm. And cozy. Maybe they should have Thanksgiving *there*. Maple could come.

"Cooper?"

She flicked on the lights and walked down the aisle to the other door and back outside. She turned in a circle, trying to hear above the herd, searching. And where was Rowsby? He didn't like to go anywhere anymore. But Jenny did. And where Jenny went, Rowsby went. Jenny had bonded to Cooper and Rowsby, like Louis to Sam in *The Trumpet of the Swan*.

The last glimmer of sunset ribboned across the pond; any minute now the high pasture would drop into the dark, as if the edge of the world was up there.

"Cooper! Coo-per!"

Jenny was a wanderer, and Ruby blamed herself, because of Maple. She took the path that zigzagged up the slope, looking out for cow patties. "Coo-per!" The gate to the high meadow was open. Oh, Jenny!

She saw Rowsby's silhouette at the brow of the hill. He started barking. Rowsby was a farm dog. He knew not to bark if it wasn't important. The hair on the back of Ruby's neck rose up. Rowsby came rushing down, barking and barking. His face was wet. She touched his nose. Sticky. She put her hand up. Ick! Blood.

"Oh, Rowsby! What did you get into?"

She stood still to listen. All she could hear were the cows below. She peered up the hill to where the sun was just a sliver at the top.

Stupid dog.

Stupid Cooper.

She pulled her sleeves down over her hands, shivering. Darkness was coming down the hill like a window shade.

"*Cooper*! Come *on*!"

Rowsby ran into the dark.

Trudging up the hill, she heard a sound. Grandpa had seen a bobcat up there. Fear twisted in her chest. "Cooper, *answer* me!" She swung around, and around again, squinting up the hill.

Was that a deer on the ground?

She ran, and tripped, and fell to her knees. She scrambled up, and ran. It was Jenny!

It was Jenny, and she'd been rolling in the same thing Rowsby had. "Oh, Jenny, what have you gotten into?"

But then she smelled it. Blood. It was *blood*. And Jenny's eye was open, looking at the sky. Not blinking. Not looking. Not anything. Something crawled across it.

Oh God, oh God, oh God. Her heart started pounding.

"*Cooper!!*" she screamed. "*Cooper!! Answer me!*"

Rowsby barked, and Ruby spun—and spun and spun. "*Cooper*!" And then she saw him. She dropped to her knees and crawled.

"Cooper!" She searched frantically with her eyes. Was there blood?

"*Cooper*! It's *me*!"

She'd never seen a face so white; it looked like he'd been crying dirt. His eyes were closed. Oh, God! Was he *dead*? But he was shaking. She took his hand. His fingers were ice cold. She fumbled to get her jacket zipper down and fought to get her arms out of the sleeves, more frantic by the second, as if only her fleece could save him.

"Rowsby, move! *Move*!" She spread her fleece over Cooper and rolled him to tuck it under his back.

He screamed and opened his eyes.

"I'm *sorry*! *I'm sorry*! *Cooper, I'm sorry*!"

"Jenny." It was just a breath of sound.

"Mommy," she whispered. She slipped her arm under his back. He screamed and screamed.

Ruby recoiled. And then she saw. The bottom of his jeans was soaked with blood. She had to look. Had to look. Had to. She gasped.

His foot was facing backwards.

She put her head down, dizzy, and bit down hard on the inside of her cheek. Stop it, stop it. Stop it! Look! You have to look!

It looked like Cooper's sock was all that was keeping his foot attached. His boot lace was tangled in it. The bottom of the boot was gone, like someone had sliced it off. Where were his toes?

She leaned over and threw up.

And she knew. She could never carry Cooper down the hill. She might hurt him more, she might even drop him. And the blood. She had to stop the blood.

Rowsby licked Cooper's cheek.

"Rowsby! You have to go home! Go *home*! Bring *Mom*! *Home*, Rowsby!"

He licked her hand and bent his ears, looking at her. He whined. She pushed him.

"*Go home*!!" She pushed him again. And again, hard. "*Rowsby*, go *home*! GO HOME!"

He looked at her, his tail between his legs, and whimpered.

It didn't matter. She hit him. "Go HOME. Get MOM." She burst into tears. It didn't matter. "*Rowsby*, PLEASE. *Oh, God*!" She pulled her foot back and kicked him.

He went.

There were *two things* she'd been taught in First Aid. Two things. She pulled her own boot off. It took a lifetime to peel her sock off. Two things, she told her hands, like another person was there giving directions.

Number one. Stop the bleeding.

She tucked one end of her sock under Cooper's leg and pulled it out the other side. Cooper cried out. She grabbed each end and slid it down below his knee. Cooper screamed.

It doesn't matter.

She pulled the ends across as tightly as she could, and Cooper screamed and screamed. Tears streamed down her face. *It doesn't matter just do it.*

"I'm sorry, I'm sorry!" And she twisted it as tight as she could. She should have a stick, they'd practiced with a stick. Tighter, said the voice. A little more, said the voice. And she pulled, closing herself to Cooper's screams and the smell of blood and if there was a bobcat, to everything except *make a knot.*

There.

Number two: shock. Keep him warm. How? *How*! She looked around.

When she lifted him, Cooper's screams shot through her like nails.

It doesn't matter.

She slid along the ground with Cooper in her lap. When she got to Jenny, she tucked him up against her. She ran back for her fleece and her boot. She pulled off the other one. Cooper had gone quiet, but she had to do it. She lifted his leg and stacked her boots underneath, tilting them to be as high as she could get them.

But he didn't make a sound. Had she *killed* him? She froze. She looked and saw his breath in the cold air. She tucked her fleece around him again, then squeezed up next to him and put her arm over him. It was up to her and Jenny. She pressed against him.

Mommy, come.

Mommy, come, Mommy, come, Mommy, come, Mommy—

Don't die. She wiped her wet face on her bloody bare arm. She was shivering so hard her teeth rattled. Don't think about bobcats.

Or bears.

Please God.

Mommy.

She should make a noise to help her find them. Think.

"Cowboy Bill, Cowboy—" It made her cry. Something else.

"Cooper, Aunt Maggie's having a baby. In June." It made her cry more. Something else.

"'We hold these truths to be self-evident, that all—people—are created equal, that they are endowed by their Creator with unalienable rights, that among them are life, liberty, and the pursuit of happiness—'"

Louder.

"'We hold these truths to be self-evident, that…'"

Mommy, come. Mommy, come. Mommy.

Chapter 14

RUBY GRIPPED THE SIDES of the chair and stared at the drops of Cooper's blood on the linoleum. She blinked and looked to the hallway, where they'd wheeled him away, and where her mother had left her behind. She didn't want to stay there with the blood, but she was frozen to the chair until Aunt Maggie came to release her, as if moving would shatter whatever was holding her in one piece.

But after Aunt Maggie came, Cooper would be wheeled back, or maybe he'd be in a wheelchair, good to go. Go to McDonald's, and Cooper would get a Happy Meal for the prize and Aunt Maggie would complain—"crap food"—and they'd laugh and Aunt Maggie would tell Cooper about the baby and on the way home Cooper would fall asleep in the back seat with his head on Ruby's lap. He'd probably have a cast. When they got home her mom would carry him to her bed and Aunt Maggie would make hot chocolate to go with the cookies she would have brought fresh from her and Sally's bakery and Ruby would tell her all about what happened. And then Dad and Grandpa would come, and she'd tell it all over again.

Who was she fooling? It was all lies.

She saw she was wearing one sneaker and one Croc. Her boots were still—

Don't. She knew one thing, though; she'd never wear them again.

Rowsby! Was Rowsby still with Jenny?

Jenny's eye.

No.

She pulled her legs up and rocked, her chin on her knees.

We hold these truths to be self-evident.

Her mom's shadow looming behind a darting light.

Mommy.

Lights coming up the hill like giant fireflies.

Remy standing in the barn door, his face chalk-white like Cooper's. She didn't remember seeing the cows or calves. Remy must have brought them into the barn. Did he wonder where Jenny was?

The snake of blood swinging in the ambulance, going from a bag hanging from the roof into Cooper.

Would Remy look for Rowsby and Jenny?

Mr. LaFountain and Grandpa used to dump the dead cows in the ravine between their fields. She and Cooper had found bones. Nowadays her dad called somebody and a truck came.

Did her dad even *know*?

Daddy's at the engine, Ruby rings the bell, Cooper swings the lantern, to say that all is well.

"Daddy," she whispered.

Suddenly he filled the doorway, his orange vest glowing. She was on him so fast he grabbed the door. He smelled like wood smoke and sweat. She buried into him.

"They told me they took him for an MRI," he said. "They said you came in an ambulance. Where's he hurt?"

"His foot—" She shook her head against his chest.

"Thank God! I thought it was his head!"

She stepped away to face him.

"No, Dad! They're doing that test to see what they can—" She'd lost her voice. Saying it made it true. "Save," she whispered.

"Save?"

"That's what they said. 'We'll save what we can.'"

"Save *what*?"

"His foot! Save his foot!"

He reeled back. "What *happened*? I thought he fell!"

"I don't *know*! Maybe a bobcat. Or a bear. It killed Jenny."

"Jenny?"

"*Jenny*! Cooper's calf."

"My God! Does Cooper know that?"

"I don't know." She saw Jenny's small body. All the *blood*. She covered her eyes.

"Look at your hands! And what the hell are you wearing?"

She pulled the enormous robe tight. "From the ambulance."

"Let's get you cleaned up."

Wally began to open cupboards and finally found a stack of towels. He held the end of one under water at the sink and wrung it out. Ruby sat like a doll while he washed between her fingers, then her palms and wrists, and pushed up the sleeves of the robe to wash her arms.

"God. There's blood in your *hair*."

He tossed the towel in the corner and took a fresh one. He gently took off her glasses and washed her face, tender around her eyes. With each touch her chest loosened more, and she began to cry, until she was sobbing and hanging onto his vest as if it were a life jacket.

Wally pulled a handkerchief out of his vest pocket. After she blew, he wiped her face again.

"Stand up," he ordered. He pulled off the robe. And gasped. "Your clothes are covered in blood!"

"Maggie's bringing clothes."

"Where's your jacket?"

"It's…" She swallowed. "How did you know to come?"

"The state police came to the cabin. We thought it was for Tommy but then they said there'd been an accident at the farm, and you'd come up here, and that it was Cooper. They brought me here and Tommy took Grandpa home. They did the lights, Cooper would've loved—"

He sat down hard.

A second later Hazel walked in, followed by a man in a white coat carrying a clipboard.

"You're here! Thank God!" She hugged Wally.

"How's Cooper?" Wally asked.

"He's sleeping," Hazel said. "They gave him a shot."

"Mr. Brown, I'm Dr. Sylvester Martin." He held up the clipboard. "We just need a couple of signatures before we proceed."

"Proceed?" Wally asked. "Proceed with what? What did you find out?"

"There's a specialist in Albany. New York. She's a renowned orthopedic pediatric surgeon—really, one of the best in the northeast—I'd want her if it were my child."

"So you can—she'll fix his foot?" Wally asked. "Good as new, right?"

Dr. Martin looked at the floor, as if it might speak for him.

But all that was there was Cooper's blood. Ruby squeezed her father's hand between hers. Not good as new. She'd *seen* Cooper's foot.

"He'll lose—he's *lost—listen.*" Dr. Sylvester paused. "He could have bled to death. Keep that in mind. Your daughter…your wife said it was your daughter who made a tourniquet." He pointed his finger at Ruby. "You saved his life by stopping the bleeding. Yes, his foot is badly compromised. But his *life*—"

The doctor abruptly sat down across from them and pulled off his shoe and sock. "Sorry, but without the scans, this is the easiest way to show you. We divide the foot into three parts: the hindfoot, the midfoot, and the forefoot. The forefoot is here." He wiggled his toes. "Your son's forefoot is gone, and the midfoot is shattered. But the whole of the hindfoot"—he cupped his heel—"might be saved, at least the heel pad, and that would make a big difference for your son's future. Dr. Harris may have a different opinion in Albany, but she's seen the scans. Your son will have to undergo a series of surgeries, and more as he grows, and he'll have some type of prosthesis, but—"

He stood up quickly and went to Wally. "Put your head down. No, way down, between your legs. I'll get a nurse."

"Get a *nurse*? You're a *doctor*!" Hazel said. She covered her mouth. "God! I'm sorry!"

"No need to be sorry. It's hard to hear." He kept his hand on Wally's neck. "I was going to say they're doing amazing things with prostheses for children. I doubt he'll have limitations, or barely any. He'll be able to do everything a normal kid can—run, even climb. In fact—"

Wally held up his hand. Stop.

"Right. Right. It's been a shock. And it's got to be scary as hell, what happened."

Wally stood up. "I need to see him!"

"Only one of you can go along. We'll keep him sedated for the flight."

"What the *hell* are you talking about?" Wally said.

"Albany, as I said. He's to be medevaced to Albany."

He said it, Ruby thought, like it was just regular. Like taking the bus.

"I'll go along," Hazel said.

"But—" Ruby began. But of course her mom would be the one to go. And she wanted her to. Just—

She remembered Cooper's chubby baby foot, so tiny, and kissing each toe. "Who's the cutest baby? Who?" She opened her eyes wide to keep from crying. "The bobcat, or whatever he saw, he must have been so *scared*. And *Jenny*—"

"The bobcat?" Dr. Martin asked.

"That's what I thought—my grandpa saw one up there—" Ruby

fumbled. "A bobcat or a bear."

Dr. Martin looked from her father to her mother. "It wasn't a bobcat or a bear, or any other type of animal." He hesitated. "Maybe your daughter would like to step out into the hall for a minute."

"No! What was it? I'm not a baby. You said yourself I saved his life!"

Her parents took her hands on either side of her.

The doctor hesitated again.

"Tell us!" Ruby said.

"It was a bullet. He was *shot.* The state police are waiting at reception to talk to you."

Winter

Bring to Cooper –
Pillow, Spiderman pillowcase, comforter, Moose
Toy Story DVDs
Moomin and Paddington books
Calvin and Hobbes
drawing book, maze book, colored pencils
fairy lights
cherry pie

Chapter 15

HENRY SHUT THE DOOR to the truck gently, as if it could wake somebody up. He opened the lopsided gate and walked along the well-worn path, noticing that most of the graves had gotten covered with leaves since he'd been there last. Mother Nature's hand-me-down quilts.

Jenny was in the lee of the lilacs. Stripped bare, they didn't make much of a windbreak, and he shivered. But Jenny loved the wind. Jenny's and Robbie's graves lay side by side like twin beds, stones for pillows. A tired American flag drooped over Robbie's. The sunflowers he'd brought in October were cleaned-out husks, raided by the squirrels and birds.

Robbie's place was flat, but Jenny's was still rounded like she had an extra blanket.

Ignoring the fuss from his back, Henry stooped and tossed the sunflowers under a lilac bush. A lone petal drifted down and he plucked it like a feather before it reached the ground.

"Hope" is the thing with feathers.

They'd visited Emily Dickinson's house on their honeymoon.

He tucked the petal into his pocket. He always wore his church coat when he visited Jenny, like they were courting.

He tugged the vase out of the hole he'd made to keep it from tipping, took out his handkerchief, and wiped the bottom of it. Not that anyone would see it from underneath, of course they wouldn't. He stuck the vase back in the hole and put in the bittersweet Ruby had given him. Its red berries were bright drops of life against the brown grass.

Before Jenny died, Ruby had liked going to the cemetery. She'd wander around, working out the neighborhood's family trees on the tombstones while Jenny talked to Robbie, catching him up. Cooper would hide behind the biggest ones to jump out and shoot at invisible enemies, just like Robbie and Wally had done when they were boys. What did their running footsteps sound like from below?

Not that anybody could hear; he didn't think that for a second.

Cooper grew more like Robbie every year, moving like he was made of springs and rubber bands. Henry's heart tripped. Would Cooper run again?

He lay down between Jenny and Robbie and folded his arms over his chest, pocketing his hands into the rough wool of his armpits. He always tried to forget the date when the men came to the farm to tell them Robbie was killed. And it had actually happened six days earlier, so every year after that he had to endure the whole week trying not to remember. But Jenny would come up every day of that week to talk to Robbie, keeping him company.

The wind had stopped. It was suddenly utterly silent, not even a bird to be heard, just his own breath. If he stayed there long enough that would grow still too. Would he see her then? Would he see Robbie? Just seeing them for a second made dying appealing, if he didn't have so much to do.

He lay until his live body betrayed him, complaining of the cold. He rolled over onto Robbie's grave, rising to his hands and knees to get up. A memory sprang up, Robbie on his back, his legs hugging Henry's waist and his arms wrapped around his neck in a chokehold.

Cowboy, Daddy!

Cowboy Bill, Cowboy Bill, shiny black pony too, I saw you go riding over the hill, I wish I could ride with you.

Cowboy, Grandpa!

A sound escaped him. He clamped his lips against it, but the truth filled his heart.

It was his fault. It was all his fault and he could never make it right.

While Cooper's calf got smarter and smarter, he'd been drinking himself to sleep at night and drinking himself awake in the morning, having his private pity party.

"Jenny!" It came out as a prayer.

~

"Welcome to the Friday meeting of Alcoholic Anonymous. My name is Tommy, and I'm an alcoholic."

"Hi, Tommy!" everyone said.

"Let's open our meeting with the Serenity Prayer."

Henry clasped his hands between his knees and stared at the Methodist Church basement floor.

"God…" Tommy began.

Everybody joined in. "…grant me the serenity to accept the things I cannot change, the courage to change the things I can, and the wisdom to know the difference." Henry hadn't said the words for over a year, but they were as familiar as any Robert Frost poem.

"Alcoholics Anonymous is a fellowship of men and women who share their experience, strength, and hope…" Tommy said.

Henry kept his eyes on the floor while more words he knew by heart washed over him.

"…honest desire to stop drinking…primary purpose is to stay sober and to help other alcoholics. We will now go around the circle and introduce ourselves, first names only."

"I'm Sam, and I'm an alcoholic."

"Hi, Sam."

"I'm Cathy, and I'm an alcoholic."

"Hi, Cathy."

All around the circle until it was his turn.

"I'm Henry. I'm an alcoholic."

"Hi, Henry!"

It resounded. He knew it was their way of saying they were glad he was back.

He hadn't had a drink in seventeen days. Not that he'd counted. When he'd opened the closet door after Harvest Festival and smelled the whiskey, he knew he had to face it, but he'd put it off and off. Just one more day. And one more, until another month went by.

Until Cooper, and his Jenny.

There'd been a moment in the woods, up in his blind. It would be simple to make it look like an accident, the slip of a foot, the shot, the fall. And it would be over. He didn't know what stopped him, but it was just an hour later that they'd seen the flashing lights coming up the road.

"We'll now go around and read the Twelve Steps."

"One: We admitted we were powerless over alcohol—that our lives had become unmanageable."

They continued around through the twelfth step.

"Thanks, everybody," Tommy said. "Before we share on this month's step, does anyone have a topic they'd like to talk about? Dan."

"It's about deer camp. I go with my cousins and, well, the beer flows pretty much starting when we get back to camp at dusk. I broke my sobriety, but I'm back now, and I have fifteen days. Thank you for listening."

Everyone applauded.

"I'm Bobby, a grateful member of AA. I know no cross-talk on what Dan said, but I just gotta say...what're they doing drinking beer at deer camp anyways? That's plain dumb. Guns and booze? Tommy, you're the sheriff, you oughta put a stop to it."

Henry almost laughed at the look on Tommy's face.

"Uh...let's keep in mind this is an anonymous organization, and keep to the concern raised. Which is...uh...which is what?" Tommy's face was beet red. "Harold?"

"Do you tell those kids in hunter safety class not to drink and hunt?"

"Look, if you want to talk about hunting, you can do it after the meeting. And if Dan wants more advice, he can get it then too, although maybe he's had enough," Tommy said.

Everyone laughed.

"Let's go to the step," Tommy said. "It's December and we're on the twelfth step. Would someone volunteer to read it again, please?"

Henry stayed afterwards to stack chairs, feeling better than he had an hour ago, which is how it always was, he recalled. He followed Tommy out, waiting while he put the key in the empty planter in the window well. Everybody in town knew where that key was. Barney Simmons even slept down there when it got too cold to camp, claiming he didn't want to take up a space at the shelter. But Henry knew that was a lie; Barney had a bottle hidden behind the water heater, or used to.

Tommy began to walk to the lit-up diner across the street, and Henry zipped up and followed like in the old days, seeing shadows moving inside the square of Christmas lights strung around the two steamed-up front windows.

They went to their old booth, and Olivia brought two cups of coffee to the table.

"What's your pleasure, gentlemen?"

She never wrote anything down. She said the day she didn't get it right someone should take her out back and shoot her.

"I'll have the pecan pie," Tommy said. "With whip cream." He patted his stomach. "Santa Claus needs to build up this belly for the kiddies next week."

"I'll have the same," Henry said.

"Whip cream on it?"

"No thanks."

She didn't leave, though. "I want to say, Henry, everybody's praying for Cooper. And we'd like to take up a collection. There's got to be extra expenses down there in Albany."

Henry was dumbfounded. Wally wouldn't want to be taking charity, he knew that much, and he guessed he wouldn't either, but it seemed impolite to say so.

"That's a generous offer," Tommy said.

"Well, good! We'll put a jar by the cash register."

"Does Cooper still believe?" Tommy asked, after she left. "I always wonder with kids his age."

"Believe?" Henry didn't know. He'd heard Cooper ask Ruby about angels last Christmas, so he guessed he did. "I don't—I—"

"In Santa Claus," Tommy explained.

Henry's voice was hoarse. "I wouldn't count Cooper out yet."

Olivia returned with their pie. "Here you go."

"You have any idea about the shooter yet?" Henry asked, after she was out of earshot.

"I'm afraid not. Some fool from out of state maybe. It's against Vermont law to hunt with anything with a magazine over six, and the LaFountains don't have anything like that, but Arnie LaFountain saw a New York truck on their road. It seems unlikely it was kids taking potshots at trees, tho' there's some evidence of that in the woods next to LaFountains' pasture. Kids get together and have shooting parties. Tho' the type of gun—"

"Their parents let them?" Henry asked.

"Might not know. But there's no shortage of fools in this world."

"You said a magazine over six rounds? What the hell?"

Tommy nodded. "Yeah. Probably an AR-10."

"What the *hell*!"

"I can't see why, for hunting—your little calf looked like—never mind. Anyway, they're getting to be popular in other states and for target-shooting." Tommy put his fork down. "Listen, I got to apologize for the Santa Claus remark. I could tell—"

"It doesn't matter. Some days you could say 'What a nice day' and the waterworks would start. No apologies required."

"I haven't been a very good sponsor over this time."

"C'mon, Tommy, you know it's on me, not you."

"But…a lot of stuff going on," Tommy said. "How are you doing?"

Henry shrugged. What could he say? "Remy LaFountain is helping with the milking." And Hazel shouldn't've made Ruby come back from Albany and go to school. But he couldn't say that.

"These first weeks of sobriety are going to be tough."

"Tougher than what Cooper's going through? It wouldn't've happened if it weren't for me!"

"What the heck are you talking about?"

"I was s'posed to change the damn latch on the gate Cooper's calf opened." Henry shoved his pie away.

Tommy was silent for a long time. "What's Step Eight?"

"It's not that easy."

"Just say it."

"It's not that *simple*!"

"I'll say it. 'Made a list of all persons we had harmed, and became willing to make amends to them all.' Are you willing?"

"What do you think?"

"Okay. You admitted to yourself you messed up, and you told me. Now tell God, or whatever you think of as God—wouldn't be surprised if it's the cows—and get started. Making amends means changing and doing what you can, and you can do a lot. Start with the damn latch. You're a fourth-generation Vermont farmer, for God's sakes, and that family is counting on you."

Tommy pushed Henry's pie back to him. "Maybe you should get some whip cream on that. You always used to."

"Can't. I get stomach ache if I don't take a pill first. It's called something or other intolerance. Dairy."

"That's pretty funny, you being a dairy farmer. Like you're prejudiced! But eat up. No matter what you think, you deserve some sweetness in your sorry life."

Chapter 16

WALLY LIFTED HIS FACE up to catch the snowflakes.

Whose woods these are I think I know. His house is in the village though. He will not see me stopping here to watch his woods fill up with snow. What kind of woods was it, where the owner lived in town? Sounded more like a woodlot. Or maybe a Christmas tree farm. But still, it was a nice poem.

If Cooper was home instead of lying in a hospital, he would have been thrilled when he woke up and saw it was a snow day. Ruby would help him pack a sled run with the old toboggan and then they'd sled until it got too dark to see. Then cocoa. But Ruby had watched DVDs all day or been on the phone. He didn't think she'd taken one step outside after feeding the chickens.

He took his hat off and shook it and wiped his face with the heel of his hand. The barn looked like a Norman Rockwell painting. The farm's dirty rough spots were all hidden under the snow. Nobody would know by looking how behind he was in keeping it all from falling down around itself. And his family wounded and divided between here and Albany.

Time was divided too, into Before and After. He tried every day to be grateful Cooper was alive, and tried to drum up some gratitude when Hazel listed the things Cooper would be able to do "someday," pretending life would go back to normal. But digging for gratitude was like trying to get water from a stone.

The real new normal was Ruby holed up in her room talking to her friends after school until Remy was done in the barn, when she'd go pour out her sorrows to Maple. Not to him, and who was he to complain? He wasn't pouring out his feelings to his father either.

The real new normal was sleeping in Cooper's bed to be close by when Ruby had another nightmare. He'd go in and find her curled up in a ball, tears streaming down her face, mumbling words that made no sense, as if she were back in the Revolutionary War, about rights and liberty, her eyes wide open and staring, fixed on horrors he could only imagine.

He'd learned it was better not to wake her. He'd lie down next to her and hum until she closed her eyes and fell into a deep sleep—until the next time.

The new normal was the whole county in their business—bringing lasagnas and cookies in tins, with names on them so Hazel'd have to return them. And they weren't even allowed to bring the cookies to the hospital. Allergies, that lady said. Issa. The "play lady," Cooper called her.

And there was Rowsby, shadowing him like he'd hidden Jenny someplace.

The blue light of his dad's TV flickered behind the snow. He should go down and check on him, but he just wanted to go inside and hole up. All of them were holed up inside themselves, their spirits gone into hibernation. Maybe they'd emerge come spring, but it was hard to see how. He felt tongue-tied and helpless against Ruby's wall of anger. If she yelled—well, he could yell too, that would be a start. The two of them could stand out here and bay at the moon. If she cried when she was awake, he could do something. But she just crept around, and made polite talk when he asked her about school or the chickens.

Hazel would know what to do, but he hadn't told her how it was; she had enough going on.

Rowsby nosed his hand and whined.

"Let's go have supper. You'd like that, wouldn't you?" He looked up at Ruby's lit-up window. Should he make her come down? Lights were turning in at their road. Probably Tommy, coming to check on him. He and Rowsby went to wait under the eave, squinting into the snow.

But it was the LaFountains' truck. It skidded a little, stopped, and the lights and wipers went off. Then nothing.

Wally stepped out under the dooryard light. He heard the squeak of the driver's side door and Arnold got out.

"Evening, Wally."

"Evening."

"Could we have a word?"

His heart sank. He didn't know what he'd do if Remy couldn't help out anymore.

Arnold leaned into the truck and seemed to be arguing with someone. Then Remy slid out the other side and shuffled behind his father to where Wally held the door to the house open. Rowsby slipped in behind them and went directly to his empty food bowl.

"You can hang your jackets on the hooks."

But they didn't; they just whacked the snow off with their caps and left their boots by the door according to Hazel's and every farm wife's rules, including Betty LaFountain's.

"Have a seat. Can I get you anything?" Wally put a tin of cookies on the table. He scooped some kibble into Rowsby's bowl. It would do for now.

"No thanks, we're good," Arnold said, and sat down at the table. Remy shifted from foot to foot, looking at the floor. A Best Buy bag dangled from his hand.

"Sit down," Arnold said to Remy, something in his voice.

Remy sat on the very edge of the chair, the bag in his lap.

So this *was* about Remy. Wally pulled out a chair and sat.

"Son," Arnold said.

Remy jumped at the bang of the water pipe overhead, followed by the squeak of a faucet.

"It's just Ruby," Wally said.

Remy looked down, and then lifted his chin and looked Wally in the eye. "It was me," he said.

"What?"

"It was me who did it."

"I don't—" And then he did. It was there in Remy's eyes, which, now he'd gotten the words out, filled with tears.

Remy talked then, turning his cap around and around. "I thought it was a deer. Cooper's calf, I thought she was a deer—you *never* let the herd up there during—I'd spent the whole day in my stand, waiting, and then coming home I saw her—like she'd shown up just for me. I believed that, like..."

Magic, Wally thought. Like magic. He remembered such moments himself, and he hadn't been as young as Remy. Believing—*wanting* to believe—that an animal *gave* itself.

Remy started to cry, like a child.

He *was* a child. Just a year older than Ruby.

"Mr. Brown, I wish—I'd do anything to go back." Remy wiped his sleeve across his face and pried a wrinkled paper out of his pocket. "I'll pay for your calf. I figured it out, what you'd make from her over the next thirty years—how much milk, how many pounds, I figured it all out, and her calves—I'll work as long as it takes, and my savings, I have a little savings, from birthdays."

Wally looked at the trembling paper, loath to touch it.

He took it. It was a list. Pounds of milk, years divided into months and weeks and days. Remy's b's and d's looped at the bottom like Cooper's. Hazel'd been working on that with him.

"I didn't see him! I didn't *see* him, I'd do *anything* to go back and see him!"

Remy started sobbing in earnest. Wally got up and grabbed some paper napkins from the counter. He put them on the table in front of Remy, and his hand hovered over his shoulder. But he couldn't put it down; he just couldn't.

Remy blew his nose, handing balled-up soggy napkins across to his father one by one, and Arnold accepted them, the way you would. The way *he* would, if it was his son.

Wally looked away from the pain in Arnold's eyes. "It was getting dark! And why the *hell* didn't you get your parents, or—what the hell *did* you do after you shot my son?"

"I never *saw* him. I never *saw* him! When I saw it was a calf I ran home and got my bike and came over. I thought about crossing the ravine, but it's icy, so—I always come on my bike, I would have been anyway, to help with the milking, with you and Mr. Brown gone. Oh, God! I'd do anything!"

"What *did* you do?"

"The ambulance was here, but no one was in it, so I ran to both houses but couldn't find anybody. Then I saw the lights coming down the hill."

Remy squeezed his head.

"I'm *sorry*! I'd do anything to go back!"

Wally blew out air. Of course, *somebody* had to have done it, it's not like he didn't know that. It was just—it was just he'd made up who had. An outsider. Some ignorant flatlander who couldn't tell a calf from a deer. Nobody he knew, and he could hate him as much as he wanted.

"Of course you would," he finally said. "Of course you would." He shook his head. "How did you figure out it was a calf?" Oh, what did it matter!

"It was how she went down. I knew from how she fell. A deer and a calf—" Remy stopped.

"What the hell were you *using*? The sheriff says it was a semi-automatic."

Remy nodded.

He didn't look away, Wally had to give him that.

"Where'd you learn to use one of those?"

Remy shook his head.

"Speak up!"

"I didn't. I mean—I don't. It got away from me."

"Where the *hell* did you *get* the gun?"

Remy gave a sidelong look at his dad. "Online."

"*Online*?"

"He met me behind the feed store."

Wally needed them to leave.

"I'm sorry, Wally. I didn't know 'til an hour ago," Arnold said.

Wally didn't have anything more to say. He could barely stand looking at them. He'd have to call Tommy St. Francis. But even if they tracked down the guy who sold Remy the gun, he'd probably just get a slap on the wrist, Vermont gun laws being what they were.

"The sheriff is expecting us." Arnold stood up. "We'll sell the rifle and give whatever it brings to you." He put out his hand.

Wally hesitated for a second, then took it.

Remy lifted the Best Buy bag. "I wanted to give Cooper something. It's called Minecraft. He can do it from—"

Wally shook his head. Not now.

Remy put the bag on the couch. "Mr. Brown, I'd give anything to go back and stop myself."

Wally couldn't bring himself to shake Remy's hand. Or hug him, that's what he really needed. But he just couldn't.

"I know that, Remy," he said. "I know you would. It was a mistake. It was just an awful, terrible mistake."

He watched until the lights turned onto the main road before stumbling to the couch. Rowsby came out from under the table. Wally patted the cushion next to him, and the dog heaved himself up and circled. Like a deer making a bed, Wally thought, although there wasn't enough room and Rowsby's tail whacked him on the ear each time around until he finally sank down with a sigh.

Hazel's new couch. No dogs allowed.

How many other ways would they break Hazel's rules before this was over?

He was going to have to tell her about Remy. And what about Ruby? He gazed up at the ceiling. Hazel wouldn't have stood for her being off by herself all the time.

He checked the clock. Almost time for Cooper's call. Cooper thought Remy could jump over the moon.

I should've punched the kid. It would've done me as much good as it would Remy.

They shouldn't sell the gun; they should smash it into pieces.

He lurched up and grabbed the tin of cookies and flung it across the room. The top flew off and cookies fell in an arc, breaking into pieces when they hit the floor. Rowsby jumped off the couch and began to scoop them up. At least he was eating again.

Wally wished he could walk down the hill and sit with his dad and watch some game, it didn't matter what, though the Bruins would be best. And when his dad muted the sound for the ads they'd talk with no particular purpose, ranging from the price of milk to the latest foolish thing the governor said. Maybe his dad would pop up with a poem. Maybe the one about the woods. He might even know why its owner lived in town.

He heard Ruby's footsteps and swung his head to watch her come down the stairs, each step angrier than the one before. Rowsby tucked his tail in and scurried under the table, guilty of eating the cookies.

If he had a tail, he'd tuck it in too.

She stopped at the bottom, crossed her arms, and glared.

"It was a *mistake*? A t*errible mistake*? He was hunting *alone*! It's against the law! There's supposed to be a grownup!"

"Not if he was on his own land."

"Cooper and Jenny were on their own land! He *cried*! He doesn't *get* to cry! *Minecraft*?" She grabbed the Best Buy bag and threw it at Wally, hitting his chest. He caught it and reached for her.

She spun away, pushing at the space between them.

"Don't!" she screamed. "Just don't! He said he'd *pay* for Jenny! Pay for *Jenny*! Her babies! How many pounds of milk? What about what a *foot* weighs—of course, it's small—so small—" She broke into sobs. "He could make a *graph*—a *growth* chart—how much it would weigh when Cooper grows up!"

She covered her face. "Daddy!"

He put his arms around her.

"I hate him," she said into his shirt. "I *hate* guns. I *hate* hunting."

"That's a lot of hate."

"Nobody should hunt! It's *mean* and—*selfish*!"

"This family's had a hunting tradition for generations and never had an accident." Why was he defending it?

Ruby pulled a balled-up paper from her pocket.

"It used to be *tradition* that people owned people! It used to be *tradition* that women couldn't vote!" She threw the paper at him. "*Read* it!"

U.S. Forest Service
1400 Independence Avenue SW
Washington, D.C.

November 29

Dear Ms. Brown,

In regard to your letter dated June 10th of this year, the Forest Ranger stationed in Rochester, Vermont, made a site visit to the gravel pit you referred to. He found that although, as you described, it is near a hiking trail, it is recessed, with a berm, and has been used by generations of Vermonters for target practice. Target-shooting in gravel pits is a time-honored tradition in Vermont, and shooting is lawful in the 400,000 acre Green Mountain National Forest, which is public land. If you wish to pursue your concerns further, I suggest you take it up with local officials who might want to post warnings in the area.

Sincerely,

Reginald H. Smythe

"Tradition stinks!"

They heard the phone upstairs, where Ruby had taken it after school.

"I can't," she whispered.

They looked at the answering machine on the kitchen counter.

"Dad! Ruby! Where are you?"

Ruby turned her back on his voice, as if Cooper might see she'd been crying.

"A dog came to visit today! Her name is Pickles, and she's trained not to bump. She's little, not big like Rowsby."

Rowsby barked once at the machine, his tail wagging furiously.

"I got two new jokes. I'll wait and tell them when you come. Ruby comes Saturday, when vacation starts, right?" His voice got low, like he had a secret. "I can't come home for Christmas. Daddy, will you tell Ruby? She'll probly cry."

Ruby ran for the stairs, taking them two steps at a time. Wally heard her voice from below. "Cooper, it's me!"

Wally stood at the bottom of the stairs. How did she do that? How did she sound so chirpy when her heart must be breaking? He'd heard Hazel do it too, and his mom. Rowsby pushed between his legs and scrambled up the stairs, more energetic than he'd been for a long time. Maybe Cooper was up there. Maybe Jenny was with him!

Wally sank to the step.

He didn't think he'd ever felt so lonesome.

Chapter 17

COOPER SAW RUBY AT the door to the playroom. It was Christmas vacation, and she'd be staying for two whole weeks! "We're decorating!" He lifted up his paper chain.

Issa had told them a special visitor was coming that day. It was probably Santa, and for Denny's sake he'd have to pretend. He was good at it. He pretended to be sleeping so his mom could take a break. He pretended he was fine when they stuck him with another needle. He pretended his pain was five instead of ten, so his mom wouldn't cry. He couldn't watch, but he pretended he could take it when they changed the dressings. And the biggest one of all, he pretended he wasn't scared each time they rolled him into the operating room for another surgery.

He was pretending so much he worried he might pretend Jenny away, instead of trying not to think about her.

Ruby walked over to the table and hugged him from the side, careful of his leg sticking out. "I can't believe you're already in a wheelchair!"

"Ruby, look!" Denny held up a paper tree, dripping with glitter glue. Denny had cancer and had lost his hair but it was coming back. He reminded Cooper of Ruby's chicks.

"That's awesome!" Ruby said.

Cooper swept the mound of paper chain into his lap and unlocked his chair.

Hazel stood up.

"I can do it, Mom." He didn't look at her, in case he'd hurt her feelings.

"Is Issa here?"

It was a man's voice. Cooper turned the chair to see if he was dressed like Santa Claus, and smacked the footplate against the table leg. He gasped.

Then his mom was there, and he turned his head into her stomach. He heard the squeak of Issa's shoes crossing the room.

"I'm Issa, the pediatric activities director. And you must be Dustin, and Amra. Welcome!"

Cooper looked up.

A girl was standing next to the Christmas tree. She had on a sports jersey with a superhero he'd never seen on it, its body covered with stars and stripes like a flag, and she wore a scarf like some of the cancer kids. She walked over to them and held out her hand.

"I'm Amra."

He tried to read the words on her shirt. *Wounded War—*

His mom took Amra's hand. "I'm Hazel Brown. And this is Ruby."

"Hi."

"And this is Cooper, and that's Denny."

"Hi, Cooper. Hi Denny! That's a pretty tree!"

"Coopuh cut it out and I did glittuh."

"I like glitter too."

"Cooper Brown! I've been wanting to meet you. I'm Sergeant First Class Delaney," the man said. He was wearing a jersey just like Amra's. "Call me Dustin."

Hazel pushed Cooper, following Issa to the couches. Cooper stared. Was Amra's foot *metal*? He looked at Ruby. She widened her eyes.

"Dustin is a member of the Wounded Warrior Amputee Softball Team," Issa said.

The metal was bent where it met the floor and went up inside Amra's jeans like the stick under the dress on his and Ruby's Harvest Festival scarecrow. Her other foot looked regular, in a sparkly sneaker with silver stars on the sides. She saw where he was looking and smiled.

"From the mall on Western Avenue," she said. "The shoe, not the foot, I mean." She laughed. "Wish it were that easy! I have a leg that looks like a real one, too, and then I wear both shoes, but this is what I use for sports." She stuck out her leg.

"Amra attended our camp last summer," the sergeant said. "She's a wicked shortstop."

"You run?" Cooper blurted.

"I *know*! I didn't believe I ever would again, after the accident. I basically thought my life was over. But I can run—and jump—and kick. And dance. Though I won't lie to you, it's not like having a regular leg, no matter what they say. But still, I'm here to say you'll be able to do a lot. And they make specialized ones, for rock-climbing and stuff. And I can wear most normal shoes on my other prosthesis." She looked over at Ruby. "Even low heels."

"Your shoe is awesome," Ruby said.

"You should get a pair when you're here!"

"How did you lose your leg, Amra?" Issa asked.

"It was a car accident. People say I'm lucky to be alive." She made a face. "I hate that."

Cooper nodded. And suddenly he was *in it*. That's the way it happened. He hadn't been thinking about it at all, and then suddenly he was in it, like he was drowning. The sound and Jenny falling, and blood—so much blood. Jenny's scream. And crawling. Trying to. Trying to crawl home.

And now Remy. It was *Remy*.

But he wouldn't cry. Not in front of this girl, or Issa, or Ruby, or his mom. His mom, especially. He turned his face toward the windows; the lights of the Christmas tree were reflected in it, like there was another one hovering in the air outside.

"Cooper, are you okay?" Ruby whispered. She took his hand. He shook her off.

"Tell us about Wounded Warriors," Issa said.

"We're all vets and amputees." Dustin hiked up his pant leg. "It's okay, I want you to look. We travel around the country playing softball against local teams, to educate the public about the resilience of wounded veterans. And we run a summer camp for kids like Amra here. Amra's dad served in Iraq, and veterans' kids have priority to attend the camp."

"Cooper and Ruby's uncle was killed in Afghanistan," Hazel said softly.

"I'm sorry. Your brother?"

"Their dad's brother. It happened before Cooper was born."

"I'm so sorry."

"Amra, the figure on your shirt looks like it's wearing prostheses," Hazel said.

"Yeah, it's great, isn't it!" Amra said. "I even wear it to school. Two years ago, I never thought I'd ever even want to go to school again." She turned to Cooper. "You're probably worried how it'll be—I was! But it'll be better than you think."

"Cooper, is there anything you'd like to ask us?" the sergeant asked.

Cooper shrugged, embarrassed. He felt stupid. He'd thought "vets" meant animal doctors.

And there were a hundred things—a million things—he wanted to ask.

"I have a question," Hazel said. "When do you take off your prosthesis? Like when you go to bed? Or other times, like in the shower?"

Dustin folded his pant leg up higher. "See where my stump and thigh meet? My stump needs airing and washing and lotion twice a day, so I don't wear my prosthesis when I'm just hanging around the house, or when I bathe, or in bed."

"I don't wear mine all the time when I'm home, either," said Amra. "For me, it's kind of like a shoe—useful for a lot of things, but not necessary for everything." She looked at Hazel. "You could talk to my parents about all of this, and how to get help paying, too. My dad says by the time I grow up he'll be able to print me a leg!"

"You mean, like on a 3D printer?" Ruby asked.

"Yeah."

"Cool!" Cooper said.

"May we see you run?" Issa asked. "I don't usually allow running, but it's for a good cause."

It was just what Cooper wanted.

"Sure," said Amra. She walked over to the windows and leaned into a running position. She looked at Cooper.

"Say when!"

"One...two...three...go!"

And she did. Running. Running *fast*. When she got to the end of the room she spun around and came back. When she stopped, she jumped up and came down, and shimmied.

And then she laughed.

It was way better than any fake Santa Claus.

~

Before she left, Amra told Ruby about a park nearby where there was a big outdoor Christmas display. "The trees are strung with lights, and there are other things, too, like Santa's sleigh and reindeer. It's amazing, you should go!"

Reassured that Issa would keep her eye on Cooper, Hazel realized that the walk to the park could be her opportunity to ask Ruby about school, and then, hopefully, pump primed, about Remy. But she never got a foothold against Ruby talking about Amra.

"Mom! Can you believe what she can *do*? Do you think she's Muslin? I mean, Mus*lim*. I mean, she was wearing a hijab, is that how you say it? Her shoe was so cool! She said she'd email, can I? You said no Facebook, but *you* email! It's like pen pals, only not olden days. Mom! Look!" Ruby pointed.

Lights winked and flickered behind a wall of bare trees bordering the park. Crossing the street, they saw there was a pond, and a pavilion next to it, lit from top to bottom by multicolored lights. Its reflection shimmered on the water, looking like an underwater castle. Old-fashioned skaters twirled in the air above it.

It was magical.

A footbridge crossed the pond and they stopped at its center to take everything in. Santa flew over the tops of trees in his sleigh, his reindeer dipping their heads up and down. Elves were passing bright packages down a line in the air. There was a merry-go-round a few feet above the ground, its horses bobbing up and down, and further along, Snoopy dancing.

"It's like we're inside a Disney movie," Ruby said, twirling. She spotted small flickering lights up on a rise. "Mom, look! It's a fairy circle!"

They crossed the footbridge and tiptoed up the slope, as if there were real fairies at the top and they could scare them away. As they got closer, they heard a voice, followed by another, a pause in between. Like a spell, Ruby thought. Then step by step, the fairies came into focus and became real people, and each person was holding a candle. They were passing a paper around and reading names, and Hazel recognized the one just read. And the next. She put a hand over her mouth. They were the names of the Sandy Hook children.

They were doing the same thing back home on the town green. She'd gone, the second year, with Jenny. December. Newtown. Sandy Hook. How many years now? She should be thinking about *them*—those other parents and the unendurable loss they were having to suffer for the rest of their lives. Not herself. She was the lucky one.

She pulled Ruby back.

"What?" Ruby whispered.

Her eyes hot with sudden tears, Hazel turned to leave.

Ruby was too young, she didn't have to know. She *shouldn't* have to know.

But Ruby stepped closer. A woman noticed her and made room and Hazel had no choice, unless she made a scene. She stepped into the circle too. A man gave them each a candle and lit them from his.

"And now we'll read the Sandy Hook Promise, written by some of the families," someone said. "We'll pass it around and take turns."

This is a Promise. To truly honor the lives lost by turning our tragedy into a moment of transformation.

This is a Promise. To be open to all possibilities. There is no agenda other than to make our community and our nation a safer, better place.

This is a Promise. To have the conversations on ALL the issues, conversations where listening is as important as speaking, conversations where even those with the most opposing views can debate in good will.

This is a Promise. To turn the conversation into actions. Things must change. This is the time.

This is a Promise we make to our precious children. Because each child, every human life is filled with promise, and though we continue to be filled with unbearable pain we choose love, belief, and hope instead of anger.

Taking it, Hazel saw that the paper was inside a clear plastic sleeve, and there were water spots on it, as if it had been in rain or snow. Last year and the year before and the one before that. Her hand trembled, and her voice shook too, as she read. It was the last promise, and she was glad. She wouldn't have to hand it to Ruby.

"This is a Promise. To do everything in our power to be remembered not as the town filled with grief and victims; but as the place where real change began."

Ruby took the paper out of Hazel's hands. She read the very last words in her clear child's voice. "This is our Promise."

Chapter 18

Lemon Fair Links

This month's appeal is for the Brown family. Needed: One foot (left, size 2) and one ankle (attached). They come in many models, colors, and materials, with a variety of bells and whistles. Like buying a car, you have your standard model that will get you from point A to point B, all the way up to the sports model, the Pro-flex-400 (only $20,000!) that would give Spiderman competition. Like the Firebolt that Harry Potter had. And a Merry Christmas to all!

Hazel sighed. She clicked on Select All and then Cut, instead of SEND. She never would have, though. Would she? It was awfully tempting.

She kept running the tab in her head: 20 percent, 20 percent, 20 percent—of the hospital, of the doctors, of the tests. Of the helicopter, *God!*—all added onto their $5,000 deductible, which they'd be paying twice, since Cooper's hospital stay would be going into the second month of the new year now for sure. And insurance would only kick in *after* they'd paid their share.

And what about the rest of his life?

Did they sell prosthetics on eBay or Craigslist? After all, kids grew out of them, like shoes. Did they get new ones for the first day of school?

Wanted: One fairy godmother.

That morning Hazel and Wally had signed a paper giving permission for the doctors to amputate what was left of Cooper's ankle. Then they went down two floors to be initiated into the world of prosthetics. Hazel could barely make herself touch them as they passed them around and wiggled their moving parts like puppet feet, although she did for Cooper's sake. And how his face lit up when the last one appeared! It was shiny and slick and high-tech—just like what a super-hero robot would get around on.

They'd been handed a badly photocopied list of nonprofits to apply to for assistance, along with two glossy for-profit company brochures picturing joyful children in colorful sports clothes kicking soccer balls, climbing up walls, swimming, and skiing. Downhill. They couldn't afford to do that before, even with perfect feet!

They'd used up their line of credit on farm expenses, and they didn't have one rich relative. A nurse told them people go on the Internet and beg. It was called GoFundMe, all one word.

"Lots of people do it in situations like yours."

The insurance company offered—"just give us the word"—to sue the person who caused the accident, except they called it an "offense." Sue the LaFountains, and make them lose their farm? That kind of thinking just fed a part of her she didn't want to feed.

It made sense when they explained it, that it's better to replace whole bone structures than taking pieces and then more pieces and then more. The foot and ankle were complicated. There were so many bones, ligaments, and tendons that would need to be rescued, repaired, replaced—again and again, since Cooper was just seven—not even mentioning skin grafts and the risk of infections. It was all surreal. Her new vocabulary had kept growing. Neuroma, phantom limb phenomenon, trans diaphyseal, Syme procedure, epiphyseal growth plate, disarticulation, elasticity, resection, viability, irrigation. And the worst: debridement. At least losing the ankle would end that!

"Mom? Mom!"

Hazel jerked. She turned to face the door and Ruby. Ruby, who'd begged her on the phone to Do Something after she'd seen the big jar at Paulsen's Store: For the Brown Family.

"Mom! It's So Embarrassing!"

"This isn't about you," she'd said, and instantly wished she hadn't. She wouldn't have been surprised if Ruby had hung up. Every phone call had been punctuated by something or other that would be different if she were home. Like Ruby reporting in a fake, just-mentioning-it voice that she hadn't tried out for the role of James Madison in the Constitutional Convention because it was "lame."

"You said you'd only be a few minutes! I need to start!"

"Five minutes more."

"You said—"

"Pinky promise. I'll be quick."

"You better be. It's Christmas Eve!" Ruby said, and left. If the hospital room door could slam, it would have.

Okay. Take two.

Lemon Fair Links

I want to thank the many of you who have been supporting our family as we adjust to new circumstances. For those of you who may not know, our son lost a foot in a gun accident right before Thanksgiving and is at Albany Medical Center. It will be several more weeks before he'll be able to come home, and then we'll travel back and forth as he is fitted for a temporary prosthesis and then a semi-permanent one. He will go through many until he's full-grown.

Hazel lifted her hands off the keys, as if her fingers might type out the truth again. Wanted, one foot for $20,000. And more. How he had nightmares, and Ruby too. How she needed to talk to a counselor, sometime when she could take a breath.

How he could be dead.

Meanwhile, Cooper and the children here have enjoyed the games and puzzles and books you've sent down (She couldn't bring herself to say his favorite was Minecraft, even though it was true. It had been the perfect gift), *and the drawings his classmates made. I've been brought to tears seeing your names on the cards, as if you've joined hands to make a net to hold us while we get our bearings. You may not even know whose hand you're holding. Just look around you as you go through your day—that's who. It's a funny feeling to think of the jars around town having our family's name on them.*

Ruby wouldn't like that last sentence. Like rubbing it in. She deleted it.

Everyone's life is touched by trauma at some time, and I'm so grateful we live in a place where we take care of each other.

I want to give a special thanks to Tommy St. Francis, the Somers family, and the LaFountains.

Remy was working in their barn before and after school not twenty yards from her house. Not to mention Betty's meals and Arnold. She never wanted to see any of them again. Never. Ever. But she would, and she knew she'd be nice about it, too.

She got up and walked over to the window and pressed her forehead against the cool glass. The setting sun lit up the hills across the river. She watched until its glow sank into the water and house lights popped on. It was Christmas Eve, and all the kids would be popping with excitement. Would her children ever feel like home was safe again?

Cooper didn't say a word after Wally told him about Remy, just went quiet like he had when she'd told him about Jenny. It cut her to the heart, holding him, helpless. It was the first time she'd failed at being his mommy, and he hadn't mentioned Jenny since. Maybe if Ruby said something—but that wasn't fair to either of them.

And last but not least, thank you to Pastor Lori and our church for feeding my husband and daughter and father-in-law. Would it be bad form to ask for fewer lasagnas?

Had she left anybody out? Probably.

She clicked SEND and closed the laptop. She opened Cooper's bottom drawer and slipped it under his socks, still in their rolled-up pairs. At least socks didn't come in lefts and rights like shoes. Just like that, Cooper has twice as many socks. Ha ha. She hadn't bought the gaudy Christmas socks they stuffed into Cooper's and Ruby's Christmas stockings every year.

She slipped to her knees and, one by one, separated each pair and threw them back into the drawer. Then she stirred them. She put her hands on her belly. Where he'd started out.

Where he'd been perfect from his little bald head to his ten tiny toes.

~

Ruby looked around in satisfaction. They'd brought in extra chairs from the playroom and Cooper's bedside table had been moved to the foot of his bed for the little tree to stand on. It looked almost real, with a string of colored lights and some of their decorations from home, but it was too bad they weren't allowed to have the one her dad and grandpa brought down, with its smell of the pine woods. The only smell was the medicine smell that hung in the air after Cooper's dressing was changed.

Her dad had brought Christmas lights that ran on batteries back from the mall with the tree, and Ruby had wound them around the bars of the extra bed, grateful that Cooper didn't have a roommate. Cooper's paper chain hung on the wall as close to the ceiling as she could reach, and she'd taped the cards from people at home below it. She'd tucked the smaller presents around the tree and put the bigger ones on the wide window sill. Her grandpa and parents sat facing the tree and Cooper was in his bed.

"Ready?" she asked.

"Ready!" they said together.

She turned off the overhead light.

And, like magic, it was Christmas.

They were silent for a long time, taking it in. Ruby looked from one beloved face to another. Cooper's face was lit by the tree and his eyelashes made little shadows on his cheeks. Light glinted off her grandpa's silver tooth. Her mom and dad were holding hands and her mom's eyes were shining as she watched Cooper's face.

Ruby's own eyes stung too, from the wonder of it all. She'd been so worried it would be horrible. Her grandpa looked at her. She read his lips. *Good job.*

"*Now* can I open a present?" Cooper asked.

They all laughed.

"Just one, and then we eat." It was what their mother always said. What they always did. Ruby sighed in relief. And they were having pizza, which only made it better in her opinion.

Cooper went right for the biggest present, of course. He hadn't figured out yet that smaller ones could be just as good or even better. And one of his was this year, for sure. She smiled inside.

Cooper tore off the wrapping paper. It was a giant stuffed Olaf from the movie *Frozen II,* his favorite of the movies Ruby had brought down from the library at home. He hugged it tightly.

"Thank you!" Cooper said into Olaf's soft belly.

Olaf was so big Ruby couldn't see Cooper's face, but she heard the happiness in his voice. Olaf had been her idea.

Her turn. Her mom handed her a small box wrapped in silver paper. It hadn't been with the ones she'd put around the tree.

Could it—? She held it for a moment and then ripped the paper away.

"Oh my God! I can't believe it!" She held the phone up to show Cooper. "Cooper, I can call you!" She looked from her mom to her dad. "I mean—can I?"

"That's one of the reasons we got it for you. I know we always said not until you turned thirteen, but with me here, and your dad off somewhere on the farm…it seemed like a good idea for you to be able to be in touch."

"But if Dad's off somewhere—"

"He has one too."

"Dad has—" Ruby started to laugh.

"Not my idea!" Wally said. "We'll see if an old dog can learn new tricks."

"Lydie put in the numbers he should have, and a couple other things he might use, and she can do that for you too," Hazel said. "But there's no Internet. Not until you turn thirteen."

"Emily will know what to do, she's had a phone for years. Oh, Mom, thank you! Thank you!" She jumped up and hugged Hazel, and then Wally, and then, filled with too much happiness for just two, Henry and Cooper.

"This is the best present I ever got in my whole life!"

Wally stepped out to meet the pizza delivery guy and when he got back they peeled off pieces as if they'd been starving. Hazel passed out cups of sparkling cider and extra napkins, wiping Cooper's chin more than once. When they finished there wasn't even a crust left.

"Can we open the other presents now?" Cooper asked.

Hazel had told Ruby that, besides not getting their Christmassy socks, she and Cooper wouldn't be getting their usual Christmas Eve pajamas either. "I hope you don't mind too much, it's just—"

"I know, Mom. Cooper can't wear things on his leg yet. It's fine." And she knew there would be fewer presents this year because of all the expenses. But her phone made up for everything!

"Your turn, Cooper!"

All their eyes were glued on him as he ripped the paper off.

He ran his hand over the smooth gray surface, puzzled. "Mom's laptop?"

Ruby opened the lid. "No! It's yours! Mom got it from school, but you get to keep it."

"It's from school?"

"They're going to send you work," Ruby said. "But the reason we wrapped it like a present is because of everything else. You can watch movies and shows and read books and play games."

Cooper looked at the blank screen. "It does all that?"

"I'll show you!"

"Can I do Minecraft on it, like on Mom's?"

For a second Ruby wanted to grab the laptop away.

"If you want, I'll load it for you," she finally said. It was Christmas.

Henry brought out the tins of cookies that Betty LaFountain and Lydie had sent along. There were frosted sugar cookie trees decorated with sprinkles, frosted chocolate reindeer, pinwheels dipped in chocolate, peanut butter thumbprint cookies with Hershey's Kisses in the middle, and Santa-shaped shortbread.

And, from Maggie and Sally, five decorated gingerbread people with the family's names iced on their chests.

Ruby lifted hers to bite off its foot like she always did, and stopped. She put it down. She'd lost her appetite. And she didn't think she'd ever be able to eat a gingerbread person again.

She settled herself on the extra bed to listen to Grandpa read the Christmas story.

"And it came to pass in those days, that there went out a decree from Caesar Augustus, that all the world should be taxed...and Joseph also went up from Galilee, out of the city of Nazareth, unto the city of David; which is called Bethlehem; to be taxed with Mary his espoused wife, being great with child."

Ruby saw that Cooper was holding Olaf, so she picked up his moose and tucked it under her chin.

"And she brought forth her firstborn son, and wrapped him in swaddling clothes, and laid him in a manger; because there was no room for them in the inn."

Her grandpa paused and looked at her and Ruby was suddenly filled with happiness.

"Glory to God in the highest, and on Earth peace, good will toward men," he finished.

How was it that, after everything, Christmas still could happen and be so beautiful? It was just like the Grinch.

"Silent night, holy night, all is calm, all is bright, round yon virgin, mother and child…"

One by one they joined their voices with Hazel's.

"Holy infant so tender and mild, sleep in heavenly sleep, sleep in heavenly sleep."

They gazed at the little tree.

Cooper burst into tears. "It's too beautiful! It hurts my heart! I miss Jenny!" He bent over, crying, and Wally and Hazel jumped up and went to him. "Do you think Jenny's with Grandma? Do you think she's taking care of her?"

"I'm as sure as the love in this room," Grandpa answered. "And that's plenty."

Chapter 19

RUBY WIGGLED HER FOOT, admiring its sparkle. She loved, loved, loved her new sneakers, exactly like Amra's.

When Amra invited her to the movies, she'd felt shy. She'd never known a Muslim person before. Or anyone with one leg. But it was the *most* fun. The mall was huge, at least four times bigger than the ones back in Vermont. She'd bought her sneakers, and she and Amra had gotten matching fuzzy socks—not Christmas ones, even though they were on sale for half price, because Muslims didn't celebrate Christmas—and found out they both liked Skittles for movie candy. They'd already emailed twice.

Principal McBride walked across the stage. "Okay, settle down!" She pointed to the screen behind her. "Today we're introducing a new safety protocol for shelter-in-place that's being taught at every Vermont school. How it's implemented, of course, will be different for younger grades. It's similar to what you're used to, but with a few crucial differences."

Ruby and Jess exchanged a look. Another lame "protocol."

The principal read the words on the screen.

"ALICE—we're not scared, we're PREPARED!"

She pointed to the enormous A. "A. *Alert*! There's a wolf close by!"

Ruby poked Jess and bared her teeth. Jess stuck her tongue out like a dog.

"L. *Lockdown*! Stay quiet and out of sight!

I. *Inform*! Tell others about the wolf!

C. *Counter*! He sees us! We need to do something!

E. *Evacuate*. Let's run away fast!

And that spells ALICE!"

"She should have pompoms," Ruby whispered.

"Glad my name isn't Alice," Jess whispered back.

Emily, on Ruby's other side, started waving her arm wildly. Ruby wanted to melt into the floor.

The principal looked impatient. "What is it, Emily?"

Emily didn't need a microphone. "Assuming the wolf is a person with a gun, I don't think it's appropriate to make him be a wolf! Wolves are *totally* misunderstood! Did you know they mate for *life*? And they've been misrepresented as villains in stories *forever*, and in Vermont people can shoot one anytime they want; there isn't even a season!"

"Well, I confess I hadn't thought of it that way," Principal McBride said. "Perhaps you would like to write to—" She studied the paper in her hand. "For now, we'll just refer to the wolf as a person, shall we?"

She pointed back to the screen. "These actions should be taken in order. Number one, anyone who sees…a *person* who is a threat, should *A*, alert everyone. Then *L*, a lockdown, would ensue, and after that, *I*, the police should be informed. This includes by you students. Don't assume the information has gone out. But *C*, meaning *counter*, is a significant change from what you've done in the past."

A new slide appeared on the screen.

"Counter: block the door with desks, file cabinets, tables." She looked back to the auditorium. "And the second list of countermeasures are to be used if an active shooter gains entrance and there are no means of escape."

Ruby squeezed Jess's fingers in a death grip. It had stopped being funny.

"Create noise, movement, distance, and distraction to reduce the shooter's ability to shoot accurately. Throw things! Swarm and rush the person. Take them to the floor and hold them until law enforcement arrives." The principal frowned. "That seems unrealistic, I must confess. But what if everyone threw things and made a lot of noise?"

"I'd be dead!" a voice called from the back of the auditorium.

People laughed.

Ruby didn't.

Principal McBride didn't like it either.

"This is not a joke! You need to take it seriously and think about it. As you go through your day today, look around. Think about how you could counter in different spaces."

The principal scanned the student body, looking doubtful. She sighed. "Okay, that's all for now. You're excused to go to your third period classes."

Students poured into the hall, talking excitedly. Ruby watched a boy sweep his arm in an arc and jerk his finger—ratatatatatata.

"It makes me sick," Jess said.

"Whoever made it be a *wolf* is sick!" Emily said.

They turned into social studies, Ruby's favorite class.

Ms. Robinson waited for everyone to quiet down. "I'm sure you have questions about ALICE, but I'd prefer not to discuss them right now. You'll have a chance to talk in homeroom at the end of the day, and we have a lot to talk about. To start off, does anyone have a question about the rights we've covered so far? Yes, Emily?"

"Do animals have rights?"

"What do you mean?"

"Wolves are being maligned all over Vermont today, in every single school! Somebody needs to stop it!"

Ms. Robinson drew her eyebrows together.

"Emily, every right we're studying started with people who cared about somebody or something like you do. There's no reason to think you can't make a difference to wolves."

"Do kids have rights?" Jess asked.

"Kids have been at the center of very important rights. A Black girl in Kansas had to walk across her town to school because of racial segregation, even though there was a school a few blocks away from her home. Her dad took the school board to court, and other parents joined him as it went all the way to the Supreme Court. The parents won, and that was the start of federal school integration."

Ruby Bridges! Ruby thought.

"Another example: An eight-year-old sued her school because they wouldn't let her service dog come with her. Her win opened the doors to service dogs, not just at schools, but in workplaces, and buses, and stores."

Ruby didn't think Rowsby would like school, even if he was there to help Cooper. He didn't like to leave the farm.

"Students are responsible for stopping schools from making them pray. 'Congress shall make no law respecting an establishment of religion.' What's that mean in plain English? Yes, Sean?"

"It means my dad gets to stay home when I have to go to church with my mom."

Everyone laughed.

Emily waved her hand. "He's probably an atheist or maybe an agnostic. An atheist doesn't believe in a supreme being, but an agnostic says it can't be known."

Having Emily as a friend was like having your own personal Wikipedia.

Ruby thought she might be an atheist. God didn't stop Remy.

"Sean should say he's one of those, and stay home," Ethan suggested. "I mean, he has the right to, right? Even if it's his parents?"

"I might get in trouble for saying it, but every person has a right to their beliefs and opinions, including children." Ms. Robinson took a book off her desk, leafed through it, and read aloud.

"'All persons are born equally free and independent, and have certain natural, inherent, and unalienable rights, amongst which are enjoying and defending life and liberty, acquiring, possessing, and protecting property, and pursuing and obtaining happiness and safety.' That's our state's first amendment," Ms. Robinson said. "Unalienable rights. What does that remind you of?"

"The Declaration of Independence," Ethan said.

"Yes! Life. Liberty. The pursuit of happiness. You children have a right to them all—your constitutions say so, both state and country."

Ruby abruptly stood up, knocking her knee against the edge of her desk.

"Ruby?"

Ruby stumbled up the aisle and into the hall. Then she ran.

She plunged through the bathroom door to a sink just in time and threw up in spasm after spasm after spasm. Her chin and hands got splattered, and her throat burned. She felt like she'd been turned inside out.

The door swished open. "Ruby?"

It was Jess.

Jess saw the sink.

"Ew! That's disgusting."

Ruby began to laugh and then she was wailing, the sound bouncing off the walls.

"I kept hearing noises! I was sure it was coming back, and I had to stay, I had to *stay*, or Cooper could die! I kept thinking about the blood, it will smell the blood! And Jenny! Jenny's *eye*. And she was *covered* in *blood*! Oh, God! Jess! I said those words—I said those words over, and over, and over, and over—"

"What words? What words, honey?" Jess put her arm around Ruby.

"'Life, liberty, and the pursuit of happiness!' So stupid!" She started laughing again. Snot ran out of her nose.

"Oh, Ruby!" Jess squeezed her as hard as she could. Then she pulled out paper towels and ran them under the faucet to wash Ruby's face.

Ruby looked in the mirror. "Ugh."

"We can hide in the library 'til lunch," said Jess, pulling out more paper towels and scooping up the remains of Ruby's breakfast, holding her breath. It would be awhile before she could eat bacon again. She wiped the sink.

"No." Ruby ducked and slurped water into her mouth and swished. She spit it out. "The librarian knows my mom."

Jess wiped the final bits away. "Why the ding-dong were you thinking of life, liberty, and the pursuit of happiness at a time like that?"

Ruby snorted. "I *know*! I know!" She snaked wet paper towels up under her arms and wiped. Her T-shirt looked like she'd sweated right through! And she'd stink the rest of the day on top of it.

They washed their hands side by side, just like they had a million times before.

"I wish you'd told me. You can tell me *anything*," Jess said to the mirror.

"I try not to think about it."

"Who wouldn't? But if you talk about it, it'll get better. That's what my mom says, anyway."

"Yeah, my mom too." Ruby turned the water off.

When they got back to the room, the class was discussing the First Amendment.

"Sally, would you read the last part again, please?" Ms. Robinson was asking.

"...the right of the people peaceably to assemble, and to petition the Government for a redress of grievances."

"An old-fashioned word, redress. What's it mean?"

Ruby had looked it up. Redress: remedy or set right.

But some things can never be set right.

"Rory."

"If a law is bad, you can ask people to sign a petition and the law might be changed."

Not if you were a kid, Ruby thought, remembering the fair.

"You could do a boycott, like the buses in Montgomery, Alabama," Jess said. "You know, after Rosa Parks got arrested."

"They didn't ride the buses for 381 days!" Emily said.

Ms. Robinson pointed to the diagram on the whiteboard. "Which branch makes laws? State and country both. Everyone?"

"Congress!"

"And who makes our local laws? Who made the rule about no dogs at Harvest Festival? There was a big fuss about it. Bernie?"

"The town selectboard. My dad's on it."

"Yes. And if you want to see democracy in action, I recommend you go to a meeting. They have a time when people can bring up problems—'grievances.'" Ms. Robinson looked up and down the rows. "Someday it will be your legal responsibility to protect and stand up for rights, but that doesn't mean you shouldn't now. Like Emily and the wolves. It might feel like it, but what you're learning about isn't old history. It's the present. It's the future. Tomorrow we'll discuss the right to bear arms, meaning firearms. Not bare arms." She pushed up her sleeves.

Ruby liked Ms. Robinson a lot.

"My dad says people want to take away our guns!" Bernie said.

"That Second Amendment is old, before there were guns like AR-15s," Ethan said.

"My dad has one of those, it's called the Shockwave!" Bernie said. "And you can't change the Constitution!"

"Why not? There've been amendments added all along, like for voting. Amendment means change."

"Time out!" Ms. Robinson made a T with her hands, smiling. "We'll continue tomorrow. For now, go to lunch!"

She motioned for Ruby to stay.

"Are you alright?"

Ruby nodded.

"If you want to talk about anything, I'll be glad to listen. Sometimes it's just good to say things to another person, even when they can't do anything. Well, listening *is* doing something, actually."

Ruby *so* didn't want to tell about throwing up.

"I heard there's going to be a fundraiser for your family at the Grange Hall. Can we help here at school, maybe make posters on Freaky Friday?"

A fundraiser! Ruby was mortified.

"Just think about it. Freaky Fridays are for you kids." Ms. Robinson touched Ruby's arm. "I know there will be adjustments… a lot of them, probably, over the next few months." She looked over Ruby's shoulder. "Jess is waiting. You'd better get to lunch. I know there's never enough time."

~

Isabel stacked up four pudding cups. "I got extras, to throw at the big bad wolf."

"That's not funny," Emily said.

"The whole thing is crazy and disgusting," Jess said. She turned to Ruby. "I forgot to ask. Do you know when your mom and Cooper are coming home? Mom wants to load up your freezer."

"Maybe by the end of February." Would he wake up crying like he did at the hospital? Somebody should sleep with him. He'd begged her not to tell their mom, and she hadn't. But should she? She'd squeezed into his bed and stuck Olaf between them, afraid she'd touch his stump, until he fell back to sleep.

"They're fitting a temporary prosthesis during February vacation, but he'll go back a few weeks later for a better one."

They'd always done something special during February vacation.

"You'll all be together again!" Isabel said. "It's like you got *scattered to the winds.*"

Isabel wrote poetry.

"More like shattered!" Emily blurted out. She covered her mouth. "I can't believe I said that!"

"Why? It's true."

They all looked down and began to pick at their food, a strange island of silence in the noisy cafeteria. Emily finally broke it.

"There's a story my rabbi told us! That word shattered reminded me. Before God made the world, everything was dark, and God said, 'Let there be light.' Then he breathed light into lots of vases and sent them out in all directions. But the light—because it came from God's breath—was too powerful for the long journeys, and a lot of vases shattered into pieces. Each piece contained a part of God's breath, and in our lives, we're supposed to look for the pieces. Rabbi Hermas said we should look for a broken and sharp thing in the world, something hurtful, and that would be a piece. We free the light by doing something to help. When enough light has been freed, the world will be healed."

"It's like that other word…redress," Isabel said. "At least I think it is. I mean, the pieces are wrongs in the world. Like that fracking. A wound to the earth!" She threw out her arm dramatically.

Wound. Ruby put her sandwich down. She turned her head, as if pulled by a magnet. Remy was standing at the far end of the cafeteria holding a tray. Looking at her. He turned away, and she saw red rising up his neck just like it did in hers when she was embarrassed. Or ashamed.

Or hurt.

She didn't know if she wanted redress or a remedy, but something needed to change.

Chapter 20

HENRY TURNED ONTO HIS side and opened his eyes. The bedroom door was a box of light, a portal into the day. He smelled coffee and blueberry muffins. The first day of school. He flung the covers off and swung his legs over the side of the bed. He'd better be up-and-at-'em before Jenny came in and scolded he'd be late. He reached to turn on the lamp.

And remembered. He leaned over, his forehead almost touching his bare, bony knees, and waited while the miserable present pushed away the past.

It was Remy who'd started the coffee, *Remy*, as he did every morning, and left a small bag of his mom's muffins. Henry could hear him talking to Rowsby. And any second he'd hear Rowsby's snuffles as he gobbled his breakfast.

There.

Jenny was gone.

By the time he'd pulled on his clothes and brushed his teeth and given a lick and a promise to shaving, Remy and Rowsby were to-the-barn gone, and the coffee was burbling its last drips. His morning pill box was perched on top of the waiting cups so he wouldn't forget. He dumped the pills into his hand and swallowed them with a gulp of water. He pulled on his coverall and cap, stepped into his barn boots, and poured the coffee, two-thirds milk with sugar the way Remy liked it. Like a kid.

He picked up the muffin bag, tucked his fingers through the cup handles, and walked out into the crisp dawn, his breath like smoke in the cold air.

The cows were waiting, and as Henry walked down the aisle he was greeted by their grievances, as if each morning, despite all the mornings before that, he might forget to milk them. It reminded him of a poem. He stopped to think.

The cat washing himself in the aisle, the one Ruby called Marmalade, stopped too, a hind leg pointing straight up, so Henry recited the poem to him.

"There is a small green island where one white cow lives alone, a meadow of an island. The cow grazes till nightfall, full and fat, but during the night she panics and grows thin as...as a ..." As a what?

Marmalade stretched up and sauntered away, off to the milking parlor for breakfast.

Henry had it. "Thin as a single hair!" he called to the cat. "She panics and grows thin as a single hair. What shall I eat tomorrow! There is nothing left!"

Rumi. That was the poet's name.

Remy had his phone on speaker as usual, and country music accompanied the rhythm of the milking machine. Remy swore the cows loved it, and who was Henry to disagree? They certainly liked Remy.

"Good morning, Mr. Brown."

"Call me Henry."

It was the same every day.

Henry set the muffins and coffee on the shelf.

He clicked his tongue and Clementine clambered up the ramp. He wiped down her teats, stretching each to get her started, his palms checking for anything that might have gone amiss overnight. He aimed the last teat and squirted milk into the bowl for the cats, and Marmalade and two others melted down from the rafters.

Henry pulled the claw over and attached each cup, turned on the machine and stood up to stretch his back.

Remy handed him his coffee.

"We're off then!" Wally called from the side door. "Don't forget Pastor Lori!"

Pastor Lori?

"Some church ladies are cleaning the house," Wally said, in a tone like he'd said it before, and more than once.

And Henry remembered. This was The Day.

Homecoming Day!

It was yesterday they'd cleared out the dining room to make room for Cooper's bed and wheelchair, Ruby insisting they replace Jenny's drapes with Cooper's Smurf curtains.

"Dad! Mr. Somers is here!" Ruby yelled. And there she was, hovering a few feet behind Wally; crossing into the barn would break her anti-Remy rule. Henry glanced at Remy, who was adjusting the vacuum hose. Pretending to.

"The keys are on the car seat," Wally told Ruby. And she disappeared.

"Why's Somers here?" Henry asked.

"We're taking his SUV so Cooper can stretch out."

Henry grabbed the muffin bag. "Here. From Remy. For your trip."

"Well, thanks! Thanks, Remy, that's awfully kind," Wally said. He rocked back on his heels. "We'll be back about suppertime."

"Don't worry, Mr. Brown, I'll be done here, and home."

"That's not what I meant," Wally said.

"I understand," Remy said.

"I—never mind." Wally went up on his toes, and down. "I gotta say,

I'm excited!" He hesitated, as if he had more. "Well! See you, then."

Henry and Remy went back to their synchronized routine, accompanied by the Highwaymen singing "*Riders in the Sky.*"

"Yippie-yi-ay," Henry sang under his breath. "Yippie-yi-ay."

Clementine rattled down the ramp and Maple took her place.

Henry poured in fresh grain for her to eat while she was being milked. She let go a stream of urine. Just another morning, just another day, good pissing, good eats, warm barn, good company, all good; did she remember her Jenny at all? Would she care that Cooper was coming home?

Henry remembered the end of the poem, and when he started to recite it Maple fixed her dark eyes on him and listened. "The cow is the bodily soul. The island field is this world that grows lean with fear and fat with blessing, lean and fat. White cow, don't make yourself miserable with what's to come, or not to come."

Cows' eyes were like souls, steady and deep.

"I like that," Remy said. He finished his coffee-milk and stuck the cup next to the others lined up on a beam. Every few days somebody—Ruby?—spirited them away, and they came back clean to Henry's house and started over.

Henry usually loved milking as much as the cows, the sounds and smells he'd known his whole life bringing in the day. But today, with Cooper coming home, his thoughts started bouncing around in his head, trying to sort themselves into something more than a poem for a cow. He needed something for a wounded boy. He took off his cap and scratched his head.

"Remy, I know you feel bad. I can't be in your shoes, but nevertheless I know it'll get better. It'll take awhile, probably a long while, but there's not much that doesn't lose its sting, given enough time." He whacked his cap on his knee. "It could've happened with any of us when we were youngsters. Matter-a-fact, we used to hunt on *your* land."

But then his anger was rising, and it was at the whole

frickin'-fucking-damn-blasted world. That took Robbie. That took his Jenny. That took his grandson's foot and calf, and along with them his confidence in the safety of his homeplace.

That was closing off Ruby's heart a little more every day. It was hard enough to raise girls in this world! And even harder to raise boys.

You're s'posed to take care of your family, fight for your country, bring home a deer, and stand up for the Second Amendment like it was holy script. But this country sent his boy home in a body bag. This country let children buy semi-automatics from a computer, of all things!

"I'd do anything to take it back," Remy said, his face turned away.

Henry jerked his head around. "Well, you can't. You just got to live with it."

Remy met his eyes. "Yessir."

Henry felt ashamed. Remy was just a kid.

"Look. It's a hard lesson, but we all hafta learn it sometime or t'other. Some things you just got to live with, and that's as much part of life as the good stuff. Alls you can do is make your amends, take your licks, and try to use 'em to be better. That's all anyone can do."

Remy turned to hook up Strawberry, and Henry saw that a tear was running down his cheek.

He turned to hook up Ariel. It wouldn't be the first time a cow on this farm got cried on.

After everyone was milked and out in the field, and Henry and Remy had washed down the milking parlor, they stepped outside. Sunlight was spilling over the top of the hill, and they all looked up—the cows and heifers, the guileless calves, the lost old man and the lost boy, the self-satisfied cats and, curled up in an empty pen by the old barn, a left-behind dog. They waited, their faces upturned like sunflowers, as the first light washed over the hill until it came to them. Fat with blessings.

~

Twelve hours later, Henry stood and watched the light on the back of Remy's bike get swallowed by the dark. He didn't want to go in and face Pastor Lori and Trudy Foley. Trudy could talk your ears off, and seemed to especially favor his.

Rowsby nudged his leg. Time for supper.

It was a picture postcard night, a star-studded sky fitting like a bowl over the cow-studded field. Would seeing them there be hard for Cooper? They wouldn't understand, but maybe he should bring them in.

Rowsby barked and ran across the yard.

There'd been an opossum nosing around the day before.

"Rowsby!"

But then he saw it: a car was turning into the driveway. Cooper!

It was over. *Over.* Cooper was home, where he could keep an eye on him.

The car disappeared behind the garage and the engine went silent. Henry heard voices. The wrong voices. Then the whole Somers family came around the corner.

Lydie was carrying a big round Tupperware container that meant a cake or pie. It was nice of her, but all the same, he wished they weren't there.

"Looks like we're not the first," Jack said, pointing to Trudy Foley's truck.

"Church ladies been here cleaning all the livelong day," Henry said, and put his hand out. But instead, Jack pulled him into a hug.

Then it was Lydie's turn. She handed the Tupperware to Jess and put her arms around Henry and didn't let go. Finally, Henry hugged her back, and, like they'd been squeezed out, tears trickled down his cheeks. Oh, heck! He stooped and scratched Rowsby around his ears.

"Let's get inside," Lydie said.

"Mommy, look! A parade!" Tyler pointed.

A line of lights was strung along the road as far as Henry could see, the front of it turning into their driveway.

Jack laughed. "Would you look at that!"

"I told everybody at school!" Jess said. "You didn't make enough cake, Mom!"

But everyone had brought a contribution.

Tommy had a pie from the diner. "Blueberry!" he called out. "Made special. Dairy free!"

Half the church was there, including little Sally Lane looking fit as a fiddle. There was the selectboard and Ms. Robinson and Principal McBride from the middle school and Mrs. Fitch, the principal from Cooper's school, and his teacher and his baseball coach and the whole Lucas family. Ethan Foley and two other boys were there, and Ruby's friends Emily and Isabel, Isabel talking a mile a minute.

"Hi, Mr. Brown!" Emily yelled.

A herd of little boys surrounded Cooper's friend Seth, who was holding something up for them to see.

Henry took a step back, and then two, into the dark. No one would miss him. And no more hugs, he couldn't take any more of those. A tongue licked his hand.

"C'mon, Rowsby. They don't need the likes of us. Cake and pie aren't good for you anyways."

~

Henry startled awake. He felt for Jenny's afghan. Something had woken him up.

"Rowsby?"

"No, Grandpa, I made him go out. He was so excited he kept jumping on me. It's me. Cooper."

Henry swung and leaped to his feet.

Cooper!

He was *right there.* Right there in Henry's kitchen, leaning on crutches that were surely too big for him. (I can fix that, he thought.) Using the counter for balance, Cooper leaned the crutches against it. He took a step and transferred one hand to a stool. He took another step, using the stool for balance.

Then Henry was across the room and swinging him up. He swung him around and then stopped, shocked. What was he thinking?

Cooper wrapped his arms around Henry's neck. "Again."

Like when he was a toddler. *Again, Grandpa! Again*!

So Henry swung him again, slowly. When he stopped, he couldn't stand up; he was too full of it all. He staggered back and sank into his chair with Cooper in his lap.

"How did you get over here? Does your mother know?"

"I walked, Grandpa! But guess what? Seth is loaning me Truman Whitby! He's in his cage in my room! And guess what else! My room is the dining room!"

Henry squeezed. "Guess what? I helped move it there!" He squeezed again.

"Grandpa! Want to hear a joke?"

"I do. I do, Cooper. I surely do."

"Okay. What do you call a very large moose?"

"Hmm, let me think—" Henry stuck his nose into Cooper's neck. Heaven. "I give up. What *do* you call a very large moose?"

"E*nor*moose! Get it?"

Henry nodded, too choked up to answer.

"Want to hear another?"

"There's nothing I want more."

"Okay. What cow lives in a haunted barn?"

Henry grinned. He'd been the one to tell Cooper that one.

"Cow-nt Dracula!"

Chapter 21

*C*OOPER COULD HEAR *A*MY'S *raspy breath next to him. The smell of the paint jars tickled his nose. He squeezed it. No noise! Biscuit's glowing eyes turned Ms. Phillips's face green. They couldn't have a real guinea pig because Amy was allergic. Ms. Phillips put her finger to her lips, Shh, even though they were already Shh-ing. Biscuit's eyes were the only light in the art closet, but they were almost as big as a paper cup, which he knew from when he and Seth taped cups on them to make them bug eyes. You could tell when Biscuit went to the next person by how their face turned green. They were only supposed to take a one-minute turn. But his teacher couldn't do anything—she had to follow the same Shh rule. Not even whispering. When it was his turn, he rubbed his cheek against Biscuit's fur and stared at his eyes. Then suddenly blood burst out. He tried to scream.*

No noise!

"Jenny!"

Wally jerked awake. He was out of the chair and to the bed in under a second, but Rowsby was there first. Cooper's eyes were wide open, but Wally could tell he was looking someplace else.

"Shh. It's okay, Cooper." He ran his hand over Cooper's hair. "It's just a dream."

He stroked his hand down Cooper's forehead and down over his eyes, an old trick from when the kids were babies and couldn't get to sleep. He stroked and stroked and stroked.

"Caw!"

Wally straightened the towel over Truman Whitby's cage. "Shh." The crow was wrestling with something, probably rearranging his collection. He took such pleasure in sneaking things that they'd taken to leaving paper clips and other shiny things around for him to find and carry off. Truman Whitby had become a part of the family, an entertaining distraction but, more important, someone for Cooper to take care of when he himself needed so much care.

Wally finally got up from his knees to go back to the rocking chair, leaving Rowsby to stand guard. It was the same chair his mom had rocked him in and, rocking Cooper sometimes, he was comforted too, as if he were both the boy and the father of the boy.

Did Cooper dream he was running, like Rowsby did? Did he have phantom freedom? He had phantom pain, pain in a foot that wasn't there. A ghost-foot.

The crow banged something, and Rowsby raised his head. He looked at Wally. *Do something.* But sometimes Truman Whitby sang under his towel and his croaky voice was worth a whole Dollar Store's collection of sparkly things, because it made Cooper laugh.

Wally heard footsteps above his head. Ruby still had nightmares. There'd been a few times when Cooper and Ruby cried out at the same time, as if they were sharing a horror in a place beyond his and Hazel's reach; they'd been taking turns, one of them with Cooper and the other in his old room upstairs next to Ruby's on the air mattress. They were exhausted.

He missed Hazel. How long would it be before they'd be back in their own bed, together?

He missed his family.

He missed who they used to be.

Coming home from the fundraiser had been hell, Ruby screaming at Cooper the second they were in the car because Cooper had told her friend Kenny that he was going to do hunter safety.

"How can you even *think* about it? Are you an *idiot*?"

They weren't used to screaming, their family didn't scream. Or call each other names. Was this the way it was going to be now? But Ruby had fun at the fundraiser, he was sure of it, even though Hazel had to shame her to make her go.

He himself had felt shy to join the men talking about milk prices and the chances for the Red Sox this year. He felt like he'd been off in a foreign country and was struggling to remember his native language. And he loathed needing their charity. Although truth to tell, if he had a bird's eye view of the big hall, with lines showing who helped who at one time or another, he knew it would be so crisscrossed it would look like a dozen spider webs.

And Cooper'd had a blast, showing off how he could do wheelies with his wheelchair and charging a quarter for kids to have a ride until Hazel put a stop to it. Wally grinned in the dark.

Ruby's footsteps again. He should go check before she woke up Hazel.

But when he got to the kitchen he saw Ruby's legs at the top of the stairs, and stepped back into the hallway. There was something furtive in the attitude of those pajama legs, despite the purple bunnies.

He watched her go to the mudroom—definitely sneaking—and pull on her jacket, hat, and boots. She took down the flashlight and a second later he heard the sound of the door being opened and closed.

He thought for a minute, then hustled to shrug on his own jacket and pull on his boots. But then he hesitated. She'd be going to the barn to talk to Maple. He could hear Hazel's voice in his head: *It's an emotional age. And all that's happened. We have to give her room.*

But there was that *attitude*. He put his hand on the doorknob. And jumped.

"Geez, you about gave me a heart attack," he whispered, pushing Rowsby back. "You can't come."

God, it was cold! His dad had been right on the money to keep the herd in. He spotted the flashlight beam lighting the path to his dad's. Not the barn and Maple. He crept behind, slipping and catching himself. He was too old to be sneaking around. He heard the click of his dad's door, loud in the thin air. When he got closer, he skidded to a stop and peeked through the window. The flashlight was directed at the gun cabinet. He watched Ruby's arm, a dark shadow, snake behind it and come out with something that gleamed. The key to the cabinet.

He was there in two strides, and when he opened the door Ruby turned and gasped, and dropped the flashlight. She put her hands up, as if he might take a gun from the cabinet and aim it at her.

"What are you *doing*?" Wally hissed. He scooped up the flashlight and aimed it at her. "What the hell are you thinking?"

She crossed her arms and looked down. But even looking down, she gave the impression her chin was up. They were having a fight and Wally didn't have a clue what it was about.

"I'm sorry I yelled," he whispered, peering around her to the dark kitchen. "I was scared, is all. You were going to open it. Why?" He turned on the overhead light.

She blinked and suddenly looked about five years old.

"Ruby. This is serious. I know you know better. I can't imagine what you were thinking. You hate guns."

She nodded.

"So what the—"

"I was just moving the Bantam rifle. So Cooper…it's just stupid!"

"Cooper?"

"So Cooper couldn't hunt," she said. "Hunter safety! And you said yes! You said he could!"

"Honey." He held his hands out. "It's a good thing. I—*we*—don't want him to be afraid. And we want him to be safe around guns."

"Not we! Not we! Mom doesn't like it either!"

"She just doesn't understand," he pleaded. "I wish *you* were taking hunter safety along with him. Every kid in Vermont should."

"Stop saying that!"

She threw the key at him and suddenly grabbed the shovel from the corner. She swung it and slammed it into the gun cabinet. Glass rained down.

They both froze.

"Don't move!" Wally said. "Don't move!" He took the shovel out of her hands and leaned it against the wall. He was breathing hard as if he'd been running, but at the same time he felt like he was moving in slow motion. "It's okay, honey. Just don't move. Are you hurt? Are you cut?"

"I wrecked Grandpa's cabinet!"

"Well, you surely did a number on it. But cabinets don't bleed. Are you hurt?"

"I don't think so." She shook her head.

"Don't shake your head." There was a piece of glass sticking into her hat like an arrow. If she hadn't worn it—

She started to cry. "Daddy!"

He plucked the bigger pieces of glass off her hat and shoulders, dropping them into his cap. He pulled her hat off carefully and tossed it behind him. He put his hand under her hair and gently combed through it with his fingers. He unzipped her jacket and went behind her, his boots crunching, and peeled it off, held it away, and shook it.

Each tender touch made her cry more.

"Now you can shake."

She shimmied, then took a giant step and grasped his fingers as if accepting an invitation to dance. Like at the fundraiser.

But she was a different person from that girl.

"What the blazes?"

His father stood in the kitchen doorway. Wally could make out the old robe he or Robbie had worn to be a shepherd in the Christmas play every year; Hazel thought she'd gotten rid of it.

Henry looked at the cabinet. "Did they take anything?"

"It was me," Ruby said. Wally squeezed her shoulders. "I was mad."

Henry scratched his head. "You were mad at the gun cabinet? It wasn't much of one, with that crazy window, but it was kind of elegant for a gun cabinet."

"No! Yes! No! I was just going to hide one gun. Then I got mad."

"Oh, well, then." Henry smiled. "I better make cocoa so you can tell me all about it."

Ruby started crying again. It was what Grandma Jenny always said.

"And take off your boots."

"Cocoa sounds just right," Wally said, and put his arm around Ruby. "You better take off your pajama bottoms too, they're sparkling. Just step out and leave them on the floor, your top is long enough to cover."

"Daddy!" She looked at her grandfather, embarrassed.

"I might have something." Henry opened a drawer and lifted out an apron covered with dancing elves.

"Grandma's Christmas apron!" Ruby tied it around her waist. It went below her knees and covered her front and back. She pulled her pajama bottoms down and stepped out of them.

"Ruby will replace the glass. Remember, Dad, when I broke the kitchen window and you taught me how to put new glass in?"

Henry frowned. "Wasn't that Robbie?" He turned the gas on under the kettle.

"Robbie broke the storm door window," Wally said.

Henry nodded. "Everybody needs to break a window sometime and learn to fix it. It's a rite of passage." He took down the Swiss Miss. "Windows can be fixed. But being mad, that's a little harder."

He lined up three cups and scooped.

"Cooper still wants to do hunter safety!"

"Uh huh. And he wouldn't be able to if one gun was gone?" The kettle began to whistle, and Henry poured water into the cups.

"It sounds dumb now."

"Worse than dumb is dangerous." Henry stuck a spoon into a cup and pushed it over for Ruby to stir. He got the marshmallows down, his back to her. "So what're you so mad about you go and bust up your great-grandpa's gun cabinet?" he asked. "Hunter safety don't seem like enough. You still mad at Remy?"

"He's over here all the time! And Cooper!"

"I told her hunter safety will be good for Cooper," Wally explained. He abruptly sat down, still shaken.

"That's not what I mean! Cooper said—Remy apologized, and Cooper said *okay*! He said okay! It's *not* okay! He didn't even have to go to jail or anything, and he's still over here all the time!"

Ruby stirred furiously, splashing cocoa down the side of the cup and over her fingers.

"That's his agreement, from that place," Henry reminded her.

"Juvenile court diversion," Wally said.

"You don't have to be *nice* to him!"

"Except we're nice people," Wally said softly. "And so are Remy and his family. And so are you, even if you break things. Sometimes nice people make mistakes that hurt people. Sometimes really bad mistakes, so bad they can't be fixed. You might, someday."

"And we'd forgive you. You'll have to forgive Remy sometime," Henry said. "But Remy has the harder job."

"What if I can't?" Ruby whispered.

"You can," Henry said. "People are built to forgive, it's in our nature. Just make it your heart's intention and leave it be, and sometime in the future you'll find out you've forgiven him without knowing it."

"I'm sorry, Grandpa!"

"I know you are. And you can start to make amends by sweeping up my mudroom. Then tomorrow I'll teach you how to put in new glass, and while we're doing it, we'll figure out something you can do instead of breaking gun cabinets."

"Okay." Ruby licked her finger. "What's the harder thing? What you said. That Remy has to do?"

Henry plopped a marshmallow into her cup. "Forgive himself. It's about the hardest thing in the world."

Chapter 22

RUBY TUCKED HER HANDS under her legs, trying to not be nervous. She twisted to see if anybody else had come. They'd put posters up, but only Jess and Emily and Isabel were there so far. Was it just pointless anyway? She could be in Albany with her mother and Cooper at that very minute, having supper with Amra and her family.

There were three selectmen: Mr. Beaupre, who had the beautiful horses; Mr. Johnston, whose son Bernie was in Ruby's class; and a man with eyebrows that looked like woolly caterpillars. Did they grow thicker when a bad winter was coming?

They were talking to Mr. Liberte from church.

Her grandfather knew them all, of course. He knew everybody. He'd even been a selectman. "Back in the day," he'd say, or sometimes "*my* day," if he was going to tell a story about it. He didn't much anymore, not since Grandma Jenny died. Except Ruby had overheard him telling Remy about the heifer who always hid her calf. She'd heard it a million times, but still.

Henry had helped Ruby put glass in the cabinet, and she'd done the other thing he said to do, too: she'd made a heart's intention right out loud in front of Maple, who she thought might need to forgive Remy too. But nothing happened.

"Angus, you know darn well it's not our business. You gotta talk to the county," Mr. Beaupre said to Mr. Liberte, shaking his head.

"I did that. And damn-all happened. I'm just askin' you to call over there and put a fire under them, not go up the mountain and sand it yourself! It doesn't seem like too much to ask."

Her grandpa shifted next to her. She glanced at his face, worried he'd get up and start complaining too. She remembered the scary time the bus slid down Slater Hill, and how he'd complained about the icy back roads and the potholes "big enough to swallow a cow." She took his hand to keep him there, just in case.

He squeezed it and whispered, "You're gonna be fine. Piece-a-cake."

She crossed her legs. It was stupid to wear a skirt. Like she was in church or something. It was just the Grange Hall with two old tables and a few rows of old wooden chairs. It was hard to believe it was the same place they'd had the fundraiser dance with the streamers and balloons. Like when Kansas turned to Oz except the other way around.

"Alright, I'll make a call!" Mr. Beaupre gave in. "My nephew's at VTrans, I'll talk to him."

Mr. Liberte got to his feet, and Ruby's stomach lurched. She was next, she was pretty sure. There wasn't anybody else there.

"That's all I'm askin'," Mr. Liberte said. When he passed Ruby he winked, like he did in church. She hated it.

"Any other citizen comments?" Mr. Johnston asked, like he hoped not. He looked at Henry.

She should have gone to Albany.

"Ruby!" Jess poked her shoulder. "It's your turn!"

She wasn't there just for herself. She was there for Cooper and Jenny and Rowsby. And all the kids in their town. She stood up, her knees knocking together. Just like in a book! Clutching her papers, she walked to the table and sat down.

The selectmen smiled at her.

Her grandfather pulled up a chair next to her and pulled the microphone over. "I'm Henry Brown, and this is my granddaughter, Ruby Brown. We live on—"

"We know where you live, Henry," Mr. Johnston said.

"For the record," Henry said, nodding to Tilda Forbes, who was typing and smiling at Ruby, not even looking at the keyboard.

"And I believe Ruby goes to school with my son Bernie." Mr. Johnston looked over their heads. "Is this some school business, then?"

Ruby swung her head around. Bernie Johnston was standing just inside the door with Ethan and Kenny. She turned back, heat rising up her neck.

She couldn't do it. She just couldn't!

"Sit down, boys, and let's hear what's going on over there at the middle school," Mr. Johnston said, looking at her.

She shook her head.

"You need to speak. For the record," her grandfather whispered.

"It's not school business. Sir."

"It's not! Well, still, we're all ears."

Henry bent the microphone toward her.

"Just speak into the top there, honey," Mr. Johnston said.

She didn't like strangers calling her honey.

She held her speech up. "I wrote it down."

"That's fine. Many's the time I wished I'd written something down, keep me from getting long-winded."

"You got that right." Mr. Beaupre laughed.

Ruby smoothed the papers. Too late now. "Dear Selectmen," she read. She swallowed. "We've come to ask you to pass an ordinance to make our town safer." Emily said they called town rules "ordinances." Had she said it right? "There's already a—an ordinance about where people can use a gun. Here's what it says." She picked up the paper Emily had printed out and read.

"A *person shall not discharge a firearm within the following specified portions of the municipality: Parcel number one, Stony Brook Woods between County Road C and the Hazen farm. Parcel number two, Babe Ruth Little League field and adjacent playground on Quarry Road. Parcel number three, Town Green. This ordinance shall not apply to a law enforcement officer of the town, county, or state, using a firearm within the course of his employment. A person who violates—*"

"Her," Tilda Forbes interrupted. "His or *her* employment, it needs to say. Davey Carlson, your very own niece is with the State Police! You need to change the wording." She glared at the man with the woolly eyebrows.

"I didn't know we had an ordinance about firearms in the first place," said Mr. Woolly Caterpillar.

"I'm just saying," Tilda Forbes said. She smiled at Ruby. "You go on, then, honey."

This time, Ruby didn't mind the "honey" at all.

"*A person who violates a provision of this ordinance shall be fined not more than five hundred dollars.*" She put Emily's paper to the side and picked up her speech. Halfway there.

Piece-a-cake.

"State laws say people can't have a gun at a school or a building doing official county or state business. Like a courthouse or the statehouse," Ruby went on. Grandpa's face when Cooper picked up his flask popped into her mind for a second. "Those are good laws and ordinances, but there are other places too. Like Lemon Fair, where kids go tubing, and Caesar's Bluff, where kids camp out, and places where families hike, like in the National Forest. And a lot of us live in the country."

Someone clapped behind her, and she stopped. Clapped! Probably Jess, but still.

"Are you finished?" Mr. Beaupre frowned. "I think I missed something. What are you asking us to do?"

"She's getting there, Will," Henry said. "Hold onto your horses."

"I always do," Mr. Beaupre said, and laughed.

Ruby searched for her place.

"There's a law that kids under sixteen must have an adult with them to hunt. That's a good law."

Isabel had said she should pause there for dramatic effect. How long? She'd wanted to say kids shouldn't hunt at all *until* they're sixteen, but her grandfather said it would be going too far.

"But there's a hole in the law, in the part about being with an adult, because kids can hunt on their *family's* land alone. We think kids should have to be with an adult on all land, including their family's, until they're sixteen.'"

Bernie's father was frowning.

Just think of Cooper. She straightened her spine. "Bullets might hurt a person or animal or pet at their own place or a neighbor's. Adults are better at paying attention and have experience about where a bullet could go. There are good reasons the law says kids have to be with adults, and those reasons don't change if they're on their own land. We would like an ordinance about that. And another one about people target-shooting near where kids are." She rushed to say the last part, that her grandfather had added. "Thankyoufor-yourconsideration."

The selectmen looked at each other.

They didn't look happy.

"Does your father know you're here?" Mr. Beaupre asked.

Henry rose halfway. "*I'm* here!"

"Just asking, Henry. Don't get het up."

Mr. Johnston looked over Ruby's head.

"Bernie, it's time to go home now. And I don't want to see you messed up in anything like this again, you hear?"

"Yessir."

Ruby looked at the table, embarrassed for Bernie, but mad too.

"Now, Ruby," Mr. Johnston said. "We're sorry about your brother. It's a sad thing that happened. Unfortunate. But sometimes, from time to time, accidents occur. And it's a sad thing when that happens to our own family, or our neighbors. No one is sorrier than us." He looked to his right and to his left, and they all nodded. "We're certainly sorry." He nodded to her right. "And to you, too, Henry."

He folded his hands on the table. "However, the individual involved was, as I understand it, perhaps poaching, poaching deer, even though it turned out not to be...ah, a deer." Mr. Johnston's mouth twitched.

Ruby lifted her chin.

"He wasn't poaching. Our land's not posted," Henry interjected. "But it will be."

"All that being said, it's not our purview—" Mr. Johnston chuckled and turned to Davey Carlson. "Poor view, that's what that boy had!" He chuckled. "Purview! Poor view!"

Henry pushed his chair back and got to his feet.

"That's enough! We're talking about my grandson here, and the animal he loved!" He shook his head. "I don't even have words. My granddaughter, and her friends, came here with respect for you and your service to their town. They did their research and they prepared. And it took courage. Courage! Are you going to return that respect? Are you going to consider their request, respecting them back, as they surely deserve?"

Ruby heard clapping behind her—Jess and Emily and Isabel. And Ethan and Kenny?

Mr. Johnston waved his hand like he was waving away a mosquito or some other pest.

"Alright. Alright, Henry. But the fact of the matter is that we both know gun laws are decided at the state level in Vermont, no matter what any town might decide. And there's the feds, too, although I don't see how it's any business of those people down in Washington DC what we do up here. When you get home, Henry," Mr. Johnston wagged his finger, "you need to ed-ju-cate this girl of yours about the Second Amendment. The legislature knows what it means, you can count on that. Those gun-control people…but that's neither here nor there." He slapped his hands down on the table, but he kept talking.

"Even if we did write up an ordinance like you kids want, it would be overturned by the state. I have no doubt about it. I can't fault you for coming in; I truly like to support young people, and I apologize if I hurt anyone's feelings."

Ruby didn't believe him about feelings. Or about young people, either. He made his own son leave the meeting. But it didn't matter. They'd lost and, humiliated, all she wanted was to go home.

"Let's look at item thirteen on the budget for town meeting," Mr. Johnston said.

As if they'd never come.

Outside, Jess and Isabel were huddled at the top of the steps, and Ethan and Kenny were down on the sidewalk with Emily—who was angry, Ruby could tell.

"Well, that was a bust!" Jess said.

"They didn't even say they'd *talk* about it!" Emily said. "They didn't even say they'd *consider* it!"

Ruby just wanted to leave.

It was all for nothing. Just stupid. Stupid, stupid, stupid. She heard the scraping sound of her grandfather working on the windshield. There was smoke drifting up from the Leavitts' house down the road. She pictured the houses and barns tucked into the valley like theirs, chimney smoke drifting up and fading into the sky. The cows and horses and sheep and chickens were tucked in, and in a little while the moms and dads would tuck their kids in too.

She turned her face up.

Why did summer stars look close and winter stars so far away?

Stars didn't care about things down here. For them, everything down here was already over. She was over, and her family, and her friends, and all that had happened, like how she'd failed.

The day before she'd gone with Jess to skate on Wilson Swamp. It was a magical place; the skinny trees and sticking-up grass sparkled with ice and the only sounds were their breath and their skates whispering across the ice. They didn't talk, but she was sure Jess felt under a spell the same way she did, like they were in a frozen fairyland.

Her whole life she'd thought she belonged. She'd always thought her family and the other families, her farm and the other farms, were the same, or enough the same to make no difference. But it wasn't true. The bullets that killed Jenny had cut them off like an island just as much as they'd cut off Cooper's foot.

Her dad was waiting at home. He'd ask how it had gone, but she knew he hadn't wanted her to do it in the first place. *Does your father know you're here*?

Ethan touched her sleeve. "If you want to take it to the next level, I'll help."

"What's the next level?"

"The state?" He shrugged. "Anyway, I gotta go, Kenny's mom is here. See you tomorrow."

"See you tomorrow."

Tomorrow her mom and Cooper were coming back from Albany, where they'd gotten to see Amra, and where he'd exchanged his temporary prosthesis for a fancy do-everything one. He'd be excited. He'd expect her to be, too.

It was hard to see stars down in Albany because of all the lights—except Venus, which wasn't a star, even if it used to be the first star she saw and wished on.

Sometimes they even come true.

Spring

Laws: Emily – Vermont, Amra - New York
facts - me
poster board, stencils, markers, pens
– Isabel and Kenny
clipboards - Mom
name of law – all
petitions – Emily write, Mom make copies
6 T-shirts (need sizes!) use egg money – Jess
candy – Ethan
baby shower present!

Chapter 23

Lemon Fair Links

This month's appeal is for Guardian Angels Shelter, for a clothes washer. Theirs has broken down, and this time permanently. They're also looking for volunteers to wash the sheets and towels until they can do it at the shelter again.

Don't forget Maple Weekend at the end of the month! Some local sugarhouses will be offering sugar on snow, pancakes, and more, and ten percent of the proceeds go to the library!

And a big thank you from our full hearts to everyone who came to the fundraiser to support our family. Our son has begun wearing his new prosthesis to school!

Hazel pressed SEND. She was overwhelmed by the generosity of their small community. Not just the dance, but the jars around town, and the checks that kept coming, tucked into cards. Every church in town had devoted their collections for a whole month! All of it had been enough to pay their insurance deduction and half of their twenty percents. They could never repay the donations, except in kindness back.

She checked the time. The kids would be home soon. Wally had taken Cooper to school but, for the first time, he was coming home on the bus. The doctor had told Cooper he'd "eventually" be able to do just about anything with his new prosthesis that he did before, and for Cooper eventually meant now. She knew it was a good thing they were home where he could be a normal boy, instead of a patient with her eyes on him every waking (and sleeping) moment. But she couldn't stop worrying.

The week back in Albany had flown by. Amra's father had taken them to a basketball game where the players were in wheelchairs. There were a few tip-overs, but no one got hurt. Cooper loved it. Would that be next?

And the kindness hadn't stopped there. Amra's parents had invited them over for supper and shared, with stark honesty, what they'd gone through after Amra's accident. While they did, Hazel could hear the kids playing in the basement, with thumps and that unmistakable ping pong ball sound, and shrieks, but Amra's parents didn't turn a hair.

Cooper's doctor said, "You'll be glad to get home and back to normal." But she'd thought *There is no normal.* Everybody goes along in life as if there is, but there are people all over who are pretending and making the best of things. She'd been living in a fool's world, sending in her donations, collecting this and that for this or that, writing Links, unaware they were about to have their turn. She felt like a veil had been lifted.

But what kind of world would it be if everyone said out loud what didn't show on the outside? They'd either be exchanging hugs all over the place—at the supermarket and walking down the sidewalk—or avoiding each other. There'd be a new syndrome: hug fatigue.

She'd read in a magazine that people should get twelve hugs a day. How did they come up with that stuff? Did they have different groups getting different numbers of hugs a day and then have them fill out a questionnaire? Eight hugs, hmm: smiling, not laughing, a few complaints. Sixteen: laughing so hard they floated to the ceiling like Mary Poppins. Let's meet in the middle—twelve!

If she got twelve hugs, she'd be blubbering all day. Everyone has their secret sorrows, and there's something to be said for silence.

Said for silence. An oxymoron!

The families she'd met at the hospital who were in it for the long, long run—some for the last run—they broke her heart.

Enough. She looked at the time.

Ruby had raced around that morning picking up and clearing everything off the table—the napkins, the salt and pepper, UNO, the stack of *New Yorkers* from the library that Hazel had brought to Albany, as if she'd read them. Ruby even put the mudroom to rights before rushing to catch the bus.

Which Hazel *wasn't* going to meet, and ruin Cooper's milestone, no matter how much she wanted to.

His teacher had said, "He's doing great! He's a pistol!"

There were gun metaphors everywhere. Son of a gun. Give it your best shot. Jumping the gun.

Shooting yourself in the foot.

And what about Ruby? Hazel couldn't pretend anymore that Ruby's behavior was just prepubescent moodiness. Her family had experienced the kind of trauma people get help for. She'd been planning to have a good old mother-daughter talk when she got back from Albany. Make a list for spring clothes. Go shopping! Have lunch! And bring things up. Bad dreams. Remy. But she'd come home from Albany to find Ruby making lists that had nothing to do with clothes, unless you counted hunting vests.

And just like that Hazel was going to cry. She lurched up and went to the sink and turned on the cold water. She would find them a therapist. Or four, one for each of them. Five counting Henry. And were there therapists for dogs? Dog whisperers.

She splashed water on her face. What was a bunch of therapists called? She held her wrists under the faucet. Worrywarts. A cogitation. Snoops. But she wanted an expert. A Wise Woman. A wisdom of therapists. The trouble was, everybody in the county knew them.

How could they pour out their hearts when whoever it was would show up at the store or family night at school?

And what would the neighbors say if they knew what was about to happen at her house that very day? At least Wally wasn't home. He'd said, "I'll leave it to you, don't let it go too far." It might have gone too far already, or will have by suppertime. What would Jenny have thought, if she knew what was going on? Did the Second Amendment come with being a farm wife, like an unwritten marriage vow?

When she turned the water off, she heard them coming up the driveway, their voices punctuated by a high-pitched shriek that only girls of a certain age made, especially Isabel, especially when boys were around. She dried her face on her sleeve and turned around.

They looked like a flock of long-legged birds, piling their bright, puffy plumage on top of the mudroom freezer and shucking off their boots—pink and yellow and purple and polka-dotted. The two boys hesitated at the door, but the girls came right in.

"Hello, Mrs. Brown!" Emily said. She plopped two large Staples bags on the table.

Jess held out a paper bag. "My mom said to say if you need anything."

Cooper grabbed the bag.

"Cooper!"

"She *said*. She said I could have one when we got here."

Hazel could smell them through the bag. Lydie's cinnamon buns. "Put them on a plate on the table and *then* you may have one. Thank you, Jess. And thank your mom, please."

Ruby slid poster board and stencils out of one bag while Isabel and Emily shook white T-shirts out of the other. Cooper took a big bite of cinnamon roll, icing sticking to his fingers and mouth. He reached out to touch a T-shirt.

Hazel grabbed his wrist.

"You'll get it dirty. And this is your sister's thing, not yours."

"But—"

"Were you invited?"

He shrugged his shoulders. Tiny shoulders.

Don't baby him. Everyone said it—the doctors, the nurses, his teacher, Issa, Wally.

"But I don't have anything to do!"

"Grandpa's at the sugarhouse getting it ready."

Cooper held up his foot. "No boots."

They'd been looking for boots that were wide enough for his prosthesis to go into, but so far with no luck.

"Oh, Cooper, I'm sorry!" But it was a lie. Hadn't she been secretly glad he couldn't play King of the Snowpile for a while longer?

"Cooper can wear *my* boots, Mrs. Brown," Jess said. "And they're Velcro, so I'll bet he can get into them." She went to the mudroom and brought out a pink boot.

"There's a daisy on the toe!"

"It's just us, don't be a baby," Ruby said, thumbing through a sheaf of papers.

Hazel went to the mudroom to look behind the freezer, where she'd thrown Cooper's old Mucks the first time they'd come home from the hospital. She pushed the jackets over and hoisted herself up. The freezer wobbled. It was half empty, no venison this year. She'd been shocked the first time Jenny asked her to get something out of it—it had been full of venison and beef from cows that had outgrown their usefulness. What had she thought? That they gave each cow a retirement party and kept her until she dropped, and then gave her a funeral with hymns?

Her mind flinched. They should do something for Cooper's calf, but she didn't want to bring it up.

She stuck her arm down and fished. She wiggled across the slippery freezer to get further down.

"Can I help, Mrs. Brown?"

She jumped like a fish, embarrassed and caught out, although for what? She pulled her arm up and slid back to the floor.

"Yes, Ethan, you most certainly can. Cooper's boots are back there, if you don't mind."

It was easy for him to retrieve the boots. No effort at all. Would Cooper ever move like that again? Holding the left boot, she returned to the kitchen and searched the top of the fridge with her hand for the duct tape. She found Doogie Thirsten's squirt gun from the bus and set it on the counter. Time to get rid of it.

"Emily, is this all there is?" Ruby held up a paper.

"You said Vermont's gun laws."

"It's just a page!" Ruby said.

"Let me see." Jess grabbed it.

"New York's, that Amra sent, are seven pages!" Ruby waved them over her head.

Seven pages of gun laws to their meager one. Hazel slammed Cooper's boot on the counter like it was to blame. But it was just a boot. Just, in fact, a *worthless* boot, the way things stood. Or didn't. Stand. She plucked the kitchen shears from the bouquet of utensils in Jenny's old crockpot.

Cooper watched.

"How will I keep it on?"

"Duct tape, for today."

"Okay," Ruby announced, in a voice Hazel hadn't heard before, that of a teacher addressing her class. "We need to do three things! The petition is one, pick a name is two, and the T-shirts and posters, three."

"That's four," Cooper said.

"Okay, smarty-pants," Jess said. "Can you draw a gun? We need one to copy for the T-shirts and posters."

Cooper grabbed the squirt gun and went to the table. He sat down, pulled over the marker jar and, after touching every marker as if the right choice might have special powers, took out red.

Hazel closed the scissors on the seam of the boot. They made a dent, but that was all.

"It says here that people can have guns in state and national parks and forests and roadside rest areas, *and* they can show them," Ruby said. "It's called open carry."

"It says here that the state decides about gun laws," Jess said. "Just like Mr. Johnston said."

"Federal law beats state laws though," Emily said.

"Wait," Isabel said. "Doesn't federal mean the whole country? So how can Vermont do that open carry if the whole country doesn't?"

"Because people here are ding-dongs," Jess said.

"Mom, do you know?"

"There aren't a lot of federal gun safety laws. Most gun incidents go to state courts, not federal court, and are decided by state laws." Or lack of. "Or it could be like the Civil Rights laws. There might be a federal law, but things go on the way they always have until enough people make a stink. Schools in some states didn't integrate for years after that law was passed."

"Ruby Bridges went to school alone for a year!" Ruby shook her paper as if it were evidence. "This whole paper is a list of things people in Vermont *don't* need to do. Listen to this: no permit to purchase, no firearm registration, no license required, no carry permits required, no assault weapon law except hunting—and we know how that goes!"

"Ruby, we'll never get anywhere if you keep getting mad!" Jess said.

"You're mad, too. Oh, here's another one! Ooh, a yes!"

Hazel winced, recognizing where that snarky voice came from. Her.

"Yes to suppressors. Vermont legalized them in 2015. What are suppressors?"

"A silencer. Like in James Bond," Kenny said. "Goldfinger, he's the man, the man with the Midas touch!"

Hazel took the sheetrock knife out of the tool drawer. They should move to the other side of the lake. Or petition New York to include their little farm. Hadn't it been part of New York before Ethan Allen got involved?

"How does this look?" Cooper asked. He held up his drawing.

Ethan took it from him. "Good. But maybe not red. If we make it black, we can put a red line across it."

"Safe storage not required!" Ruby continued. "It's crazy!"

"A lady at the fair wouldn't let Ruby sign a paper about gun locks," Cooper said.

Hazel swung her head around. The fair? This started at the *fair*?

"Mom, what's background checks?" Ruby asked. "It says here that background checks are 'not required for private sales'."

Hazel turned around and rested her back against the counter. "There's a federal law called the Brady Bill. There was an attempt on President Reagan's life, and an aide of his, James Brady, was shot and paralyzed. The bill—it became federal law—says everyone who's convicted of a serious crime and anyone who's judged to be mentally ill by a court is put on a list, and when someone goes to buy a gun, the store checks to see if their name is on the list. If it is, they can't buy a gun. But it only applies to federal gun dealers unless a state makes it a law for other purchases."

Hazel hugged Cooper's boot to her chest. They were *kids.* Kids. When she was Cooper's age, she ran around the neighborhood with a Super Soaker. Nowadays she might be shot if it was black. And if *she* were Black? Like Maggie's and Sally's baby would be.

"People buy guns at gun shows or from a neighbor, or yard sales, or off the Internet, and don't have to have one," Emily said.

"Like Remy," Ruby said under her breath.

Hazel looked quickly at Cooper, tracing over his drawing in black. Had he heard? She picked up the sheetrock knife.

"Why would anybody care if their name got checked?" Isabel asked. "I mean, unless they were a criminal."

"My uncle says background checks is like making people register their guns, 'cause their names get written down," Kenny said.

"So what?" Emily asked.

Kenny shrugged.

Jess shook out a T-shirt. "We better get going. We'll put Cooper's drawing in the middle and—"

Cooper grabbed the squirt gun and aimed it at Kenny, who leaped up and ducked behind Isabel, who squealed.

"It's not funny!" Ruby said. She grabbed the gun and put it back on the refrigerator.

"Why does New York have all those laws, and not Vermont?" Cooper asked.

"Because everybody here hunts," Kenny said.

"But the things we're talking about don't change hunting except for kids on their own land," Jess said.

"Don't people hunt in New York?" Cooper asked.

"The deer-hunting population in Vermont is actually less than ten percent," Emily said.

"That's all?" Kenny asked.

The phone was ringing. "Cooper, will you get that?" Hazel pulled the sheetrock knife down the seam. The rubber resisted, but then the blade cut through. Too much about guns. Time to get Cooper out of there.

"We need a name," Isabel said.

Cooper was there, holding the phone up. "It's Mr. Johnston, he wants to talk to you."

Everyone stopped to listen.

"Hello? Yes, this is her mother."

They all watched, trying to make out why Bernie's father would have called.

"Well, I don't see—well, I—actually, I don't—they *did* get permission, and—"

Cooper leaned against her.

"Mr. Johnston, I appreciate your service to the town, I really do. But I don't think this is your business. These *children*, as you call them, reserved a table, and age is *not* a factor, nor their reasons. They are part of this town and that's all that is required. I'll see you at town meeting, and hope you have a nice day." She went to put the phone back and realized she was shaking with anger. How dare he. How dare he!

The "children" were all staring at her.

"What did he say, Mom?"

"It doesn't matter." Just change the subject. "But Isabel's right, you should have a name. And it should include the word law." Wake up and smell the coffee, Kyle Johnston. The "children" are coming to town.

"Jenny's Law," Cooper said softly.

"What did you say, Cooper?" Ruby asked.

"You should call it Jenny's Law. Like that law Mom said. That was named for that man. He didn't even die."

"Oh, sweetie!" Hazel went back to the boot to hide her face.

"I think that's a great name, Cooper!" Ruby finally said. "Jenny's Law."

"I'll write it right now," Jess said, and picked up a stencil.

"Those kids got shot at that school," Cooper said. "*They* should get a law. It could've been me and Seth, if that guy lived here. There isn't any lock on the art closet."

Hazel's knife skidded off the boot and sank into the countertop.

There was a knock on the door.

There isn't any lock on the art closet.

"Just a minute!" Who would knock? Everyone just stuck their head in the door and called out.

It was Remy.

"Mrs. Brown, I wonder if you know where Mr. Brown—I mean, Henry—is?"

"He's at the sugarhouse."

"Oh, okay. I came a little early, and thought we might have a couple games of cribbage." Remy looked over her shoulder.

"How about we say *everybody* has to do hunter safety, even if they don't hunt?" Kenny was saying.

"That's what my dad says. I'm gonna start next week!" Cooper said.

"That's just dumb!" Ruby said. "Remy LaFountain did hunter safety, and what good did *that* do?"

Remy's eyes met Hazel's for a second, and then he looked away.

She didn't know what to say.

She had to say *something.*

"You've been a good friend to him," she blurted. "To Henry."

Remy touched the brim of his cap. "Not as much as he's been to me. Sorry to bother you."

But he wasn't looking at her, he was looking behind her. Hazel turned her head and saw Ruby looking right back, with a look she had never seen before, half defiance and half despair.

The mudroom door clicked, and Hazel swung around. Remy was gone.

Chapter 24

RUBY STRIPPED OFF HER purple leggings and tossed them on the growing pile on her bed. She needed to look *older*. She needed to look *serious*. But pretty, too.

She flung herself down, spread-eagled like a snow angel.

"Did your clothes have a tantrum?" Hazel asked at the door.

Ruby sat up. "Nothing works with the T-shirt!"

"Move over."

Hazel began to sort the pile of discards, bottoms to the left and tops to the right, and came to Ruby's green leggings. "Green for Vermont." She pulled out the blue turtleneck. "Green mountains, blue sky!"

"Mom! Besides, that shirt makes me look puffy."

"Puffy?"

"My cheeks."

"I think the blue brings out your eyes. But *puffy*! We can't have that!" Hazel held the shirt away as if it stank and dropped it back on the bed.

"It's not funny."

"It's a *little* funny that you're worrying about what to wear under a T-shirt with a gun on the front." Hazel held up another turtleneck.

"Here! Leaves!"

"They're shamrocks."

"Okay, I give up." Hazel perched on the edge of the bed. "I came up to ask something."

Ruby looked at her warily. "What?"

"About Remy."

Ruby put the T-shirt up to her face, hiding behind it.

"I know," she mumbled. "I shouldn't have said about hunter safety. But—"

"Did you say it on purpose? Did you *want* him to hear?"

"I was mad. It's how I *felt*!"

"But to hurt Remy on purpose...Ruby, that's just plain mean. I know you saw his face."

"Not as mean as shooting off Cooper's foot!" But Ruby was shaken. Her mother hardly ever scolded her. "I know! I'm sorry! Grandpa said if I decided to forgive Remy, it would happen. But it didn't!"

"Did Grandpa say it would be easy?"

"Kind of. I don't know."

"Did being mean to Remy make you feel better?"

"Kind of. But bad, too."

"Oh, honey." Hazel took the T-shirt out of Ruby's hands and shook it out. She spread it across her legs and smoothed it down. "What Remy did was...comes from...living in this culture and being ignorant and young and inexperienced and...and self-centered. The way thirteen-year-olds are. He probably seems older to you, a year feels like a lot at your age, but I clearly remember being thirteen, and it wasn't easy."

"You didn't go around shooting things, though!"

"No, but when Maggie got really sick with strep throat I told her she'd probably never talk normally again and *definitely* never sing, and she believed me."

"You did? Oh, Mom, that's awful!"

"It was. I was jealous at all the attention she got. As for you, I think things have just been too much. My being gone so long. Not to mention nightmares. As for shooting things, that's exactly why you're doing all this, isn't it? To keep kids like Remy safe from making mistakes with guns?"

"He killed Jenny, Mom!"

"I know. I *know*! Of course I know. I'm mad too. But still—just for a *second*, imagine how you'd feel if you'd done what Remy did." She pulled Ruby down next to her and took her hand.

Ruby leaned in. "You're mad too?"

"Not at Remy. How can I blame him? He's a child who's been raised to think having a big gun makes him a man. I'm mad at a world where people care more about their damn guns than their kids and other people's kids."

"Mom!" Her mother never swore, except at the chickens.

"I think forgiveness is more of a journey than a destination. It sounds like you've started on it, and maybe the next step will come clear. Anyway, we need to leave in fifteen minutes. And I wouldn't talk about guns in the car. Your dad's—"

"Is Daddy mad at me?" Ruby asked in a small voice.

"No! The important thing is he's proud you're doing what you think is right." Hazel paused in the doorway. "Now pick out some dazzling outfit."

Ruby finally settled on the green leggings and the blue turtleneck. She pulled the no guns T-shirt over her head and down. It almost reached her knees. What was Jess thinking? Oh, well. This wasn't about her anyway; this was about kids being safe from guns.

That awful Mr. Johnston would be there, and Woolly Eyebrows too.

She lifted her chin. They had a right. The Constitution said so.

She tugged a clipboard out of her backpack. She held it up and pretended she had a pen, looking at the mirror.

"We want rules to make guns safer around kids," she said to her reflection. She tugged at the turtleneck. Maybe it did bring out her eyes.

"Would you sign our petition? It's called Jenny's Law."

She wondered what her grandmother would say about it all.

But she knew.

There's only ever going to be one of you, so be your best you.

She'd have to tell Remy she was sorry.

~

Town meeting was a day off from school. It started at ten in the morning and went until five, and at noon there was a break for lunch. The school gym was divided by the volleyball net. One side was for the town meeting and the other side was for the potluck and people at tables with handouts. Stand Up for Racial Justice and the solar panel people were there. And between them was their table! The poster Jess had hung from the edge of the table looked great.

Grandma Jenny had always brought her wild rice and chicken casserole and butterscotch-chip cookies that Ruby helped make.

But Ruby didn't have time for feeling sad. They had work to do.

Isabel was putting out the fact sheets and Ethan was dumping Hershey's Kisses into bowls. The idea was that people would come for the candy and pick up a fact sheet and sign their petition.

Jess pulled the clipboards out of Ruby's backpack and began to attach the petitions.

Ruby picked one up.

Jenny's Law

BE YOUR BEST YOU

We, citizens of Vermont, request that the Vermont Legislature take up the following, in the interest of the life, liberty, and happiness of Vermont children:

1. *If a child under 18 lives in a home, all guns and ammunition must be locked up, in separate places, or each gun must have a thumbprint trigger lock. Locks should be made available free at gun stores, daycares, schools, and doctors, paid for by a special tax on ammunition and gun purchases.*
2. *Kids must be 16 to hunt without supervision on their family's property.*
3. *If you have had a restraining order for domestic violence, you may not have a gun in your home with children, ever, even after the order has been lifted, even locked away.*
4. *Everyone using a gun must take a gun safety course.*
5. *Being safe around guns should be taught yearly, appropriate to age, at schools, preschools, and daycare centers.*
6. *There will be no hunting or target-shooting within a mile of schools, playgrounds, parks, playing fields, and other places where kids are invited or encouraged to be, including hiking trails in the Green Mountain National Forest.*
7. *Anybody who sells a gun on the Internet to someone under 21 will be fined $1,000, and all gun purchases must have a background check, even if it was from the Internet or at a yard sale.*

It looked real. It *was* real! Emily was a genius!

Senator Somers said they needed three hundred names to have their petition considered, and each petition had places for twenty, so they'd printed fifteen petitions.

"I'm ready!" Emily said, holding up a pen. "Larry's Lumber" was written on the side. The man who owned that business was Kenny's uncle, the one who didn't want background checks. Ruby bet he didn't know why Kenny wanted so many pens!

"I'm nervous," Isabel said. "What if nobody signs? What if somebody gets mad!"

"Look at Kenny!" Jess pointed.

They watched Kenny showing his clipboard to an elderly lady. She looked surprised, but she took it. She shook her head, frowning. She was going to say no, Ruby just knew it.

But then Kenny handed her a pen.

"She signed!"

Kenny looked over at them and made a mark in the air. One down. Two hundred ninety-nine to go.

Ruby grinned at Emily. They walked to the double doors where people were coming in, carrying covered bowls or Tupperware containers. Some looked at Ruby's shirt, puzzled. Nobody stopped.

She saw Remy and his mother entering, and turned her back so as not to be seen.

"Your face is all red," Cooper said, and took the clipboard. He grabbed the pen from her hand and walked over to a couple with a baby. Except for a little hitch in his walk, you'd never know one foot was made of plastic.

He held out the clipboard. "Would you sign my petition to make Vermont safer for kids?"

The mom scanned it. "Sure." She wrote her name.

The dad was struggling with the baby's snowsuit. "What's it for?"

"It's for gun safety rules." The mom made a face at the baby, "That's right—no guns for you!" The baby grinned, showing one tooth.

The dad took the clipboard. "Who's Jenny?"

"My calf. She got shot."

"That's awful!"

"It was," Cooper said.

The dad signed. Ruby left her clipboard with Cooper and went to the table for another one. Ethan was standing behind it.

"Want a kiss?" he asked. He picked up a bowl and held it out.

She could feel herself blushing. She saw Ms. Robinson coming in and rushed over. "Ms. Robinson? Would you sign our petition? It's to—" What had Cooper said? "It's for gun rules to make kids safer."

Ms. Robinson scanned it. "Wow! This is impressive." She dug a pen out of her purse, juggling a bag of apples.

Ruby took the bag. "There's information at our table," she said.

"Ethan said you were working on something, but I had no idea it was this extensive," Ms. Robinson said, following Ruby. She picked up their handout. She began to read aloud. "One in three homes with children have guns. 4.6 million children live in a home with an unlocked, loaded gun. Eighty percent of unintentional firearm deaths of children under 15 occur in a home. 7,957 children and teens are shot every year, and almost 2,000 die, 693 from suicide. Another 166 survive an attempt. Nine out of ten of these were with guns accessed at their own or a relative's house.

'*Every single day* - like today - 22 children are shot!" She looked at Ruby, shocked. "Everyone should know this! Where'd you get these numbers?"

"From the Brady Center to Prevent Gun Violence."

"So what's your plan? I mean, after you get your signatures?"

"If we get three hundred my dad said he'd sponsor a resolution to make a state study," Jess said.

"You know, this is just the kind of thing Freaky Fridays are for.

May kids sign your petition?"

"We never talked about it," Ruby said. She remembered the petition at the fair. "Probably not."

"It could send a powerful message, kids petitioning the legislature, even if it's not strictly legal. And even if it doesn't go as far as you hope, you'll have educated a lot of people. I'd be glad to be your Freaky Friday advisor. I mean, it goes hand in hand with what we've been doing in class."

"I don't know," Ruby said.

"Well, I think you should talk about it. Meanwhile, I'd better find a seat and do my due diligence. Keep the apples."

"Thanks! Apples might attract a different crowd," Ethan said. "Nobody except kids have come to our table so far. Except for you."

That changed with the lunch break, when people were waiting for the potluck to start. But it didn't mean everyone wanted to sign a petition. Some said, "I'll have to think about it," or "Good luck in *this* state." One man told them to keep their hands off his Second Amendment, like it was his own private right, or he'd written it himself.

Cooper came over, holding out his clipboard. "I filled it!"

"Wow! That's great, Cooper!"

"I need money."

"What are you doing, bribing people?" Ethan asked.

"What?" Cooper looked worried.

"He's teasing," Ruby said. "Why do you need money?"

"For a cupcake."

"Ask Mom."

"I did."

"Have another Hershey's Kiss."

Half the names on Cooper's list were kids. Seth had signed, and Jess's little brother! Ruby realized that she didn't even want to ask Jess's dad if kids counted; they should count more. And Cooper's was their first full petition! Even if it had chocolate fingerprints on it.

She blinked. Remy's name was the next-to-last one. She looked around. He was at the dessert table. She took in a big breath.

Just do it.

Her stomach flopped.

She could just write a note.

Just *do* it.

She looked around. He was leaving the table.

Be your best you.

She wound through the crowd and quickly, before she changed her mind, tapped him on the shoulder, and he spun around.

When he saw her, he looked horrified. He thrust a cupcake at her and she took it automatically. He turned away.

She grabbed his sleeve. "Wait. I need to—" *Just say it!* "Listen—this—" She motioned to their table. "It's not because of you. I mean, it is, sort of, but it's about a lot of things."

"I saw the petition."

"Right." Say the rest. *Say it.* "I'm sorry for saying that about you and hunter safety." Her face was on fire.

"I get it. You hate me. I do too."

"I don't hate you!" And Ruby realized with surprise that she didn't. "You shouldn't either! I mean…I *did*, but…but I *don't*…I'm just…it's just when I see you, I think about it."

"I think about it too! All the time." He turned away. He turned back. "I'm sorry!" He rushed toward the double doors while she stood there as if her feet were glued to the floor. And then he was gone.

She gave the cupcake to Cooper.

After the budget was voted on and the gym had mostly emptied out, they counted signatures.

"That's twelve and fifteen, and, let's see, six plus four plus eight and another ten—" Emily counted in her head. "Fifty-five."

"Some are kids," Jess said.

"You know what Ms. Robinson said about getting kids to sign—we could get a *lot* at school!" Emily said. "And we could go on Instagram!"

Cooper walked up. Ruby saw he was favoring his prosthesis.

"Cooper! You got the most names!" Jess said.

"Can I do it again?"

"We haven't decided what's next," Ruby said.

"Dad left with Grandpa, but Mom's bringing the car out front so I don't have to walk so far."

"Oh, Cooper, I'm sorry!" Ruby grabbed her jacket and backpack. "Call me," she said to Jess, and followed Cooper to the double doors. A man passed them, bumping into Cooper. Cooper cried out.

"Cooper!" She glared at the man's back. "You almost knocked over my brother!"

The man swung around and pointed his finger at her chest. "I hope you have a bulletproof vest under that T-shirt." He jerked his finger. "Bang, bang." He laughed and went through the door.

Ruby turned to stone.

"Ruby?" Cooper whispered.

She put down her backpack. Cooper stared at her, his eyes wide. She pulled on her jacket and, her fingers stiff, fumbled to zip it up.

She wanted her father.

She took in a big breath and let it out. She put her arms around Cooper.

He pulled away. "Come on! We need to tell Mom!"

Ruby swung her backpack up and stopped. "No. We can't. We can't tell anybody. If we tell, they'll stop us." She grabbed Cooper's arm. "You have to promise!"

Cooper pulled away again. "No. Mom needs to know."

"He's just a bully!" Ruby said. "You don't back down to a bully!"

"I was *scared*."

"*He's* scared—he's scared we'll take his stupid guns away! He's just a big bully! Cooper, *please.* You want to keep helping, right?"

Cooper stared at her.

"Please."

"Okay."

Ruby took his hand. "Good. Let's go home. You need to take your foot off."

Chapter 25

COOPER HAD IMAGINED DESKS like at school, and boys like him sitting at them. But instead, they were at the firehouse, and he was the only kid there who wasn't in high school.

"Okay, that'll wrap it up for this week. Leave your homework on the table and my deputy will collect it." Sheriff St. Francis winked at Cooper. "But before you head out, let's review the four primary rules of firearm safety. Cooper, would you read the first one?"

Cooper opened his study guide to the first page. He'd practiced them with his grandfather.

"One. Watch that muzzle! Keep it in a safe direction at all times."

"Stacy?"

"Two. Treat every firearm with the respect due to a loaded gun. It might be loaded, even if you think it isn't."

"Dan."

"Three. Be sure of the target and what is in front and beyond it. Know the identifying features of the game you hunt. Make sure you have an adequate backstop. Don't shoot at a flat, hard surface or water."

"And Carlos."

"Four. Keep your finger outside the trigger guard until ready to shoot. This is the best way to prevent an accidental discharge."

Cooper wanted to show Ruby that there were rules, but he thought he'd better not. Number three would just make her mad. Instead, he kept his study guide at his grandfather's and did his homework there too.

"Next week we'll study the types of actions firearms have, and their mechanisms," the sheriff said. "Anyone who can't take apart and put together their firearm has no business hunting. You'll be handling a single-shot bolt-action rifle, so study pages five through eight. Have a nice evening, everybody."

As he collected the homework, Cooper worried. It was easy to make diagrams and be the sheriff's "deputy." But in just one week he'd be holding an actual real gun, one he was supposed to use to shoot live things, not barrels of water or old rusty vans. When that moment came, what if he chickened out? Sheriff St. Francis would be sorry he'd let him do hunter safety, and his father would be ashamed.

The sheriff drove Cooper home each week and then visited his grandfather. The two men had been friends since kindergarten, and Cooper tried to imagine the sheriff as a little boy. He'd seen pictures of his grandpa from when he was little, but all he could picture was the sheriff as a tiny Lego guy in his brown uniform and shiny black shoes.

Cooper stretched up on his good foot and pulled his jacket off the hook. Remy's and his dad's big black coats hung side by side: LaFountain A., LaFountain R. There hadn't been one fire since he'd started hunter safety, not even a chimney fire from an "idiot flatlander," as his grandpa called somebody who had one. But riding in the sheriff's car almost made up for it, because he got to sit in front, not in the back where the criminals sat behind a fence.

"Can't put you in the cage!" the sheriff laughed. "What would your mother say?"

But Cooper knew what she'd say, and it wasn't that he could sit up front, although she'd agree that it was filled with wonderful things like the spotlight and the siren and the airhorn and handcuffs. Cooper got to see a deer the week before. It stood in the road like a statue, eyes gleaming red until the sheriff turned the lights off and it jumped into the woods, dark as a shadow.

There was a box that showed how fast cars were going and a breathing thing like Amy used at school. Except this one showed when somebody was drunk and driving. They'd have to sit in the cage and could get put in jail if they flunked it. Cooper worried about Grandpa. He didn't drive the bus, but he drove the truck all the time. Whenever Cooper took out the vacuum he was careful not to look and see if the bottles were still there. Because if they were, would he have to tell somebody?

He buckled himself in.

"Ready to ride?" The dashboard lit up like the inside of a spaceship and the radio crackled and hissed. The sheriff smacked it with his fist.

Cooper loved it when a voice came out of the night and then was gone again, like it came from another spaceship that drifted out of their orbit. Sheriff St. Francis had only answered it once so far, when a lady's voice said a car had gone off Quarry Road into the swamp. The sheriff asked did they need help, but to Cooper's disappointment they didn't.

"How's your sister's petition going? I wouldn't say no to a few gun safety laws myself, but that'll be our secret. Don't want to lose my job!" The sheriff signaled and turned out of the parking lot.

Cooper tried to puzzle it out, and finally asked. "Why would you lose your job?"

"I'm here by the goodwill of the voters. No one bothers to run against me, but if it came to a contest between some NRA Second-Amender and me, I'd probably lose, things being how they are these days."

"What's N-R-A mean?" He'd seen stickers on trucks and there was a whole booth of stickers and shirts and other things at the fair.

"It stands for National Rifle Association, and the Second Amendment of our Constitution gives us the right to bear arms. To carry firearms. Some say that means any kind of firearm and that it applies to everybody. Others say it was written for militias, like the Green Mountain Boys past and present—you know, the National Guard—and has nothing to do with personal firearms. Those are the two extremes, but most people are in the middle. They're all dead now, the folks who wrote it, so anybody can say what they want. But the NRA has five million members, and that's a lot of saying."

"Don't you like them? The N-R-A?"

The sheriff laughed. "Actually, I'm a member. But I don't like how they bully people who want reasonable gun laws. When I was growing up the NRA was all for gun safety. And, frankly, I think the whole mess about the Second Amendment being so precious was cooked up by gun manufacturers. But that's just one man's opinion."

"Do you think Jenny's Laws are—" he fished for the sheriff's word—"reasonable?"

"Haven't seen 'em. I guess I best take a look, actually, in case some fool decides to get all wrought up, even if it's not gonna go anywhere." The sheriff glanced at Cooper. "Don't tell your sister I said that."

The words "bulletproof vest" popped into Cooper's head almost every day. *Bang bang.* Was that man an N-R-A? He wasn't sure what "rot up" meant, but he was pretty sure that man was.

He scratched hard at his knee. Sometimes that helped when that ghost pain acted up. He stared into the darkness. "If I tell you something will you keep it a secret?"

"I guess it depends. You'll have to trust my judgment. But I won't tell anyone without informing you first."

They passed the LaFountains' turn-off. Almost home.

So Cooper told him.

Sheriff St. Francis slowed down and turned into their driveway.

He stopped.

"You must have been scared."

Cooper looked at his feet. He nodded.

"I guess you didn't tell your mom and dad. That's the secret part?"

Cooper nodded.

"They need to know. And you want them to, right?"

Cooper nodded again.

"Want me to go in with you and you tell them now? Get it over with?"

Cooper's stomach suddenly didn't feel too good. Maybe he could start with his mother. "Yes, please."

The sheriff put the car back in drive. When they got to the house, he put his hand on Cooper's shoulder. "You did right telling, son."

"Ruby's going to hate me."

"She might be relieved."

But Cooper didn't think so. And they walked into an argument.

"But, Mom! It's just for this one thing! I won't do anything else. I promise! The way it works is you send it to *your* friends and they send it to *their* friends and Emily's mom said her name could be the name that people see. Nobody would see my name at all!"

Ruby leaped to her feet when she saw Cooper.

"Cooper, you won't believe it! We already have over one hundred names, and Emily—"

"How was hunter safety?" Hazel interrupted. She looked at the sheriff. "Everything okay?"

"Fine." Cooper sat down to take his boot off. His grandfather had sewn in a piece of rubber from an inner tube to widen it. When Cooper asked how he learned to do it, his grandpa said, "If you farm your whole life, you learn to make do."

"Mom, *please*!" Ruby begged.

"I'll talk to your dad."

Ruby gave Cooper a triumphant look.

"Isn't Daddy home?" he asked. His heart lifted. But just then his dad and grandfather walked through the door.

"How was hunter safety?" Wally asked.

Cooper glanced at the sheriff. "Good!"

"So what's up? Did something happen in class?" Wally squatted down to help Cooper take off his prosthesis. "Did you wear your boots all day? You know—"

"I forgot."

Ruby looked at Cooper sympathetically. "I'm going to my room."

"I wish you'd stay, if you don't mind," Sheriff St. Francis said.

Cooper couldn't meet Ruby's eyes.

Wally went to the drawer for a clean dishcloth. He soaked it, wrung it out, and handed it to Cooper.

As if he'd wash his stump in front of the sheriff!

"So, Tommy, what's on your mind?"

"Something that occurred at town meeting."

"You promised!" Ruby glared at Cooper.

Cooper looked at the sheriff. See?

"Go ahead, Cooper," the sheriff said.

"There was a man," Cooper said. "A *mean* man."

"He was just a stupid bully," Ruby corrected. "It wasn't a big deal. He just *said* something mean."

"What did he say?" Hazel asked. "Cooper?"

Cooper watched Ruby. "He said, 'I hope you're wearing a bullet-proof vest under that T-shirt. Bang bang.'"

"What? I don't understand," Hazel said.

"She had on the gun T-shirt. He pointed his finger and went bang bang."

Hazel looked at Ruby. "My God! Who was it? Did you know him?"

"No! Or I would've said! Really! But I didn't, so there's nothing anybody can do."

"This gun mess stops *now*," Wally said. "It's enough."

"Daddy! We can't! We're doing Instagram and YouTube Kids!"

"YouTube!" Wally said. He looked at Hazel. "This. Is. Over."

"That man was just a bully! Ruby Bridges had to face much worse every single day, and she stood up to it because her parents had faith in her! They knew it was for an important reason. Daddy, don't you see?" Ruby pleaded. "It's important! Peter was just sixteen!"

"Peter?"

"Daddy! How can you forget? Jess's cousin! He *killed* himself! *God*!"

"Can you describe this bully?" the sheriff asked.

"He had a earring," Cooper said. "Like a animal tooth."

Henry turned around and headed for the door. "Everett Peele."

The sheriff put his hand on Henry's arm. "Sit down, Henry. I got this. Peele. I could've guessed. He claims that tooth is off a catamount."

"Will you lock him up?" Cooper asked hopefully.

"I'll take away his guns, to start with."

"Then we can go on!" Ruby exclaimed.

"No," Wally answered. "You cannot 'go on.'"

"But, Daddy!"

"They've put so much work into it," Hazel said. "Is this about your daughter or your precious guns? She has as much right to object as you do to shoot things!"

"Some nut-job threatened our kids! Do you think he's the only one out there?" Wally began to pace, a bad sign, Cooper knew. "We live in the country. People have guns. Most people are like us, but...you've *always* been unreasonable about guns! First you think anybody who has one is dangerous, and then when someone really is, you want her to go *on*?"

Hazel stepped in his path. "Yes! I am! I am 'unreasonable.' Somebody should be! Our kids have to do lockdowns! And I *hate* the NRA, and now I've said it! You can bet Everett Peele is an NRA member!"

Cooper and Ruby looked at each other, shocked.

Their dad held his hands up. "*I'm* an NRA member! Are you blaming me too?"

"No! Of course not. No! I'm just sick of—"

"Stop! Stop it! Just stop it!" Ruby jumped between them. "I won't do it anymore, okay?" She put her hand on Wally's chest. "Just stop fighting," she whispered.

The sheriff interrupted. "I best be going. I'll see you at the meeting, Henry."

And he left. To get the bad guy, Cooper thought with relief. He was glad he'd told, even if Ruby would hate him forever. Cooper stared at his dad. His dad was an N-R-A.

Was everybody? "Grandpa, are you a N-R-A too? Is that the meeting you go to?"

"NRA? No, no, it's a meeting to help me not drink. Alcoholic Anonymous. AA."

"Not drink?" Ruby asked.

"When I drink alcohol I can't stop, so I go to meetings to get support," Henry explained. "Support not to."

"Oh, Grandpa!" Ruby ran over and flung her arms around him.

He looked at Wally. "How about if I'm with Ruby when she does her petition?"

"You could come to Freaky Friday!"

"AA's at noon, so I'll be in town anyways," Henry said.

"But no gun T-shirt," Hazel said.

"Daddy, please?"

Wally frowned. "I do hate a bully. And I guess I know when I'm outnumbered. But nothing outside of school. No petitioning anywhere else."

Ruby almost knocked Wally down with her hug.

Hazel put her hand on Cooper's head. "Oh, sweetie, you must've been scared!"

And Cooper lied. "I wasn't scared at all." It looked like things would be okay. Except for his foot. He was feeling that ghost pain bad.

Chapter 26

HENRY STAMPED DOWN THE sticky snow to make a path for Cooper, following behind with the other half of the buckets, the spiles and tools rattling inside them. It was a heavy load, but Cooper insisted he could do it. Rowsby slipped around them and bounded into the woods, his happy tail wagging back and forth like a flag. His old joints welcomed the warmer temperatures as much as Henry's did.

"Seth says there's no such thing as a coydog!" Cooper said.

It was a continuation of a conversation that had started at the sugarhouse and moved with them on their tractor ride to the woods. There'd been a picture in the paper of dead coyotes piled up in the bed of Roger Clark's truck, and Roger with his rifle across his chest like he was a sheriff in a town in the Old West who'd saved everyone from vicious predators. It upset Cooper and Ruby, and made Henry sick—hunting with no purpose except to get the highest kill count.

"Coydogs have about died out," Henry said. "But I can testify they were real." He stopped at the first tree and put down his buckets. He knew when he woke up and heard the drip, drip outside his window: tapping day. The perfect sugaring formula was a string of freezing nights and warm days. It didn't happen perfectly every year, and he was grateful it had this year; regular routines were balm on the wounds of the last two years.

His dad would roust him out of bed, yelling, "Sap's running!" He'd done the same with Wally and Robbie, and Wally did the same with

Ruby and Cooper. They hoped for a school day, because they got to take the day off, but this year Ruby had chosen to go to school. Henry himself had to be in town for AA and her Freaky Friday meeting, so they had to shake a leg.

"Tell the story, Grandpa."

"What story is that?" Henry teased.

"You know. Gluskabe."

Cooper locked his knees and leaned toward their first tree. It was always the same one. He spread his fingers over the bark, and Henry could swear he saw the old maple sway toward him, like a cat wanting to be scratched.

"Okay. One spring day Gluskabe was walking in the woods and came to an empty village. But it wasn't just empty; it was a mess. All the fires were out, and the gardens were choked with weeds."

He stomped down the snow around the tree.

"Then he heard a sound, a moan, but not one of pain, more like Yum and Mmm, Mmm, Mmm. He followed it to a stand of maples. And there were the villagers, on the ground beneath them, sucking on broken-off maple twigs like straws. Mmmm, Mmmm."

Rowsby bounded up and circled the tree, looking for the perfect spot.

"Their stomachs were big and round and sticky-outy and their chins were sticky with syrup. Shaking his head, Gluskabe trudged to the top of the highest mountain, Mozodepowadso, which means moosehead. We call it Mount Mansfield now, but that's another story. Gluskabe sat down and told the Creator what he'd found. And after listening, the Creator gave him careful directions."

Henry pushed Rowsby gently away. "Go find your own tree."

Rowsby cocked his head, grinning. The sap was rising in the old dog, too.

"When Gluskabe got back to the village he found the biggest birchbark bucket and went to the river. It took many trips over many days, but he finally filled every maple tree to the top with water. The people whined and complained, 'Our sweet drink is all watery!'"

Henry said it in his whiniest voice.

Cooper laughed.

"'From now on you will have to work for your sweet drink,' Gluskabe said. 'You'll have to keep a fire and boil down the watery sap. It will take patience, but your reward will be healthy lives, and you will appreciate the maple syrup as the gift that it is.'"

"I like that story." Cooper took the drill out of the bucket.

"Don't forget to—"

"Slant the drill up. I know, Grandpa."

Avoiding last year's tapholes, Cooper pressed gently. There was a second of resistance and then he was in; he pulled the drill back quickly. He stuck his little finger into the hole and came out with a sticky shaving, holding it up for Henry to see.

"Looks good."

Cooper handed the drill to Henry. He picked up the hammer and a spile.

"Be sure to—"

"I know, Grandpa. Tap, not pound."

They went from tree to tree, Henry drilling and hanging the buckets and Cooper tapping in the spiles. When Rowsby ran around Cooper's legs, throwing him off balance, Henry resisted grabbing him. He wouldn't have helped Cooper before.

"So you saw one?" Cooper asked.

"Saw one what?"

"A coydog. Did you see any?"

"What do you think a coydog is?"

"Half dog and half coyote."

"I did more than *see* coydogs, I petted them. When I was about your age, we had a dog named Daisy. She lived in the barn and brought in the cows for milking. Your great-grandfather started talking about getting her spayed—you know what that is?"

"No puppies."

"Well, Daisy had her own plans, and showed up in the family way. And one morning, there she was, nursing a half-dozen bald pups back in a stall. And she'd chosen the right stall, too—Maudie's, who wouldn't hurt a flea. Those pups were so cute you wanted to squeeze the heck out of them. But then we noticed something funny. When their coats came in, half were black and sleek like Daisy. But the others were tan, and their coats were thick and coarse. My dad said they had different fathers."

"They had different *dads*?" Cooper was all eyes.

"Yup. Daisy must've mated with each of them just a few minutes apart. Anyway, after a while the tan ones' playing was so fierce, we had to separate them. One bit through my skin, but their under-fur protected them from each other's bites. So what do you think they were?"

"Coydogs?"

"Yup. And that's how I came to pet coydogs."

"Did you keep any?"

"We kept one, but not a coypup. Rowsby's great-great grandma, she must've been. My Mom named her Ruth after a lady in the Bible who said 'Whither thou goest, I will go, and where thou lodgest, I will lodge.' Because Ruth wouldn't let Maudie out of her sight. But that's a story for another day."

"You tell good stories, Grandpa."

"Got a lot to tell, at my age." Remy had said he should write them down.

"What about the other puppies?"

"We found homes for them, but I heard later—" He stopped.

"What?"

Henry fondled Rowsby's ears, as if to soften what the old dog was about to hear.

"One of the coydog pups got shot after it grew up. Some fool mistook it for a coyote."

"What if they shoot Rowsby?"

"Rowsby doesn't look anything like a coydog."

"But what if they *did*? It *could* happen!"

Henry put his hand on Cooper's shoulder.

"Have you been worried?"

Cooper nodded. He shrugged off Henry's hand, but couldn't hide the tears filling his eyes.

"After we buried your calf, Tommy—Sheriff St. Francis—and I posted the entire farm. Forty signs in all."

"You *buried* Jenny?"

"Nobody told you?"

Cooper wiped his eyes. "I thought—"

"You thought Watsons came with their rendering truck? We'd *never* do that with your Jenny! She's buried in your Grandma Jenny's trillium."

"Stars of the woods."

"Maybe you'd like to have a funeral for her when they come into bloom." Henry put his hand on Cooper's head. "Does Ruby worry about shooting too?"

"She's just mad. Sometimes she's mad at everybody!"

"How about you? Are you mad?"

Cooper shrugged. "No, it's just—"

"Spit it out."

"It's school. The kids aren't mean, but I can't keep up. They said I'd be able to do whatever I want, but I can't. If I do too much it hurts. They lied!"

Henry looked over Cooper's head. The trees had been through

every kind of storm, but they couldn't tell him what to say except *things take time*, and those aren't words any red-blooded little boy wants to hear.

"I'm not going to deny it's hard," he ventured, "but I don't think they lied. Look at that friend of Ruby's, that Anna girl, she plays baseball."

"Amra."

"What?"

"It's Amra, not Anna, Grandpa." Cooper sighed.

It was maybe the deepest sigh Henry had ever heard.

"You got more to get off your chest? Might as well leave it all here with the trees. They have deep roots. They can take it."

"It's my own fault!" Cooper swayed and put his hand on a tree trunk for support. "I taught Jenny to open gates! If I didn't she'd be alive!" And just like that he was crying. "I miss Jenny!"

Henry gathered him up.

"And if *I* had changed the *latches*..." Henry hugged Cooper tightly. Two peas in a pod. "I'm the grownup here. And I promised I'd change that latch, and I didn't." *Because I was drinking.* But he couldn't say that. "Because I was drinking and feeling sorry for myself."

Cooper leaned away. "I don't blame you, Grandpa." He wiped at his cheeks.

"Then don't blame *yourself*."

"Then don't blame *your* self!"

"If you try, I'll try. Let's shake on it."

Cooper put his hand out.

It was so small. And taking it, Henry could see there was more. "What else is on your mind?"

"I don't want to keep doing hunter safety." Cooper searched Henry's face. "I don't *want* to shoot a deer."

"Well, who says you have to? But you're gonna have to finish hunter safety for the safety part."

"I have to?"

"You do. You don't have to hunt, although there's nothing wrong with it, and for the most part people who hunt have more respect for animal life than many who don't. It's a heck of a lot better than keeping animals cheek by jowl in warehouses, that's for sure. But that's another story. Anyways, I haven't shot a deer for—oh, going on ten or so years now."

After Robbie was killed he'd lost the stomach for it.

"You haven't?"

"Nope. Many's the time I've seen one, sitting in my blind, but I just keep still and watch. Sometimes we look at each other, and that's worth—well, it's worth a lot. It's not that I'm against hunting, not at all. But no matter what anybody says, it's your choice, Cooper, to decide to take an animal's life or not. And it's nobody else's business."

"But Daddy wants me to hunt with him."

"Doesn't matter. And anyhow, more than anything, what your daddy *always* wants is what's right for you kids. Bottom line."

Henry picked up the drill and paused. "Listen!" He watched Cooper's face and knew the instant he heard it.

Ping.

Ping.

Ping.

The sound of sap striking the bottoms of the buckets.

Then Cooper pointed.

A half-grown deer stood in a slice of sunlight not twenty feet away, looking straight at them, as if she'd come to share the moment the sap started to flow. Cooper leaned against Henry.

"I love you, Grandpa," he whispered.

"And I love you, Cooper. More than words can ever say."

~

Henry had just enough time before Ruby's Freaky Friday meeting to make the second half of his AA meeting. Afterwards, as he was getting into his truck, Harold Able called to him.

"I don't have but a minute. I have to get over to my granddaughter's school," Henry said.

"Wally's girl?"

"Ruby. She's at the middle school now."

"Well, she's what I want to talk to you about! Her and that senator's kid—well, *him* being anti–Second Amendment doesn't surprise me—or that other girl, that crazy girl." He stuck his finger in Henry's face. "Your own son *died* for it, and there's a lot of folks upset about what those kids are up to. I thought you ought to know." He shook Henry's hand. "See you next week."

Henry got in the truck and pulled into the street, upset. And ashamed. *That crazy girl.* He should've spoken up. And *Your son died for it.*

Bullcrap.

Robbie didn't die for Harold's or anybody else's damn rights—he died for *nothing*, not a damn thing. And Harold didn't have a clue what "those kids" had to deal with. They went to school every day thinking they could get shot!

There was a crowd in front of the school. A fire alarm? They'd had to be silent back in his day. This one looked like a party. Spring fever; the sap was rising and they'd busted out!

Henry parked and crossed the street.

They were chanting. He cocked his head to make out the words and saw Ruby. She was wearing that T-shirt, breaking Hazel's rule. A lot of kids were wearing them.

"Say it loud, and say it clear!
Jenny's Law is needed here!
Say it loud, and say it clear!
Jenny's Law is needed here!"

Then, as if in response, "*Show me what democracy looks like! This is what democracy looks like*!"

Ruby waved. "Grandpa!"

"Mr. Brown! Mr. Brown!"

It was Ms. Robinson, trying to run in high-heeled shoes, a hand on her head as if to keep her hair from flying off.

"Good afternoon," Henry said, wishing he had a fancier hat than his old John Deere to doff. "Doff" was an old-fashioned word, but there was something about what was happening that made him feel giddy, as if there'd been a rebel hibernating inside him waiting to spring free. *Say it loud, and say it clear! Jenny's Law is needed here*!

"Mr. Brown! What did you know about this?" It was an accusation.

Henry held his cap over his heart. "Not a thing. I swear."

"Well, we can't have it! We just cannot have it! I'm all for—for activism, but—"

Henry saw a van with the WXCZ logo on its side coming down the street.

It was about to get better.

"Grandpa!" Ruby and Jess ran up. "Isn't it wonderful? It's a *walk-out*! They're doing them in Burlington and Montpelier too, and maybe even more places! Emily put it on Facebook and Snapchat and Instagram!"

"It's gone viral!" Jess said. "Wait 'til Dad hears! He'll *have* to bring it to the legislature now!"

Henry grinned at Ruby. He hadn't a clue what those snap or gram things were, but if it made her happy, he was happy too. They'd needed some happiness for a long time.

"Oh, boy." Ms. Robinson looked from Ruby to the school to the van and back to the school. "I'm going to be in big trouble!"

Chapter 27

WALLY PICKED THE TWIG out of his hair and examined it. The bud was chewed off. He looked up. Mister or Missus Porcupine was up there snacking on spring. He smiled, but only for a second.

His mind had been spinning, trying to make sense of it, but it sure looked like somebody had knocked down three fence posts on purpose. And of course three cows had crossed the brook and wandered down to the road, the ones Remy called the Noseys because they stuck their noses into everybody's business. They'd probably stuck those noses into the brook too, which was full of runoff from the LaFountains' pesticide-treated fields. He'd have to quarantine them and report it. He could lose his certification temporarily. And their reputation as a trustworthy organic dairy.

"Okay, ladies! Time to come home!"

A car came around the curve. Hazel?

She pulled up and opened her window. "What happened?"

"Somebody pulled down some fence posts."

"What? What do you mean, 'somebody'?"

"I don't know what I mean. It's just three posts, but I have no way to know if the cows drank from the brook. I'm gonna have to quarantine them and dump their milk. Where are you off to?"

"I got a call from school—no, not Cooper, he's fine. Ruby. Ms. McBride wanted me to come in 'as soon as possible.' She said it was about Freaky Friday."

"Another problem from that damn crusade of hers."

"Wally! How do you think Ruby feels when you talk like that?"

"I don't talk like that in *front* of her. I stay neutral."

"There's no neutral to Ruby; neutral means against! I better go. Good luck with those three! They look like they're trying to hitch a ride to town."

He laughed.

And he had to admit, whatever he might think about Jenny's Law, Ruby was happier. He'd even caught her talking to Remy. When she saw him watching, she looked embarrassed, but Remy whistled along with the radio all through milking. He'd never done that before.

~

When Ruby got to the office, her mom was sitting on the bench waiting. Oh, no! She should've told about the walkout, and now she'd be in double trouble, home *and* school. The door to the office opened, and Principal McBride stuck her head out.

"Good! You're both here! Come into my lair!"

It was a lair, with no window, and messy with sports equipment and stacked up files and lost and found boots and jackets and hats. A spider plant dripped off a filing cabinet. Grandma Jenny said they scooped up bad air. There'd probably be a lot of bad air in a principal's office!

Ms. Robinson walked through the door. She held her hand out to Hazel. "I'm glad you could make it." But she didn't look glad. She moved boxes from two chairs to the floor and everyone sat down.

"Thank you for coming right away," Principal McBride said to Hazel. "It's about the walkout. What did Ruby say about it?"

Puzzled, Hazel looked at Ruby. "You mean Freaky Friday? Ruby's grandfather said they went outside," Hazel said tentatively.

"Did he say *who* went outside?"

"I assumed it was the petition group." Hazel turned to Ruby. "It wasn't?"

"It was!"

Principal McBride tapped a pencil on the desk. "Along with every student at first lunch."

Ruby pulled her sweater sleeves down over her hands.

"What do you mean?" Hazel asked.

"The whole cafeteria got up and walked out at the same time, like one of those—what are they called? Mashmobs."

"Hashmob," Ms. Robinson said.

"Flash mob?" Hazel asked.

Ruby curled her fingers. It was nothing like a flash mob! It was a *protest.*

"And all without a word. The lunch aide said it was spooky how silent they were. But right outside the doors they started chanting."

"You mean, like a march?" Hazel asked.

"It was a walkout," Ruby said under her breath.

"They called it a walkout," Principal McBride said. "But yes, exactly. She's got the makings of an activist, that girl of yours."

Ruby thought her mom's mouth twitched. Did she think it was funny?

"It was on the evening news," the principal said, "and half the town saw it. The calls started at suppertime and didn't stop until I turned my phone off at 10:30. They started up again Saturday morning."

"I had no idea!" Hazel said. "Why didn't anybody call us? I mean, on the *news*? You'd think—was Henry there when this—walkout was happening?"

"He showed up in the middle of it and claimed he knew nothing about it," Ms. Robinson said. "But I think he enjoyed it."

"Claimed?" Hazel echoed.

"He didn't know," Ruby said. But she could tell he was proud of her.

Hazel turned to Ruby. "What did you chant?"

Ruby was embarrassed. It felt dopey to say it here all by herself.

"Say it loud and say it clear, Jenny's Law is needed here," Ms. Robinson said.

"Oh, Ruby!" Hazel said. But she was smiling.

"And we can't have it," the principal said. "I think a lot of the kids went along for the novelty of it all."

"We've been studying our rights," Ruby said softly.

"Including their right to protest," Ms. Robinson added.

"Nobody had to come. They *wanted* to," Ruby said.

Hazel squeezed her arm.

Principal McBride looked from Ruby to Hazel. "Well, it's out now in the adult world, and you can bet some parents are having talks with their kids about the *Second* Amendment. I just never thought it would go this far. I've been told that we've been de facto sponsors of Jenny's Law by giving it time on Freaky Fridays, and we're not allowed to take a position on anything political." She held up her hands. "We're going to have to drop it."

"*Drop it*?" Ruby blurted.

"Well, the school's part, yes."

"But don't you support what they're doing?" Hazel's voice rose. "Do you *like* doing that awful ALICE thing? And what about that boy at the high school with his father's gun in his locker? Jenny's Law would have prevented that!"

A bell rang in the hall.

Ms. Robinson stood up. "Ruby, I feel like I owe you an apology. I hate that this is happening." She put her hand on the doorknob and then turned around and leaned against the door as if she wanted to keep something from entering. Or maybe leaving.

"I've loved teaching the Constitution and Bill of Rights all these years. They're important, and if I could make it happen, I'd make every adult learn about them too. But everything's different now. *Everything.* What you kids live with because of guns is scary and wrong."

She looked directly at Principal McBride. "I don't say these things in front of the kids, but I get so mad! We've had two suicides in our school families in the last two years! We both know there are kids in this school who live in homes where domestic violence takes place and guns are in the house. After there's another school shooting someplace, you can feel the fear for weeks and weeks. Not to mention that boy at our own high school with his father's gun. And we expect these kids to learn? You need to feel *safe* to learn!"

She looked at Hazel and back to the principal. "And now ALICE. I wish every adult in this state had to go through it! Pretending there's a bad man outside your door who wants to kill you? Every child in this country is a victim of gun violence just going to school every day thinking about it! And those video games at the fair that are basically target practice with automatic weapons! And their score is based on how many they can kill in the shortest time!"

A bell rang.

"I'm sorry," Ms. Robinson continued. "But it's all true, and nobody, *nobody* in this state is doing a thing about it except these brave middle school kids! Ruby, I'm so proud of you I could bust, and if it costs me my job—well, so be it." She went out, closing the door behind her with a small bang.

Ruby and Hazel and Principal McBride were silent, shocked.

"Will she? Will she lose her job?" Ruby finally asked. "Because of me?"

Principal McBride shook her head. "Not if I have anything to say about it."

"We should go to the school board!"

Principal McBride looked ready to weep. "Oh, Ruby, I wish it would help! But the school board were the first ones to call me and complain."

~

Going to the house after getting the Noseys back in and the fence mended, Wally was lost in thought. Hazel and Ruby and Cooper, and even his dad, had been traveling down a road he'd never seen before. It wasn't on any Vermont map, that's for sure, and it all started with Cooper's calf. Death was the way of things on a farm; it was natural, like the rhythms of the year. But it wasn't supposed to come from your own neighbor, from a boy he couldn't even stay mad at.

When he walked into the house he was taken by surprise. The kitchen was decorated for Cooper's birthday party, and his cake was on the counter, eight striped candles waiting to be lit. It had completely slipped his mind. The cake was chocolate, and three layers, but not a special shape like his mom had done. His favorite had been the Millenium Falcon. So Hazel had given up, and that was a good thing. Now that Cooper was at school she could make time for her writing. Which reminded him: he'd promised to fix the rickety leg on that old desk she'd found.

He took last night's lasagna out of the fridge and brought it to the table. Hazel would've made him heat it up. She never understood that some leftovers were best cold. He moved a stack of presents to the side. Dogs in party hats. Like in that book, what was it called?

He took a forkful and fingered the folder that had been underneath the presents. His mother's name was written on it. He opened it. It was filled with newspaper clippings. What—

Oh. Jenny's Law.

Coyote hunt attracts protesters
Accidental shooting kills 4-year-old

NRA says it's a culture war
Governor vetoes waiting period
Burglary fabricated to justify domestic shooting
Man threatens girlfriend with gun in front of her children

Wally put down his fork. He'd lost his appetite.

AR-15 found in student's car

This was what Ruby was reading, instead of Nancy Drew or whatever girls read nowadays.

New school lockdown protocol
Stolen guns sold for drugs
Teenager commits suicide
Teen threatens schoolmates online

Did she go through the paper every day?

Fatal shooting follows argument
Deferred sentence for gun threats
School shooting plot discovered
Drunk driver points gun at teens

Had it always been like this?

Machine gun target-shooting gaining in popularity
Gun deaths outnumber vehicle deaths

Had *Hazel* seen all this?

He felt like he should move Cooper's presents off the table, and far away from the awful words.

HAPPY BIRTHDAY COOPER swayed over his head. Blue party hats were stacked inside of each other in the middle of the table.

Go Dog Go, that was the book.

Do you like my hat? I do, I like your party hat.

Wally heard the door. Henry, with Rowsby. He quickly closed the folder, as if he'd been looking at something R-rated. That's what it felt like.

Rowsby made a beeline for the table and locked his eyes on the lasagna.

Wally put the plate on the floor.

Henry dumped the mail down and pulled a piece of paper from his pocket. "This was in the mailbox."

Wally read it out loud. "Stop your kid or you'll pay for it." He felt like he'd been punched.

AP: Kids Take on the NRA

A group of middle-schoolers from a Vermont farming community have sparked a children's crusade to get gun-safety laws enacted in a state once described as "safe and happy and armed to the teeth" by the *National Review*.

After an online petition garnered over 10,000 student signatures and prompted school walkouts in over a dozen towns, a supportive senator arranged for the students to present their case tomorrow to the Vermont State General Assembly before they adjourn for the year, in hopes that legislators will form a group to study gun injuries and deaths and come back with a plan.

One of the students' goals is to keep guns out of the hands of children, and to that end they are asking the legislature to pass a law making it mandatory that guns be locked up or have gunlocks on them.

Chapter 28

RUBY HAD GOOSEBUMPS. THE big room was packed, and the entire back part was filled with kids! The balcony was full of people wearing hunter orange, which had become the symbolic color of those opposed to gun laws. The representatives were at their desks, and the senators were in chairs set up down the middle. She and Jess and Emily were sitting on a platform, and there were chairs set up for their families facing it. Aunt Maggie looked like she'd swallowed a basketball! Jess's mom was there, but not Tyler. That was good, because he'd want to sit on Cooper's lap and that would be a problem later.

She was still shaken up at how Isabel's parents wouldn't let her speak at the last minute, scared she'd be targeted by people like that horrible Everett Peele. Isabel should never have told them. At least Ethan and Kenny were there.

And Remy, too.

She and Emily and Jess had come early with Jess's dad to "get the lay of the land." It reminded her of the fair and leading Jenny around so she would feel comfortable when Cooper brought her into the big tent. Two tents would fit in this room!

Before she left, her father had said he was proud of her, and she'd held his hug to herself all the way up to Montpelier. Her mom said, "If you get nervous stop and breathe."

Her grandfather said, "Your grandma would be proud of you."

Cooper just patted his pocket.

BANG!

The Speaker of the House hit the podium with her gavel.

BANG!

"Go home!" a voice shouted from the balcony. People started to stamp their feet.

Ruby grabbed Jess's hand. It's just bullies, she reminded herself. Senator Somers had warned them it might happen.

Bang! Bang!

"Silence, or you'll be escorted out!" The Speaker waited. BANG! "It doesn't happen often—"

BANG!

"—that our legislative bodies come together, but the same rules that apply to any citizen testimony apply today. There will be—" Bang! Bang! "That's enough!"

Ruby looked at Jess and Emily, shocked. How could grownups act that way? If kids did, they'd be made to leave. Maybe even be suspended.

"*Again*, the same rules that apply to any citizen testimony apply today. There will be no applause or other forms of response to what is said. And please turn off any devices you have that may beep, sing, neigh, or cause any other noise that technology has come up with."

Everybody laughed.

"And now, let me present Senator Jack Somers."

"Go home!" the same voice yelled, and other voices joined in, chanting.

"Go home! Go home! Go home!"

BANG!

"Thank you, Ms. Speaker!" Senator Somers had to shout over the noise. He looked up to the balcony, and Ruby saw a man in a uniform walking down an aisle. "No, let them stay! They're going to learn something here today, and I wouldn't want them to miss it." He turned and smiled at Jess and Ruby and Emily. "Sitting up here, I recalled that it was children in my home district who proposed the painted turtle as our state reptile, and it was passed unanimously!" He faced out again. "But—not to say painted turtles aren't important—today is a little different. Today's resolution is supported by children from *every* county. And now I'd like to introduce one from mine, Emily Roleaux, who will speak first. Emily?"

"Piece-a-cake," Ruby whispered as Emily got up from her chair. She watched her walk carefully to the podium in her new clogs. Clop clop clop. She hoped Emily couldn't hear how loud they were; she'd hate it.

They'd decided to dress up, but not too much.

"Not like graduation last year," Jess had said. "More like picture day."

Ruby had outgrown her graduation shoes, but wouldn't have wanted to wear them anyway. They came from another life, before everything had happened.

"Emily, how many kids support Jenny's Law?" Senator Somers asked. "Just speak normally into the mic."

Ruby worried. Emily never spoke normally.

"I have to turn my phone back on!"

There was a roar of laughter.

Ruby felt bad. Emily didn't say things to be funny.

But Emily held her head high and read from her phone. "Eleven thousand, three hundred and twenty-two!" She put her phone into a pocket and took a card out of another one. "Do I start now?"

Senator Somers bent the microphone away a little. "It's all yours."

Emily read from the card, looking down. "Article One of the Vermont Constitution says, 'All persons are born free and independent and have certain inherent and unalienable rights, amongst which are the enjoying and pursuing and obtaining of happiness and safety.'"

She looked up for a second, and then back down.

"We want better gun safety so Vermont kids can enjoy, pursue, and obtain happiness and safety. It's our right." She turned the card over.

"Article Seven says, 'The government is…instituted for the *common* benefit, protection, and security of the people…and *not* for the particular emolument or advantage of any single person, family, or set of persons, who are *part only* of that community, and that the community hath an indubitable, unalienable, and indefeasible right to…alter government, in such manner as shall be…judged most conducive to the public weal.' Weal means *good*," Emily explained. "*Public* good."

She looked up again and stiffened.

Oh-oh. Ruby crossed her fingers. Too many faces! Don't look at their faces! Look up! Look at the ceiling!

"A lot has changed—" Emily faltered. "A lot—"

Cooper waved, and Emily locked onto his face.

"A lot has changed since the Constitution was written. Like cars, and who can get married, and smoking and pollution. When those things have changed, the Vermont legislature has made new laws to keep people safe and help them pursue and obtain happiness. Like seatbelts and car seats and no smoking inside."

She'd poured the words out in one big breath and had to pause, but didn't take her eyes off Cooper.

"But you have *not* kept up with how *guns* have changed people's safety and happiness! Guns are not the same as they were, but you've listened to a *part only* of the people! When the government said everyone had to have car seats for their children, some people didn't like it, but did that stop the government from making cars safer for kids? No! When the surgeon general said smoking wasn't just bad for the smoker, did that stop the government from making people smoke outside? No!"

Ruby wanted to stand up and cheer.

"You skipped one!"

A man in the balcony was standing and pointing at Emily.

"You skipped the *Second* Amendment! Don't they teach that one? I don't pay my taxes for your fancy schools to ignore my rights! And I have the goddamned right to bear arms, it says so right in the U. S. of A. Constitution, right after my right to speak, and I'm speakin'!"

People around him clapped.

Emily stood there, helpless.

The man waved his arms around. "What a bunch of sissies! If somebody broke into your house to steal so's they can go buy their drugs, what are you gonna do, call 911 on your *devices*?" He laughed and looked around for approval. "I'll shoot first and ask questions later!"

People around him began to stamp their feet.

The Speaker went to the podium. "Sit down! You're out of order!"

Bang! Bang!

Emily pressed her hands over her ears and turned around to face the wall.

The man crossed his arms, a big grin on his face.

Wally stood up and turned to face the balcony. "Have some respect! These are children!"

"*You* have some respect!" the man said. "Like respectin' my rights!"

"I'll respect you plenty down here! I dare you to come down *here* and say those things! That's my daughter and her friends up there. And I'm proud to say so!" Wally said, shaking off Hazel's hand. "And I—and all the rest of us—should feel *ashamed* of ourselves. Because we left it to her! To these kids—who have more courage in their … in their little *toe* than the rest of us combined."

"This is stupid!" The man turned around and stomped out the door.

Emily fled back to her chair and folded up with her head on her knees.

"I didn't finish!"

"You said the important things," Jess whispered. "That's why that bully got so mad."

It would have been Isabel's turn, and Jess had volunteered to combine her part with her own. When she got to the podium she waited until you could have heard a pin drop.

"Um. My name is Jess Somers and I'm thirteen years old. My town is small, but I'm affected by guns like kids all over the state, and I'm going to tell you how." She held up her paper.

"Our schools have lockdowns called ALICE. Each letter stands for something we have to do. A is *alert*, L is *lockdown*, I is *inform*, C is *counter*, E is *evacuate*. It's practice for if a shooter comes into our school. The teacher locks the door and we sit on the floor next to a wall or in a closet and wait." Jess looked at the rows of senators. "And think." She paused.

"We think about those little kids in Newtown and the kids at Parkland who got shot. We think about how somebody can shoot our whole class in less than one minute. We think about C. C for Counter. It means if a shooter gets in the room, we're supposed to throw things and even attack him. A thirteen-year-old is supposed to attack a man with a semi-automatic weapon. I think you should think about that for a minute."

She shifted her gaze to the rows of representatives.

"When a lockdown happens, you don't know if it's real. One time when we had a lockdown, I was stuck in the girls' bathroom and when somebody opened the door, I stood up on the toilet so nobody could see my feet and shoot me. I think you should think about what that feels like."

She waited. She looked up at the balcony.

"Our end-of-year hike got cancelled because people were target-shooting near the trail. And last summer—last summer—my cousin shot himself and he died. I mean...on purpose."

Everyone gasped.

"He was sixteen. The gun he used hadn't been locked up." Jess's voice had risen and choked off. Senator Somers stood up, but as if she could see out the back of her head, Jess shook it. No.

"It was my uncle's gun, and he has to live with that for the rest of his life. I know a girl whose brother was shot by someone playing with a gun. He's paralyzed, and the boy who did it is in a prison so far away his family can hardly ever visit him."

Ruby looked at Cooper. He'd said it was okay, but now it was real. Their mom's arm was around him.

"Last fall, just before Thanksgiving, my best friend's little brother and his pet calf were shot by a boy hunting with a semi-automatic rifle he bought online."

Someone in the room cried out.

"No, he's okay! I mean, *he's* doing okay. But his calf died."

She didn't say the rest, about his foot. She skipped ahead.

"I'm not going to list everything from my town, because some are private and I don't have permission. But they're things you all know about because they happen in your towns too. Like a domestic violence threat with a gun. Another suicide. The state police coming to school because of a threat on Instagram. An accidental shooting. Another mass shooting happening someplace and being locked into our schools with no recess for younger kids, in case there's a copycat."

Jess held up her paper. "We kids live with this every day. Some of us just hear about it, and it's scary. Some of us have something happen to us or somebody we love, and it changes us forever. This is the world we're growing up in. Look around you. If we counted them up, all the guns that people in this room have, how many would there be? And why do you have them anyway? You think to yourself that nothing will happen to you or to your family. You're safe. You're careful. But things do happen. You can *help* or you can make it *worse*, but there aren't any sidelines. And it's time to put kids' safety over having guns. Thank you for listening."

Somebody clapped, and then more people.

Somebody booed. And then more people.

Bang! Bang!

"We will clear the chamber! I mean it!" the Speaker called out.

Ruby was so proud of Jess she could burst. But now it was her turn. Emily took her hand and squeezed, and Ruby squeezed back, grateful. Emily didn't like to be touched. She was suddenly filled with optimism.

They were doing this! Her knees didn't knock even a little, and when she got to the podium and put her paper down and smoothed it with her hand, she realized she didn't need it. She knew what to say.

"My name is Ruby Brown. I'm from Lemon Fair and I live on a dairy farm."

She counted silently to five. She looked around. It actually looked like a "sea of faces." But she knew where Remy's was, and he was giving her two thumbs up.

Grandma Jenny would say it was icing on the cake. A piece-a cake with frosting on top.

Okay. Go.

"When our school went outside after the lockdown Jess told you about, kids were running around play-shooting like they were practicing for when they could have *real* guns. I think it made them feel safer, like they had power. Gun purchases go up after a mass shooting. It's said that people buy guns because they're worried they're going to lose their right to buy them. But I think it's because the mass shooting was scary and getting a gun makes them feel like they have some power—like the kids on the playground."

She looked at the balcony. "My dad wears an orange vest to be safe when he hunts." She paused. "But you're not hunting now, so why are you wearing them? I think it's to show you're on a team. You want to look big and scary by being in a group. But I'll bet you have kids and grandkids and hug them and aren't scary at all! I'll bet you've had tragedies in your life and cried. Some of you lost somebody because of a gun. Some of you loved someone who took their own life. Why do you want there to be sides? You want us to be scared of you, so you stamp your feet. Against children! How did that feel?"

She aimed her finger and jerked it. "Bang bang! Kids are taught to divide people into good and bad. Our country's history teaches that view, all the wars and the Wild West showing heroes and not what really happened. Kids are *attracted* to guns; our country teaches them to be from history and TV and movies. Kids get real-looking toy guns for their birthday. If kids find a gun, they shoot."

She looked at Cooper and nodded.

He slid to the floor and walked carefully to the platform, and she saw that he was wearing the new purple high-tops he'd gotten for his birthday. When he reached the step, he hesitated.

Ruby wanted to help. But he'd never forgive her. He finally stepped up with his good foot and swung the other one up behind him. He grinned at her and turned around to face the crowd. He waited then, just like they'd practiced, until everyone was looking at him. He was careful to look over everyone's heads, like Ruby had instructed; if he looked at their mother, he wouldn't be able to go through with it.

He pulled Doogie Thirsten's squirt gun out of his pocket. He held it up. He pressed the trigger and there was a satisfying gasp. But then everything fell apart. Ruby watched in horror as people threw themselves to the floor, screaming. No one saw the water shooting out like a small geyser and falling on Cooper's head.

A policeman crashed into Cooper, yelling and twisting his arm, and suddenly Grandpa was wrestling with the policeman. It all happened in seconds, while she'd just stood there watching.

She ran to Cooper and stooped down.

"What the *hell* were you doing?" Wally lifted Cooper to his feet, half-shaking and half-hugging him.

"We wanted everybody to see—you know, a kid with a gun," Ruby said. "I guess it wasn't such a good idea."

"You could say that."

Their mom was crying. "Oh, God! Oh, God!"

Cooper looked at Ruby. "Did I do okay?"

"You were perfect," she whispered.

"I guess we should adjourn," Senator Somers said. He had his arm around Jess, and Emily stood behind them.

"But we're not done!" Ruby said.

"Ruby!" Wally said.

"Please, Daddy! Or it's all for nothing!"

Hazel pulled Cooper over and held him tightly. "Cooper could have been hurt badly!"

People were getting to their feet and brushing themselves off.

Ruby pointed at the policeman. "You hurt my brother!"

"Ruby! You apologize right now!" Wally said.

"He's the one who should apologize, to Cooper!"

"Ruby, that's enough," Hazel said.

"Please, Mom, please sit down," she pleaded.

"Honey—"

"Mom, please! It's our one chance!"

The sound in the room was deafening.

"Mom, please. Daddy! You always say to keep our commitments!"

Wally held his hands up in surrender. "Hung by my own words." He shook his head, but Ruby thought his mouth twitched. He took his handkerchief out, wiped the water from Cooper's face, took his hand, and followed Hazel back to their seats.

Ruby picked up the gavel. BANG!

"Look at yourselves!"

BANG!

"You're supposed to be the grownups!"

BANG!

"We get one life, *one*!" Ruby looked at Maggie for a moment. "Think about a baby! Everybody wants it to be happy, they would do *anything*. People act like being alive is *easy*, like…like it's nothing special, and then there's a shooting and you're all 'We have to do something!' and then you do *nothing*! Again, and again, and again, and again."

She struggled for the right words. "Everybody is born so precious and—and unique! And everybody dies. My grandma died, and my brother's calf. Why would you want to make it *easier*? Does it have to be *your* school that makes you change? Does it have to be *your* kid? It's time to put us kids first! Things are different now! It's not okay anymore to keep buying guns like they're your favorite toy! Guns are not toys! It's just selfish!"

She looked at her mom, and stopped to breathe.

"Some of us who are kids now will grow up and get guns like they're toys, or to feel safe. Some won't even wait to grow up. But we can't be safe. Because of all the *guns*! Some of us who are kids now, some of us will shoot somebody someday. It might be by accident, or it might be on purpose, it might be someone else or it might be our own self. But it will happen."

She was determined not to cry.

"You're thinking your excuses not to do anything, how people have a *right*, like that man said." She raised her chin. "But we don't care, because guns have gone too far. We care about Jess's cousin and my brother, and being scared at school or shooting somebody by accident. We care about suicides."

Jess and Emily were suddenly next to her.

"Your Second Amendment needs to be amended—things are *different* now! What's going on now is destroying what the founding fathers wanted, the first, most important thing: 'We hold these truths to be self-evident, that all people are created equal, that they are endowed by their Creator with certain unalienable Rights, that among these are *Life*, *Liberty*, and the pursuit of *Happiness*.' What happens when one group's idea of what that is doesn't go with another's? There wouldn't be fights about it if you put your kids first."

She smiled at Cooper.

"I asked my brother what we should call this. He said we should name it after Jenny, his calf that was shot. She was named after our

Grandma Jenny. She used to tell us—"

Stupid tears!

"She said, 'There's only ever going to be one of you, so you be your best you.' One of everyone. One Peter, Jess's cousin. One Cooper, my brother. One of everyone you love. Just one. No replacements. One of *you*."

Jess took her hand.

"One of each kid who's died from a gun. What kind of memorial is hiding in a closet? Practicing for when it happens again? Practicing to hide? To be shot? Their memorial should be *less* guns, not more! Their memorial should be *no assault weapons*! Their memorial should be *gun locks*! At least do *that*! You've done *nothing*. There are so many things we can't control. Like cancer. But guns, you can. You make laws to keep kids from *vaping*, but not to keep them from guns."

Ruby wiped her cheeks with the back of her hand. "You're *hurting* us. My brother has had to be brave. He's eight years old! Can you be brave too? If it was just you, if you weren't in a group, what would you want to happen? If nobody would know, if it was secret, would you vote for gun safety laws then? Be brave."

She took Emily's hand.

"That's what we came to say."

June 5

Dear Ms. Somers, Ms. Brown, and Ms. Roleaux,

Thank you for addressing the Vermont General Assembly. Your remarks were educational and certainly gave us food for thought! It was clear you had done your homework! Unfortunately, this is not the time for Vermont to take up more gun laws.

It's heartening to see young people engaged in civic activism, and I would not be surprised to see any one of you at the Statehouse again, perhaps representing your town!

Respectfully yours,

Susan Hood

Speaker of the House

Chapter 29

VERMONT IS SO SMALL that for the map Henry Cooper Brown made in second grade, he only needed half a poster board. But to Cooper, Vermont was exactly the right size, especially his part of it. He drew two squares for the two houses and a smaller one for the sugarhouse. He drew two rectangles for the two barns and a sprinkle of dots with skinny legs and tiny triangle wings for the chickens. He drew a circle for the pond, buckets for the sugar maples and spiky triangles for the pine trees near the road. He drew brown ovals with tails for the cows and big twisty antlers on the deer, to make sure it was clear which was which.

Cooper thought about things like that, how a calf could look like a deer, but he didn't like to. He thought how for an animal there's just that day but for people there's before and after, and sometimes he wished he was an animal. And he thought about other things too, like was there Heaven and did calves and dogs go there, and why don't turtles watch over their babies, and why do crows like bright things, and why was a circle of flying turkey vultures called a kettle, and did they think of it as home, and who named it that? His home was named No Frills Farm.

If a turkey vulture were looking down at No Frills Farm one Sunday in June, she'd see splashes of white in the lush green woods, as if there'd been a star shower and, upon landing, the stars had bounced and pooled together.

And circling the star pool she'd see a kettle, but flying closer would discover it was made of human beings, the big ones and the small ones—one so small it had to be held—and they were holding hands. A dog was dancing in and out of their legs, and a black bird, one of those pesky ones, was flitting around their heads. And inside the star pool there was a small mound with fresh grass and apple chunks sprinkled on top.

If the wind was just right, she'd hear their song.

> *For flowers that bloom about our feet, for tender grass so fresh and sweet, for song of bird and hum of bee, for all things fair we hear or see: Giver of all, we thank thee.*
>
> *For blue of stream and blue of sky, for pleasant shade of branches high, for fragrant air and cooling breeze, for beauty of the blooming trees: Giver of all, we thank thee.*
>
> *For this new morning with its light, for rest and shelter of the night, for health and food, for love and friends, for everything that goodness sends: Giver of all, we thank thee.*

"And so it has been and, God willing, will continue to be, for generations to come," Henry said, and squeezed his grandchildren's hands.

Summer

white T-shirts
(Emily - small, me, Jess - medium,
Amra, Tisha - large)
rubber bands, blue, yellow, red dye
red white and blue glitter nail polish
flashlights , glow sticks, sparklers
pink cowboy boots, contacts
Cooper at camp – 10 postcards, 10 stamps
100 petitions, 20 white poster boards,
500 buttons – 2 inches

the end

Author's Note

The morning 20-year-old Adam Lanza walked into Sandy Hook Elementary School and killed twenty children and six adults, I was in my own elementary school with kids who, like the kids in Newtown, were looking forward to vacation. Like everyone, I was stunned and devastated. And I was sure that Congress would finally act to ban assault weapons and pass other gun safety laws. How could they not?

They didn't.

Another Vermont teacher, Ann Braden, started GunSense Vermont, with the goal of passing common sense gun laws in our state, and I joined. In the spring of 2015 just one law out of those we'd been petitioning for got passed, and a week later I woke up in the middle of the night with the outline of a story in my head. I quickly scribbled it down. I felt like someone—the kids I'd taught and loved?—had given me an assignment: write a book, call it ***Jenny's Law***, and—one more thing—include a calf. A brown one. That's how specific it was. How could I refuse?

Jenny's Law was in its final draft when 19-year-old Nikolas Cruz killed seventeen people and injured seventeen more at Stoneman Douglas High School in Parkland, Florida on Valentine's Day in 2018. Walkouts sprang up in schools all over the country. The day for the walkout in our small town ended up being a snow day from school, but nevertheless over two hundred students plus other community members gathered to call for gun safety laws. Kids went to the capital to talk to their legislators, and when a teen-ager threatened his former high school, our Republican governor made an about-face and signed four common sense gun laws. He was re-elected that November by a wider margin than before.

That summer, a group of students from Parkland who'd founded the non-profit March for Our Lives came to Vermont and I accompanied local teens to hear them speak—kids who'd been the same age as the Sandy Hook victims in 2012. It was inspiring to see kids speaking up for gun safety laws, but sad too, that they had to. Some of what they were doing was in my story before it happened in real life, and I struggled with what to change. Had the book become irrelevant? How to honor the kids? I rewrote it for kids, and then rewrote it for adults and finally decided to leave it as it was before. It wasn't up-to-date, but it represented what kids are dealing with in this country.

And now, just before ***Jenny's Law*** goes to the publisher, families in Uvalde, Texas have been shattered by still another mass shooting. Nineteen children and two teachers! How are we going to stop this?

Nelson Mandela said "May your choices reflect your hopes, not your fears."

I offer this small story in the spirit of hope.

Many people have helped bring the Brown family and their community to life—my writing groups and friends, my sisters Jeanie and Kathy, my daughter-in-law Maura, my son-in-law JP, and youth. My grandchildren Milo and Callie have given me critical advice from their perspectives. I thank everyone from a full heart. I am blessed to have found my copy-editor Louise Watson, my book designer Jenny Lyons, Rachel Fisher at Onion River Press and my cover artist Claire Tebbs close to home. Each of them contributed valuable advice, and their unique care and expertise transformed ***Jenny's Law*** from a document on a laptop into the book it is. I'm very grateful.

My husband Gerry, my daughter Poppy, my son Tor, and my sister Anna Rose, have given me constant encouragement. Without their faith in me and the story, ***Jenny's Law*** would never have gotten to publication. Thank you.

Resources

Many counties and states offer gun safety courses. Vermont's listings for hunter safety courses can be found at the Vermont Fish and Wildlife site.

The following organizations are working to make communities safer from gun violence.

Americans for Responsible Solutions is a nonprofit political action organization founded by Gabby Giffords and her husband Mark Kelly that encourages elected officials to stand up for solutions to prevent gun violence and protect responsible gun ownership. It merged with the **Law Center to Prevent Gun Violence**, which writes amicus briefs to defend gun-control laws that are challenged, and are "a think tank for solutions to the gun-violence epidemic."

The Brady Campaign advocates for policy and for the government to enforce laws already on the books. It has a number of local chapters, and its website is a reliable source for information about gun deaths and injuries.

Coalition to Stop Gun Violence is an umbrella group of 48 religious, social, and political organizations that are fighting to pare back concealed-carry laws and prevent gun-related suicides.

Everytown for Gun Safety advocates for required gun safety courses, background checks, keeping guns away from domestic abusers, and tougher gun-trafficking laws, and supports various congressional candidates. An arm of **Everytown, Moms Demand Action for Gun Sense in America**, is active at a grassroots level.

GunSense Vermont is a nonpartisan group that works with students and survivors using evidence-based practices to advocate for laws that reduce gun violence. Its non-profit arm, **GunSense Vermont Education Fund**, educates Vermonters about gun violence, including suicide, homicide, intimidation, and domestic, and works to facilitate civic engagement to reduce gun violence.

March for Our Lives, born out of the tragic school shooting in Parkland, Florida in 2018, is a youth-led movement dedicated to promoting civic engagement, education, and direct action by youth to eliminate the epidemic of gun violence.

New Yorkers Against Gun Violence focuses on protecting residents of New York, particularly youth, from gun violence through legislative advocacy and education designed to encourage action, influence public opinion, and lead to policy change.

Newtown Action Alliance was founded by residents of Newtown, Connecticut following the tragic shooting at Sandy Hook Elementary School in 2012. They are "dedicated to reversing the escalating gun violence epidemic in this nation through the introduction of smarter, safer gun laws and broader cultural change."

Sandy Hook Promise is a national nonprofit organization led by several family members whose loved ones were killed at Sandy Hook Elementary School on December 14, 2012. Their intent is to "honor all victims of gun violence by turning our tragedy into a moment of transformation. By empowering youth to 'know the signs' and uniting all people who value the protection of children, we can take meaningful actions in schools, home, and communities to prevent gun violence and stop the tragic loss of life." **Sandy Hook Promise** has created programs for schools that people can advocate for and volunteer in.

States United to Prevent Gun Violence is an affiliation of 30 state gun-violence-prevention groups working to make communities safer through common sense laws and anti-violence education.

Violence Policy Center was founded by a Newtown resident and "works to stop gun death and injury through research, education, advocacy, and collaboration."

CPSIA information can be obtained
at www.ICGtesting.com
Printed in the USA
LVHW030609111122
732851LV00002B/183

9 781957 184081